TRAGEDY AT TWO

TRAGEDY AT TWO

Ann Purser

severn House

This title first published in Great Britain 2009 by
SEVERN HOUSE PUBLISHERS LTD of
9–15 High Street, Sutton, Surrey, England, SM1 1DF,
by arrangement with the Berkley Publishing Group,
a division of the Penguin Group (USA) Inc.

British Library Cataloguing in Publication Data

Purser, Ann.
   Tragedy at two. -- (The Lois Meade mysteries)
   1. Meade, Lois (Fictitious character)--Fiction.
   2. Cowgill, Hunter (Fictitious character)--Fiction.
   3. Cleaning personnel--England--Fiction. 4. Murder--
   Investigation--England--Fiction. 5. Romanies--Fiction.
   6. Detective and mystery stories.
   I. Title II. Series
   823.9'14-dc22

ISBN-13: 978-0-7278-6855-8   (cased)
ISBN-13: 978-1-84751-209-3   (trade paper)

For Emily, who brightens our lives.

All Severn House titles are printed on acid-free paper.

Printed and bound in Great Britain by
MPG Books Ltd., Bodmin, Cornwall.

ONE

Exotic gypsy girls in bright, swirling skirts and flashing
gold coin necklaces stamped to the dancing rhythms of music
played by a swarthy young man on a lively fiddle. Lois Meade
looked across at her husband, Derek, and her mother, both sound
asleep in the sitting room, in spite of the television. She smiled and
got silently to her feet. She would take just a few steps. . . . She
swayed to the beat, and her feet began to move.

Derek and Gran slept on. Lois lifted her arms and began to
circle the furniture. She hummed the tune, now wilder and faster.
There was excitement and danger in it, and the promise of something wonderfully triumphant. As she twirled around the sofa,
she had her eyes shut in imagined ecstasy. And so tripped over
Derek's feet.

"You all right, gel?" he said, rubbing his eyes. "We don't want
that ruddy noise, do we," he said, and pressed the off button.

Lois Meade was a sensible mother of two grown-up sons
and one daughter, and lived in Long Farnden, a small village in the
heart of England. She had been born in the nearby town of Tresham,
married Derek, an electrician, and having left school as soon as
possible with zero qualifications, she had become a cleaner, choosing
jobs outside town, in the villages around.

Lois was ambitious, provided there was no studying involved,
and she and Derek scraped up enough money for the mortgage on
a solid, substantial house that had belonged to one of her clients in
Long Farnden. Here she set up a cleaning business, wittily named
New Brooms. "We Sweep Cleaner" was the motto emblazoned on
her white van. The business had taken off, and though Lois continued
to have weekly staff meetings in her office at home, she was soon
able to rent a main office in Tresham.

All very praiseworthy and straightforward. But Lois had been a
rebel in her youth, and had even spent a night in a police station
cell for refusing to give her correct name and details when she and

her gang had been picked up for disorderly behaviour. She had quite cheerfully admitted that she carried a knife for self-protection in a school that had a reputation for being rough.

Now a law-abiding wife and mother, she still sometimes had a rebellious itch, needing the excitement that came from sailing close to the wind. For a few years now, she had been involved in gathering information helpful to the law.

In other words, she was an informer, working with the police. But not quite that, she would be at pains to point out. An amateur sleuth would be more accurate. She took no money, worked only on cases that interested her, or—as in her last involvement—where her own family was in danger. And probably the greatest incentive, she would be loath to admit, was that she worked only with Detective Chief Inspector Hunter Cowgill.

At the moment, she was having a fallow period. No ferretin', as Derek called it. She had only the efficient organising of her business to think about. Her team of cleaners, including one young man who also took on interior décor commissions, was handpicked and knew their jobs inside out. All gathered at a meeting once a week at Lois's house, and Hazel, one of the longest serving, manned the office in Tresham.

"I was enjoying that," Lois said now, frowning at Derek. "It's me gypsy blood."

"What gypsy blood?" Gran said sharply. She had an uncanny knack of being able to listen when apparently asleep. "There's no tinkers in our family!"

Derek laughed. "What about Lois's dad?" he teased. "He had dark skin and that nose he's passed on to our Douglas. Definitely a gyppo's nose, that." He got to his feet and went over to help Gran to her feet. "Come on," he said, "time we all went to bye-byes."

Lois sniffed. "Time you stopped saying that," she snapped. "We got no children now, don't forget."

"Ah," said Gran, "but it might not be long."

"I'm off," said Lois, but Derek stared at Gran.

"You know something I don't?" he said.

"Douglas and Susie, o' course."

"Blimey, they're not wed yet. Give 'em a chance."

Derek went to the window to draw the curtains back ready for morning. "Hey, Lois!" he called. "Come down here. Something's going on outside!" He put out the lights, and the three of them stood at the window, peering out. A car had drawn up outside their gate, and the interior light was on. A man was speaking on a mobile phone. Then he began to get out of the car, and Lois caught her breath. As the door opened, she saw who it was.

"It's him!" she said. "What a cheek, at this time of night! It's Hunter Cowgill. Come on, let's creep upstairs and pretend we're asleep. Quick, Gran! He's coming up the drive."

By the time the soft knocking began at the door, Gran was safely in her room, and Lois sat hand in hand with Derek on the top stair.

Cowgill did not go away. He knocked louder, and then called through the letter box. "Sorry, Lois, but it's urgent. Derek? Could you open up for a minute?"

Lois put her finger to her lips and turned to Derek. He was making a strange face, his eyes half-closed. Then he sneezed, twice, muffled as best he could. Then, after a loud gasp, a final explosion at full volume.

Lois got wearily to her feet. "It's a fair cop," she said to Cowgill as she opened the door. "You'd better come in."

TWO

Derek put on the lights in the sitting room and looked at Lois. "I don't suppose you want *me* here," he said. It was a statement, not a question. "I'll be in the kitchen. Shall I put the kettle on?"

"No," Lois said firmly. "This won't take long."

Cowgill nodded. "I'll be as brief as possible," he said, and waited until Derek had gone out and shut the door behind him.

"Sorry about this," he began, but Lois interrupted him.

"Cut the apologies," she said. "What d'you want? It had better be important."

"It is. Your daughter Josie's partner has been found badly beaten up in a ditch on the way to Waltonby. He's been taken into Tresham

General, and Josie is with him. I promised her I would tell you straightaway."

"Rob? Beaten up? Oh, dear God, no! What on earth was he doing out there at this time of night?"

"Seems he could have been there a while. A passing motorist spotted him and alerted us. Are you all right, Lois?" he added. She was very pale, and did not look too steady to him. He got up and called through to the kitchen. "Derek! I think we need that kettle on after all."

"I want Derek in here. Without the tea," said Lois, shaking herself.

Cowgill went over the facts again, and saw that Lois had taken Derek's hand for reassurance. "It is up to you both whether you want to go to the hospital straightaway," he said. "Josie looked shattered, of course. She might be glad of some support."

"Is his life in danger?" Derek asked. Rob was not his favourite person, but he'd been Josie's partner for some time and Derek respected that. He had noticed that the relationship had cooled off lately, partly because Cowgill's nephew Matthew Vickers, also a policeman and lately transferred to the Tresham force, had shown considerable interest in Josie. Derek was not blind. He could see the way the wind was blowing.

"I couldn't tell you how seriously he is hurt, I'm afraid," Cowgill answered. "No doubt Josie has been told."

"Of course we'll go in to the General," Lois said. "Good job we'd only just gone up. Have you any idea who could've attacked Rob?" she asked Cowgill. He shook his head. "Not yet," he said.

"Rob's a bit of a wimp," said Derek carefully. "Not so good at defending himself, I'd say."

"Oh, come on, Derek," Lois said. "Let's get going. Your van or mine?"

Josie was sitting in a huddle by the hospital bed, where Rob lay unmoving, with monitoring equipment pipping away beside him. She looked up as she heard her parents approach, and Lois's heart lurched. "Oh, Josie," she whispered, and put her arms around her, "It's all right, duckie," she said, "Mum's here."

"And Dad," Derek said, putting his hand on Josie's shoulder. A nurse brought up two chairs for them, and they sat down. For some time they sat without speaking, holding hands. Lois had not looked at Rob's face, but now steeled herself and glanced over at the bed. His eyes were swollen and bruised, and the rest of his face was like a piece of raw steak.

"The bastards," Derek whispered. He leaned across to Josie, who was now sitting up straight and staring fixedly at Rob. "Don't worry, me duck," he said. "We'll get 'em."

Now the nurse returned and beckoned to Josie, who disappeared with her into the corridor. Lois looked at Derek with raised eyebrows. He shook his head and shrugged. Rob didn't look at all good to him, but with all that bruising and swelling it was difficult to guess how bad he was in himself.

Josie reappeared and sat down again. She looked at Lois and her chin quivered. "He's got a chance," she said quietly. "That's all they can say at the moment." Then a tear ran down her cheek unchecked. "It's all my fault," she blurted out, and the dam burst.

It was getting light by the time Lois and Derek left the hospital. Lois had not wanted to go, but the nurse had assured her they would look after Josie. She had said there was no point in them losing sleep when they had to work the next day. "Or I should say today," she said with a smile. "You'll be able to get three or four hours in if you go straightaway," she had said firmly, and now they were on the way back to Long Farnden.

"What did she mean, it was all her fault?" Lois asked.

Derek shook his head. "Search me," he said. "The only thing I can think is that they had a row and Rob stormed out."

"And got into a punch-up with a gang for no reason at all? Not very likely, is it? As you so tactfully put it, Rob is a bit of a wimp. He's a mild chap and wouldn't pick a quarrel with anybody, let alone a marauding gang."

"Could've been just one drunk on his way home. Big bloke, took offence at nothing, like they do. Rob didn't stand a chance. That's my best guess."

Lois opened the door wearily and found Gran in her dressing gown sitting at the kitchen table, head on her hands, fast asleep.

"Sshh!" Lois whispered to Derek, but Gran was waking up.

"There you are, then," she said. "Tell me the worst."

"All I'm telling you at the moment is that Rob's got a good chance, and is in good hands."

"Thank God." Gran struggled to her feet and reached automatically for the kettle. "You two get off up to bed and I'll bring you a cup of that calming rubbish Josie sells in the shop. She swears by it, but I bet it'd take more than tea that smells of cats' pee to calm her right now."

But by the time Gran had boiled the kettle on the Rayburn and taken up the tea, Lois and Derek were asleep, arms around each other. Gran felt her eyes prickle, and went sadly to her own bed. She looked at her photograph of Lois's dad and wished more than usual that he was still alive.

THREE

The pub in Long Farnden had recently been given a major makeover, which included renaming it. Most of the locals were dead against it, and sent a petition to the brewery asking for the original name to be kept. They might just as well have appealed to the man in the moon, said Derek, who had been a prime mover in all this.

"It's not enough that we have to sit on silly little wimmin's chairs," he'd said. "Now a new sign goes up without our say-so, callin' it the Toad and the Washerwoman! What's that got to do with anything in Farnden? And this new landlord's useless."

Now he had only one worry on his mind, and looked morosely at the empty glass in his hand. He had been sitting there for an hour or so, gaining comfort from his friends. Gran had not argued for once when he said he'd have a pie and a pint to save her cooking lunch.

The new vicar, having said all the right things to Derek, got to his feet and left. The regulars ignored him. New landlord at the pub, new vicar in the church, it was all too much for them. Not that they were likely to be too bothered about the new vicar, except that he was one of those who drop in to the pub for a half of cider now and then, and so crossed their paths.

"Recruiting, they say," said Sam Stratford, husband of one of Lois's cleaners. Sheila had been with New Brooms for a long time, and Sam had more or less retired from farmwork.

"Wasting his time, then," Derek said, looking at his watch. The new imitation old clock on the wall chimed a tinny two o'clock. At this point the door opened and a couple of dark strangers came in. Silence fell, and all heads turned. One of the two men was young, the other in his forties. They were tidy-looking, but different. More colourful, somehow, thought Derek. And watchful.

Sam leaned across to whisper in Derek's ear. "Tinkers," he said, not too quietly, and others around the table turned back to their drinks and nodded. Conversation gradually resumed, but nobody spoke to the two newcomers.

"Foreigners, maybe," Derek answered. "Can't understand a word they're saying."

Sam shook his head. "Gyppos. Probably down on Alf Smith's land. You know—they come every year. Romany speaking. Serves them right if they get treated rough. When in Rome do what Rome does, as my Sheila says. O' course," he added, "they might come from Rome, if y' know what I mean. They'd still be foreigners."

"They'd be Italians, wouldn't they?" Derek said. They gave up, and an apprehensive silence fell as the older of the two men came over to the locals' table.

"G'day," he said in a deep voice. "D'you know of any work goin' round here?"

Derek and the others looked at each other. Finally Derek said, "What kind of work?"

"Anything, we can do anything. We're not afraid of hard work."

"Not what I've heard," muttered Sam under his breath.

Derek saw the man's hands clench into fists, and answered swiftly. "I reckon there'll be some work on Thornbull's farm soon. If we ever see the sun again, that is. The rain's holding them up somethin' shockin'."

The man asked where the farm was, and Derek gave him directions. "You stand a good chance there," he said. "The Poles and them don't come over as much as they used to do. Get better wages at home, they reckon."

"Where're you from, mate?" Sam said.

"Up the road," the man said.

"Campin' on Alf Smith's land, are you?" Sam's voice was hostile.

"Yeah, but we'll be moving on to Appleby."

"Sooner the better," said Sam, getting up to go. "A bit stuffy in here," he said, turning to his friends. "See ya, boy," he grunted to Derek, and without looking at either of the strangers, he stalked out.

"He's not feeling too well," Derek answered in as loud a voice as he could manage. The message had been only too clear, as he could see from the gypsies' faces.

The conversation at the table resumed, but this time on a hot village topic. "How's Rob, then?" one of the locals said. Derek shook his head. "Dunno," he said. "Josie's still keeping vigil, poor gel, and Lois has gone to sit with her. I'm excused, as Lois says I can't sit still for five minutes an' am not much use, anyway."

"Is he conscious yet?" one of the others said. They all knew Josie from the shop, and were genuinely sorry as well as curious. "Can he tell them anything about who attacked him?"

Once again Derek shook his head. "Don't know" he said. "He was still out for the count, last I heard. I'll know more when Lois gets home." He looked at his watch and drained his glass. "Better be going," he said.

"Watch y' back, boy!" chorused his friends.

Lois did not leave the hospital until late evening, and now, nearly home, slowed down at the thirty limit sign. She was in very low spirits. There had been no change in Rob's condition, and Josie had looked half dead herself. The nurse had promised to insist that Josie have some sleep in a side room, and Lois had left the hospital reluctantly. She was worried about Rob, of course, but her main concern was Josie. She had mentioned to her that between them she and Gran were keeping the shop going, but Josie had hardly seemed to listen. The only thing she repeated in the hours that Lois was with her was that it was all her fault.

The lights of the van picked up a moving shape, and Lois braked hard. It was a dog, and it vanished through the hedge into the field where Lois knew there were gypsies. She could see dim lights coming from the caravans, and wondered if she should go and make sure the dog was not hurt.

She drew into a gateway and stopped the engine. It was muddy as she got out, and she cursed. Before she got to the caravans, a tall man came towards her, silhouetted against the moonlit sky.

"What d'ya want?" he said.

She could see he had a dog on a leash. It was growling and showing its teeth.

Lois explained, and the man shook his head. "It'd be the whippet," he said. "Fast as the wind. That'd be all right. You on yer own?" He sounded concerned as he asked the question, and Lois answered quickly that she was on her way home and her husband would be expecting her. She was later than planned, she explained. Then she wondered if saying that was a good idea. Either he was suspicious of intruders, or he was planning to kidnap her and sell her into white slavery.

The man put out his hand. "D'you want to come over and see the lady who owns the whippet?"

He turned away and set off before Lois had a chance to answer. She hesitated, and then followed.

FOUR

Lois is late, isn't she?" The day had passed slowly for Derek, and soon after he came home he had fallen asleep in front of the telly until troubled dreams had startled him awake.

"She said she might be," Gran replied without looking at him. "She was going to stay with Josie as long as possible."

"Hope the delay is nothing to do with Rob getting worse. Should we phone the hospital?"

Gran didn't answer, but cocked her head to one side. "Isn't that the van? Sounds like she's home."

Sure enough the back door opened and Lois came in, looking pale and tired. Derek went up to her and gave her a hug. "Not a setback, is there?" he whispered in her ear. She shook her head.

"I've been off with the raggle-taggle gypsies," she said.

"Lois! What d'you mean?"

"She's trying to frighten us," Gran said, dishing up food and insisting they all sit down while it was still hot.

"No, no, come on, Lois," Derek insisted. "Did those gypsies bother you? Where did you see them?"

"I nearly killed one of their dogs. It ran straight out in front of the van. I stopped, of course. I saw it limp off through the hedge. Thought I'd better look for it. You're supposed to report it, aren't you? Anyway, I went in the field where they've got their vans parked, and one of 'em came across to speak to me."

"I'll kill 'im!" Derek said, getting to his feet.

"Sit down and don't be ridiculous!" Lois said. "He was polite, and asked me if I'd like to go and see the woman who owned the dog, to make sure."

"You didn't go, surely?" Gran was looking alarmed now.

"Shouldn't we start our supper?" Lois replied, and began to eat.

At the hospital, Josie had never felt so tired, but would not leave Rob's bedside. She stifled a yawn, and went over once again in her head what had happened that night. If they hadn't had that terrible row, he wouldn't have stormed out and walked off in the dark to God knows where. He'd been out for hours, and then there'd been the call from the hospital. If he'd stayed at home with her, he wouldn't have been attacked and dumped in a ditch for maybe hours before he was found.

She thought back to what he had said before disappearing into the night. He had once more suggested they get married, and she had refused to give him a definite answer. Then he had lost his temper and said if she had cooled off in their relationship she might have the decency to say so. He had repeated his accusation that she was having a secret affair with "that cop Vickers," and called her a tart. And then he had gone, slamming the door behind him. She should have had the courage to tell him exactly how she felt. She was fond of him, of course, but he was about as exciting as the man who came round with the fish. She supposed they had got too used to one another.

How could she look at him now and think these thoughts? She yawned again and her eyes closed. She swayed on her seat, and the nurse caught her in time.

"Come on, Josie, let's go and find you a bed for a few hours' sleep. You'll be no use to Rob in this state. You'll want to be bright and chirpy for him when he wakes up."

Josie stood up. The heart monitor pinged steadily, and there was no sign of him waking. His face twitched occasionally, and that was it. She went with the nurse to the door and stopped. The pinging had become uneven. The nurse had gone on ahead, and Josie in a panic called her back. Before Josie had reached the bed, the pinging had stopped and a continuous sound pierced the silence. From countless television programmes, she knew what that meant.

"Help, for God's sake! He's dying!" she screamed, and then staff seemed to come from nowhere and the room was full of activity.

Derek was making sure the doors were all locked and bolted when the telephone rang. It was Josie and she could hardly speak.

"Dad? He's gone. Rob's gone."

"Who is it?" said Lois, and with one look at Derek's face, knew it was Josie. She took the receiver from him and listened to her daughter's stumbling account of how everything had been tried but nothing could bring him back to life.

"Stay where you are," Lois said. "We'll be there in no time. Is someone with you?"

A nurse came to the phone and assured Lois that they would look after Josie until they could pick her up. "Drive carefully, now, Mrs. Meade," she said. "Arrive alive."

Under the circumstances, Lois thought this was probably the most tactless thing she had ever heard said by anyone.

FIVE

With Josie safely back in Farnden, tucked up in bed in her old room, the night passed in fitful sleep for them all. Josie had taken pills the hospital gave her, and was troubled with nightmares, all of them involving darkness and violence. Gran took the photograph of her smiling husband and put it on the pillow next to her, and Derek and Lois spent the night waking each other as they surfaced from troubled sleep.

Next morning was a bad time for them all. Derek said he might as well go off and finish the job he was doing in Waltonby, and Lois and Gran sighed with relief as he went off in his van.

"Best keeping himself occupied," Gran said. "You and me can see to all the necessaries, Lois."

The telephone rang. Lois sighed. She knew who it was, and went into her office to answer the phone away from Gran's sharp ears.

"I was expecting a call from you earlier," Lois said, and Cowgill replied that contrary to belief, the police were not without sensitivity.

"How is Josie?" he asked, and winced as Lois said what the hell did he expect when the girl's longtime partner had been brutally murdered?

"Right. Please tell her how sorry we are. I need some help, Lois. Rob was, as you say, brutally attacked and left for dead. Now the poor fellow has died, and that is murder. We need to move quickly."

"Before they get on the road?" Lois said.

"What d'you mean? Who? Do you know something, Lois?"

"Only that one or two nosy parkers in the village have already assured me that it was one of the gypsies camped outside Farnden. I know nowt, and wouldn't be so stupid as to jump to such an obvious conclusion."

"Nor would I, Lois. I think we need to meet, but I realise this will be difficult for you. It is just that you and your family can probably give us a good start in our investigations."

"A good start! You mean you've not started yet? Good God, man, Rob was attacked more than twenty-four hours ago!"

Cowgill frowned. "You know as well as I do, Lois, that I used a figure of speech. Of course we began as soon as the news came in." He paused, and she did not reply.

"So," he continued, "I'll be with you at twelve noon. If Gran and Derek could be there, so much the better. Goodbye."

And goodbye to you, too, Lois said to herself. She realised she had pushed Cowgill too far. She should know by now that he could be totally professional when required, even with her. But the sound of someone being violently sick in the bathroom put Cowgill from her mind, and she rushed upstairs. It was Josie, and she had

awoken, not remembering for a few minutes. Then the whole night-
mare had come back to her with a vengeance, and she vomited as
if she would never stop.

Lois coaxed her downstairs, and with Gran managed to persuade
her to have a cup of tea and a piece of toast and Marmite. "You
always used to like Marmite when you were a little girl," said Gran.
"It'll be easier if you can get something inside you. Here, Lois," she
added, "you'd better have some, too. It's going to be a long day."

"Longer than you think," Lois muttered under her breath. She
had somehow to break the news that Cowgill would be coming to
question them. In the quietest possible voice she told them, and
was surprised when there were no objections. Josie was obviously
still numb, and Gran came from a generation of working-class people
who did not argue with a policeman.

A call to Derek's mobile made sure that he would be at home
at twelve noon, and Lois sat back, trying to organise her thoughts.
She knew almost nothing more than that Rob and Josie had had a
row, he had stormed out of the house, and had been found several
hours later in a ditch on the Waltonby road.

There was, of course, something else. She had told Derek and
Gran no more about her encounter with the gypsies, but there had
been more to tell. After the man had invited her to go and see the
owner of the dog, she had followed him across the field and up to
a caravan that gleamed white in the darkness. He had knocked at
the door and an elderly woman answered it. Her hair was braided
neatly round her head, and her apple cheeks shone. Dark eyes
peered out at Lois, and when the man explained, she had insisted
on Lois going in to see the whippet, sound in wind and limb and
contentedly in its basket.

"This is Athalia Lee," the man had said, and Lois was cordially
invited to sit down. "Would you take a cup of tea with us?"
Athalia had asked. "It was kind to come and ask after the dog.
One of these days he'll cause a real accident, then there'll be
trouble." She looked at the man, who smiled. "More than usual,"
he said. "They'd have us out of here quicker than you could say
knife." He saw Lois wince at the word, and frowned. "You're
safe enough here, y' know, missus," he said.

Lois commented on the good smell coming from the bubbling
saucepan, and the conversation drifted awkwardly into other
subjects, but it was Lois who was ill at ease. The other two were

warm and comfortable. Finally, having drunk a good cup of tea, Lois said she had to go, and Athalia had seen her to the door. "Come and see me again," she'd said. "I'll tell you how to make a good stew. I'll not put the evil eye on ya, y' know!"

Now, as the minutes ticked slowly past in Gran's kitchen, neither of them spoke. Lois was surprised at how sad she was at the thought of the gypsies being blamed without reason. A more practical point struck her. She realised just before Cowgill knocked at the door that now she would be able to approach Athalia Lee for help if she needed to.

As the doorbell rang, she decided she would think twice before telling Cowgill of her visit to the gypsies.

SIX

Josie sat with Lois and Derek on the sofa, and Gran fussed about making coffee. Hunter Cowgill had taken a comfortable chair next to Josie, and his note-taking assistant sat inconspicuously by the window.

"Shall we wait until Mrs. Weedon comes in with the coffee?" Cowgill said kindly. "Then we shall all know what's being said. Sometimes a memory from one person will trigger another."

"I've told you all I know," Lois said, and Derek took Josie's hand. "We don't want her upset," he said. Cowgill was not his favourite policeman, owing to the number of times he had involved Lois in dangerous cases. But he had to admit that Lois had been keen to be involved. It was like a hobby to her, he had decided, and had lost count of the number of times he wished she had taken up knitting instead.

"Here we are," said Gran, coming in with a tray. Coffee was handed out, and then they settled down to answer Cowgill's questions. But first Cowgill told them what he and his colleagues had discovered already.

It seemed that there had been no knife wounds. All Rob's injuries had been caused by fists or boots, or a heavy stick or club. No witnesses to the attack had come forward.

"What d'you mean by 'club'?" Lois said. "A golf club? Or a weight lifter's club or . . ." She couldn't think of any other kind.

"A blunt instrument, you could say. Something heavy with an even heavier end to it."

"A baseball bat," Josie said, as if suddenly emerging from a dense fog. "Could've been that, if Rob had come across thugs looking for trouble. He would've tried to defend himself, but he wasn't strong and wouldn't have had no weapon." Her lip began to wobble, and Derek squeezed her hand.

"Try not to think about it, duckie," he said.

"We've got to think about it," Josie answered, and looked at Lois. "After all," she said, "Mum is our own private sleuth. Between us we'll get 'em, whoever he or they were." Lois nodded and turned to look at Cowgill, who could see tears in her eyes. Oh Lord, he thought, this is going to be a tricky one. No hopes of a cool, dispassionate Lois this time.

Nothing very useful emerged from this first session, and Cowgill drove back to Tresham trying to sort out what had been said. The most useful contribution had been Josie's suggestion of what might have been the weapon. He could not at this stage believe the encounter had been deliberately planned. As far as he could see, Rob had not had enemies. A mild sort of chap, with perhaps not enough drive or ambition for Josie, who was growing very like her mother. He smiled to himself. Heaven help anyone who crossed the path of the pair of them! Then he thought of his nephew, Matthew Vickers, keen young policeman and probably more than interested in Josie Meade. How soon before he heard from him?

Lois, too, was thinking hard as she drove into Tresham to call in at the office in Sebastopol Street. For her, Josie's suggestion had set off a useful line of thought. First, sort out the kind of people who might own or have access to the kind of weapon likely to have been used. Right. A golf club. Easily available, but carrying one in a casual encounter? Nervous widows kept one under the bed, but she'd never heard of hoodies carrying golf clubs, or evil gangs in Tresham arming themselves with natty putters.

So had Rob been weaving his way home in the middle of the road when a defeated golfer had failed to get past him, stopped his car and beaten him up with a handy club? Or had some young oaf, fresh from a team victory in a baseball game and on his way home, yelled insults at Rob who had tried to engage him in a befuddled argument? The alcohol level in his blood had been high. But a *baseball* game? Where? When?

Lois sighed. What else might have been used. A heavy stick with a gnarled knob at the end of it? Such as might have been cut from a scrubby roadside wood? One well polished from frequent use, and quickly wiped clean of the blood and hair sticking to it. Washed in a stream . . . running through the wood . . . known by a group of travelling undesirables who had been camping nearby? Oh, blimey, she muttered sadly to herself. This scenario was, of course, much the most convincing. Well, she was sure the police would be coming to that conclusion swiftly, and as she turned into Sebastopol Street, she made up her mind to take another direction. She pulled up outside New Brooms office, and went in to see what Hazel had for her to deal with.

Matthew Vickers had come into the police station later than usual. After a couple of days off duty, he had taken an instruction to visit an old man who claimed a gang of kids had persistently banged on his doors, both back and front, and had disappeared before he'd managed to get to his feet. Then, the last straw, his home help had stepped in a pile of excrement shoved through the letter box. Matthew had soothed the old man, taken details and promised to put a stop to the harassment.

"And when I've put a stop to that, the little sods will have moved on to some other vulnerable oldie," he said aloud to himself. He was in a gloomy mood returning into the office, and was deeply ashamed of feeling uplifted for a second on learning of the murder of Josie Meade's partner, Rob.

"Is the governor in?" he asked, and was told he had just arrived back from Long Farnden.

"Right, thanks," said Matthew. As he left the room, his colleagues looked at each other. "Guess where he's off to," said one. There was no answer, but general laughter.

SEVEN

As Gran knew only too well, the worst period for the bereaved is after the funeral and when all the attendant tasks have been dealt with. Suddenly there is a vacuum which nothing can fill, however many friends you have and however many clubs and activities you decide to join. You still have to come home to an empty house, with nobody to talk to. She had been in this position herself for some years until Lois had suggested she move in with them. Gran had burned her boats, sold her bungalow and followed the family to Long Farnden. It could have been disastrous, but they had all worked at it, and on the whole it had been a good solution.

Perhap Josie would come back to live at home permanently. She and Rob had made a nice little nest over the shop, but it could be lonely for her now. And she might feel safer in the house with the rest of them. It might be alarming if she heard burglars trying to break into the shop.

"Josie, dear," she said, as her granddaughter got up from the table after lunch, "have you thought of staying with us, at least for a while? And where are you going now, duckie?"

Gran had noticed Josie had an umbrella in her hand. It was pouring with rain outside, the sky heavy and threatening.

"To the shop, of course," Josie said firmly. "And thanks for worrying about me, Gran. But the shop is my life now, and I'm used to being independent. I don't think I'd fit in back at home for any length of time now. Goodness knows what a muddle that Floss is making of the takings!"

"She's a very nice girl, and a good cleaner. It's nice that she and Ben have got that little house by the church. And now he's got a job in Tresham, thank goodness. I know she wanted to stay in the village."

"Being a good cleaner doesn't make her a good shopkeeper, does it? It was nice of Mum to lend her to me, but I'm off now. Getting back into harness will be the best thing."

"Well, if you're sure." Gran marvelled at how much Josie sounded like Lois. They were so alike, and yet seemed to get on well together. Perhaps the girl was right. A house with three bossy women in it would be an uncomfortable home for Derek!

Contrary to her expectations, Josie found the shop immaculately tidy, the till full of small change, and the safe securely locked. Floss had an attractive overall to keep her clean while cutting ham and cheese and handing out ice creams and sweets to sticky-fingered children.

She looked startled to see Josie back so soon, and rushed to get a stool for her to sit on. But Josie waved it away and said she was not ill. She even managed a smile for worried-looking Floss.

"I'm here to help," Josie said. "You're obviously doing brilliantly, and I'd be glad if you could stay for a week or two. There's bound to be a lot of kerfuffle with the police and I'll be called away now and then. I'll make some coffee for us." She vanished upstairs, and Floss was almost in tears herself when she heard muffled sobs. It was probably the first time Josie had come back home since Rob's murder.

It was all round the village, of course. Everybody knew it was murder, and everybody had a firm idea of who had done it. Most had decided on a no-good gypsy, but a minority favoured the gang of youths who congregated in the evenings at the swings and slides in the play area of the recreation ground. They weren't allowed there, but that made little difference. So far, they had drunk their drinks and smoked their smokes without bothering anyone else, and they had been tut-tutted over but left alone. All teenagers go through a bad patch, the village agreed, and this was relatively mild. But there was always one, the gang leader, who wanted excitement.

"And for excitement, read violence," said the vicar, Keith Buccleugh—or Buckluck, as he was known in the village—to his wife, Marjorie. "What do you think, dear? Should I offer to talk to them, man-to-man? They might open up to me, and give us some clues as to what really happened."

He really believes it, thought Marjorie, looking at him fondly. But she knew he would end up as mincemeat if he approached the hooded ones and she said mildly that perhaps they should leave it to the police now. She was sure they would come to him if they needed his help.

"I suppose Mrs. Meade will be recruited again," he said glumly.

"She has quite a reputation now. Ah, here comes Josie. I asked her to pop in when she felt like it. Shall we have a coffee ready, Marj?"

For thirty married years she had hated that diminutive, but had never wanted to hurt his feelings by saying so. Sometimes she looked back on those years and realised she had spent far too much time protecting him from hurt feelings. A vicar needed to be tough, and Keith had never been. An overprotected and much loved child, he could never see unkindness coming. He really believed that everyone was basically good. What about original sin? He had shaken his head and not replied.

Josie had left the shop with the intention of spending, at the most, ten minutes in the vicarage. At this stage she could do without the vicar's sugary condolences, but she wanted to do the right thing and so, arming herself with the excuse that she had to get into Tresham to see Hazel at Mum's office, she rang the doorbell.

"Come in, come in," said Marjorie, "Father Keith is just on the telephone. He'll be with us in a couple of minutes." This was how he liked to be known, and it had taken some doing for the village to adjust.

"Morning, vicar," Josie said, as he joined them. She was led into the sitting room, and as she sat down she mentioned her Tresham appointment. "But it is nice to sit and listen for a bit," she said politely. "I've done nothing but answer questions for days."

That should put a stop to old nosy, she reckoned, and sat back and smiled.

"Of course, Josie. It is my job to give you words of consolation, but this morning you can forget I'm a vicar. Think of me as just another customer of the shop, and we can chat."

"Oh, and that reminds me," Josie said, fumbling in her pocket, "I brought you a present." She handed over a bar of the unsweetened dark chocolate he loved, and after that the ten minutes grew into half an hour, and Josie finally got up to go, thinking that he was not such a brainless twit as she had thought. He gave her a peck on the cheek and said he was always ready for a chat and a bar of chocolate, day or night, whenever she felt like it.

"Sweet girl," he said to his wife, after she had gone. "We must do all we can to help. There are more ways than one of gathering information."

In New Brooms's office, Hazel was talking to a client, so Josie went into the room at the back that doubled as storage and kitchen. She stood looking out of the window that overlooked the neat paved yard at the back and across to the new leisure centre going up on the old warehouse site. When Hazel came in to say the client had gone, Josie realised she had been staring out and registering nothing.

"The swimming pool will soon be finished, they say, so we can go and have a dip after work," Hazel said. She looked closely at Josie and took her hand. "Come on, sit down and I'll bore you with the latest exploits of my precious daughter, who is, as you know, a genius. You don't even have to listen. And I shan't ask you a single question."

"Acting on orders from Mum?" Josie said.

"How did you guess?" Hazel replied.

EIGHT

Lois had been to see a client on the outskirts of Tresham, and as she took a shortcut down Sebastopol Street she saw Josie's car parked outside the New Brooms office. She had not intended to stop, but now pulled up. Neither Josie nor Hazel saw her coming, and were guiltily startled when Lois seemed to materialise from nowhere.

"Speak of the devil," Josie said wearily.

"Hi, girls. Just thought I'd check to make sure all's well. You okay, Josie?"

On an impulse, Josie turned and gave her mother a hug. "As well as can be expected, I suppose," she said. "Did you want to talk to Hazel? I'm off home now."

"Were you going to ask me something, Josie?" Hazel said. She was aware that her friend had arrived, said nothing very much, and was now leaving.

"Can't remember," Josie replied. "See you back at the buildings, Mum." She walked towards her car and Hazel said, "Looks a bit lost, doesn't she."

"I'd do anything to help her," Lois said. "But I can't bring him back."

"We can find the sod who killed him."

"I mean to. But whoever beat him up might not have intended to kill him."

"So what's the difference?" Hazel said fiercely.

"In law there's a difference. But Rob's dead either way. That's all we need to remember. All of us."

"Gypsies are like large, scruffy birds," said Father Keith on a duty visit to the pub that evening. He was enjoying himself, and had had more than his usual half pint. "Alighting in a familiar nesting place, making use of what Mother Nature provides for them, and when she fails, they use their ingenuity to arrange for humans to supplement supplies, sometimes unknowingly."

"It's stealing! No need to wrap it up in poetic language," Andrew Young said fiercely to the loquacious vicar. Andrew was the latest recruit in Lois's cleaning team. The abiding topic was still the murder. No consideration was given here to the possibility that it might be manslaughter.

There was a chorus of agreement with Andrew, and the vicar judged it time to drink up and be on his way.

"Stupid bugger," said Sam Stratford. "Lives on a different planet from the rest of us."

"Hoping to," said Derek and everybody laughed.

"But seriously," Andrew continued. "I don't know why they haven't been moved on weeks ago."

"Police won't go near them unless they have to," Derek said. "I remember my Dad saying about that site on the other side of Tresham that if a bomb dropped on the lot of 'em the crime rate in town would go down by half."

"Even if they do get moved," Sam said, "they leave sackfuls of litter behind. And not in sacks, either. Some other bugger has to clear it all up."

The door opened, and Sam groaned. "Surely himself hasn't come back for more," he said.

But it was the same tall gypsy who had asked for work, and he came straight across to Derek. "Thanks, mister," he said.

"What for?"

"We got work at that farm. Good bloke farms it. We're not always trusted. Anyway, thanks." His dark face warmed, and he smiled at Derek.

"S'okay," Derek said in embarrassment, and turned his back. The others glared at him. "Doesn't do to encourage them," Andrew said quietly to Derek.

The gypsy, whose name was George, went to the bar and ordered a drink. He stood alone drinking unhurriedly and then walked slowly out of the pub. As he left, he looked back at Derek who, astonished at himself, waved a hand in farewell.

"For God's sake, boy!" said Sam. "You'll be asking us to join the Friends of Farnden Dids next!"

"What's Dids?" Lois said, when Derek reported what had happened. To his surprise, Lois seemed pleased that he had made a fool of himself. In fact, she thought he'd not made a fool of himself. The others were the fools. He had thought of not telling her anything, but everything came back to Lois in the end. So he told her everything except sending them up to Thornbull's. John Thornbull was Hazel's husband.

"Where've you been all these years, Lois?" scoffed Gran. "Dids is short for didikyes. Gyppos to you and me."

"They're gypsies or tinkers to me," Lois said.

"Oh, don't you start," said Gran. "Tolerance is all very well, but you have to speak from experience, and they're a dirty rough lot. Always have been. They don't respect our laws. Worse than foreigners."

Neither Lois nor Derek said anything more, and the subject was changed.

"Josie phoned a couple of minutes before you got in, Lois," Gran said. "She's sleeping back over the shop tonight. I tried to persuade her to come here, but you know what she's like once she's made up her mind. Anyway, I said we'd expect her for breakfast. I want to make sure that girl's getting food inside her. Bereavement can cause weight loss, you know. And she's thin enough already. She'll need her strength."

"Maybe I'll just pop down and make sure she's all right," Lois said.

"You might get a flea in your ear," Gran said.

"She's my daughter," Lois said.

Before she got to the shop, Lois could see a car, not Josie's, parked outside. As she got nearer she saw a man sitting inside. She stepped into the shadows and waited. After a few seconds, the man got out and stood looking up at Josie's window. The curtains were drawn, but a light showed that she was there. Lois's heart beat faster, and she wondered whether she should go back for Derek. But no, there wasn't time for that. Then the man got back into the car, started the engine and drove away. As it passed under a street light, Lois was sure she recognised the face of the driver.

NINE

Hazel Thornbull arrived home to find her daughter Lizzie in bed and asleep, and her husband John dozing in front of a discussion programme on television. She walked over and kissed the top of his head.

"Sorry to trouble your beauty sleep," she whispered in his ear, "but did you remember to shut up the bantams?" Hazel kept a few bantams in the garden, not for the eggs, as they were not very good layers, but as pets. She loved the feathery silkies, and they all had names.

John jumped up and said, "Of course I did. Um, what did you say?"

"Never mind," Hazel said. "Day go well?"

"Not bad. Them dids are good workers. Don't say much, but just keep their heads down and get on with the work."

"Gypsies?" Hazel said. "What, that lot from outside the village?"

"So they said. I asked them if they were moving on, because if they were they were wasting my time. I need workers who'll last the season."

"And?"

"They said they were staying as long as they could. The tall one actually laughed, and said you could never tell when the polis would evict them, but they were behaving themselves and hoped to stay until Appleby. He was quite a nice bloke. Had a sort of dignity about him."

"Rubbish!" said Hazel loudly. "You can't trust them round the corner! You'll probably regret it, John."

Then Lizzie appeared at the door looking worried and clutching Floppy Doggie, and had to be reassured that all was well and Mummy and Daddy were not quarrelling and it was time to go back to bed and sleep.

"You know everybody thinks it was one of those gypsies killed Rob, don't you," Hazel said, when all was quiet again. "Not everybody," John said. "Now things have cooled down, now the Farnden branch of the Ku Klux Klan have decided not to go with a fiery cross to torch the encampment. A lot of people realise that it was much more likely to have been oafs drugged up and on their way to Tresham. Rob was drunk and was probably wandering around all over the place. And even he could get belligerent in his cups."

"Rob? Josie's Rob?"

John nodded. "I've seen him," he said. "One night in the pub he was goin' on about some policeman who fancied Josie, said he was taking advantage. Drownin' his sorrows, was Rob. Landlord tried to stop him at his fifth pint, and that's when Rob turned nasty. It was quickly settled, but we were all surprised."

"I wonder if Lois knows about this," Hazel said quietly. "Or if she's been told that those two are working up here for us."

"Nothing to do with her," John said firmly. He was not keen on Hazel getting involved in Lois's ferretin'.

"Of course it's to do with her," Hazel snapped. "Rob was nearly her son-in-law."

"But he wasn't, was he? Maybe that's part of the picture. Anyway, I don't want you mixed up with all that."

"I know, I know," replied Hazel. "We Thornbulls keep ourselves to ourselves. I'm off to check on Lizzie," she added and disappeared.

As she went up the stairs on tiptoe, she resolved to ring Lois first thing tomorrow morning.

As it happened, next morning after breakfast, when Hazel was just on the point of leaving for work, deciding it would be better to talk to Lois from the office, there was a knock at the farmhouse door. She opened it quickly and was confronted by an upright figure, an elderly woman, with a basket over her arm and lace mats spilling over the edge of it. A gypsy, realised Hazel, taking in the long skirt, dark face and greying braided hair.

"Buy some lace, dear?" said the woman. "All handmade by experts. Very cheap compared with what you'll get on the market."

It so happened that Hazel had learned lace making with her mother-in-law at WI classes in the village, and she could see with one eye that the mats were machine made. "No thanks," she said. "And I'm in a hurry, so if you don't—"

Before she had finished speaking, the woman had turned around and was walking at a measured pace through the yard and out into the road.

"—if you don't mind, I have to go," shouted Hazel at her retreating back.

Ten

The telephone rang, and Hazel rushed into the office and picked it up.

"Morning Hazel," Lois said.

"Morning Mrs. M!" Hazel puffed her reply, and Lois smiled.

"Anything in the post?"

"Just the usual," Hazel replied, rapidly opening envelopes. "Two requests for New Brooms's services, and . . . um . . . one asking about our interior décor expert. Shall I pass that on to Andrew, or do you want to look at it first?"

"Make me a copy, and then pass it directly to him. Anything else?"

The morning call was routine, but Hazel seemed reluctant to sign off. After a pause, she began to speak. "Just, um, well, John and me were talking last night. He's hired a couple of them dids from that site by the road. Seems they're there illegally, but old Smith who owns the land doesn't bother about them. Some say he's got gypsy blood himself, way back."

"So what's wrong? Have the two done something bad?"

"Um, no. But I don't like having them so close to the house when we've got a young child. You hear such awful things . . ."

Hazel trailed off, aware of an icy silence. Then Lois replied.

"Yes, well. Perhaps you could give 'em a chance, Hazel. I've no doubt John will keep an eye on them. Was there anything else?"

Hazel hesitated. She sensed she had offended Mrs. M, who seemed to be sticking up for gypsies in general. Hazel couldn't think why, when it was more than probable they beat up her Josie's Rob until he snuffed it. Still, it might be important.

"There was one other thing," Hazel said. "It's about Rob. I can hardly believe it, but John saw it with his own eyes." She paused, but Lois said nothing, so she continued. "Seems he was in the pub one night, and had had a skinful. Drowning his sorrows, John said. When I asked what sorrows, John said Rob was telling anyone who would listen that Josie had a cop lover who was taking advantage of his position. He said he'd teach the pair of 'em a lesson if he could catch 'em together. They were making a fool of him, Rob said, and he started swinging his fists at all and sundry when they laughed at him."

"So what happened?"

"The landlord calmed him down. John says everybody was really surprised. Rob is such a mild character usually. I thought you'd better know, in case it's helpful in finding out who killed him. If he had violence in him, an' that." Her voice trailed off.

"I don't know what to say, Hazel. I can hardly believe it myself. Not Rob, surely? Still, if John saw it all, it must be true. I'll sound out Josie and see what she says."

"Don't tell her it came from me!" Hazel said in alarm. "We're good friends, see, and she needs me at the moment."

"I'll say it's gossip," said Lois dryly. Of course it was gossip, but she'd have to investigate nevertheless.

Soon after this conversation, when Hazel had time totake off her coat and sort the post properly, she thought over Mrs. M's reaction. Surely she'd have been more worried if Rob had been violent? After all, if he had been beating up Josie, it was cast-iron certain that Mrs. M would have been down there giving the wimp a sorting out he would not forget. Maybe she did know, and was keeping quiet. Hazel picked up the phone to make appointments for Lois to visit the two new potential clients. Then she put it down again. A figure appeared at the door and seemed to hesitate. Hazel saw that it was Josie, and rushed to the door.

"Hi! Come on in. I was just making a coffee. Want some?"

She all but dragged Josie inside and sat her down in a chair. After they were settled, Hazel smiled kindly and said had Josie remembered what she wanted to ask last time she came in?

"What last time?" Josie said. She looked around the room as if she hadn't seen it before, and began to hunt around in her bag.

"Have you lost something?" Hazel asked quietly. She could see that Josie was still in a daze. Probably on tranquillizers or something, she thought.

"Here, Hazel. Have a look at this. I've not shown it to anyone, least of all Mum. Just between us, huh?" She handed Hazel a crumpled piece of paper and Hazel smoothed it out. She peered at the scrawled message. There were dirty splotches on the paper, and the pencil had clearly been blunt.

"Read it out," said Josie, staring at Hazel's face.

"'Them dids got yore Rob. A well wisher.'" Hazel held the paper by one corner and dropped it in her wastepaper basket. "That's the best thing to do with that," she said, thinking privately that she would show it to John. That should convince him.

Josie got up and fished the paper out again. "I don't think so, Hazel," she said. "This may be mischief-making, but on the other hand it may not. I know most of the village want to see the back of the gypsies, and they may be right. Mum knows a bit more about them than she's telling, so I'm not showing her this. God knows, they might be dangerous, and she's a great one for rushing in where cops fear to tread."

"So what use is this? Might just as well chuck it. The last thing we need in Farnden is a lynch mob storming the encampment." Or our fields, she added to herself.

But Josie stuffed it back into her bag, and changed the subject. "How's Andrew Young getting on with his interior décor? Many takers for his skills? He's a nice bloke, Mum reckons."

Hazel replied that he was doing well, and customers seemed to be very satisfied. She wondered how she could return to the subject of Rob and his possible violent streak. How on earth *could* you ask someone if your lately murdered partner had ever beaten you up?

"I expect Mum and Dad will be looking around for a suitable substitute for Rob," Josie said flatly.

"Josie!" Hazel was shocked. "Of course they won't. They would never be so insensitive. And anyway, Mrs. M doesn't interfere in people's private lives. Unless it affects the business of course. Whatever made you say that?"

"If they won't, Gran will," Josie said, and this time Hazel was relieved to see the trace of a smile. "Maybe she'll match me up with Andrew Young. Good for business, that would be. Shop and New Brooms all under Meade management. That should please Mum. She is a bit of a control freak, you know."

Hazel was incensed. She knew it was really none of her business, but she launched into a great defence of Lois. "And as for interfering, did she ever mention to you what the rest of the village suspected? That the customer was more than right when he happened to be a young and handsome police sergeant?" She could have bitten her tongue out, but it was too late. And in the end it was the answer to her difficult problem. Stung into a tearful outburst, Josie stood up and yelled at Hazel.

"Mind your own bloody business, Hazel Thornbull! I expect it was you and your village chums who made sure Rob knew about my so-called secret assignations with Matthew Vickers down in the old cottage! God, nothing's private in Farnden! If you and the gossips hadn't been so busy, Rob might be alive today!"

Hazel watched as Josie flung out of the office, scattering papers and leaflets in all directions. Well done, she told herself, what a splendid friend and listening ear I turned out to be.

ELEVEN

The parish council assembled in the newly restored Reading Room for its monthly meeting. The usual cross section of people, including Derek Meade, were all democratically elected and all were present, except one. Young farmer John Thornbull, husband of Hazel, had sent a message saying he would be late. A cow was in difficulty calving and he'd have to see it safe.

The chairperson, Mrs. Tollervey-Jones, was sympathetic. "I am sure we all understand," she said. "We shall hope to see John soon. There is an item on the agenda which would be best discussed with him present."

"Gypsies," said Sam Stratford gruffly. His father had been a popular parish council candidate for the villagers whose families had lived in Farnden for generations. Sam now lived in Waltonby, where there was no parish council, but a parish meeting, and he was the Waltonby representative in Farnden. It was generally held that he was a good bloke, spoke his mind, and was well endowed with common sense.

"Thank you, Sam," said Mrs. T-J. "We will have a full and frank discussion on the matter later."

Minutes were read and agreed. Matters arising included the serious recurring problem of Miss Truelove's knickers. These were of Directoire design, and periodically vanished from her washing line and were found draped over a thorn bush down the fields. It was a traditional village sport for the kids living nearby, and though everyone knew who the thieves were, no one stopped them.

The only one present at the meeting with a straight face was Mrs. T-J, who promised to pursue the matter personally. And even she hid her face with vigorous nose blowing when Derek said they'd never catch a knicker thief. Too clever by half, he said.

They were nearly at the end of the agenda when John Thornbull arrived, full of apologies. He was welcomed, and sat down next to Derek.

"You can catch up later on what's been decided so far, John," Mrs. T-J said, "and now we have the last item to discuss."

"Gypsies," repeated Sam Stratford.

"Thank you, Sam," Mrs. T-J said, in the voice of a nursery school teacher. She gave a brief account of the gypsies' arrival on Smith's scrubby piece of ground by the road, said they were camping illegally on grounds of health and safety, but Smith refused to evict them, or even authorise their eviction. It was the duty of the parish council to represent the whole community, and they had to treat this matter as urgent. Many people in the village had complained. Many were connecting their presence with the recent case of violence to a parishioner, namely Rob Wilkins.

She paused and looked at Derek. "I should, of course, have started by expressing our sympathies to your daughter at the cruel loss of her, um, er, partner," she added. "Perhaps you would convey them to her?"

"Can we get on, Chairman?" said Sam Stratford. He could see that soon there would be no time to get down to the pub before it closed. And he was not leaving until the matter of the gypsies had been dealt with.

"Perhaps you would like to give us your views, then?" replied Mrs. T-J icily.

"Simple," pronounced Sam. "Evict 'em. Easily done. One of them companies that does it in twenty-four hours."

"And who pays?" said Derek. "Old Smith wouldn't stump up. He likes them being there. I suggest one of us goes to see him. Points out the problems with the village, and the further steps we can take."

"Such as what?" said Sam.

"Oh, there's plenty can be done," chipped in the latest member of the council, an incomer lawyer from the new houses in Blackberry Gardens.

"No need for that," said Sam. "If nobody's willin' to pay, I could get a few together who would do the job for nowt. *And* the dids'd not come back," he added grimly.

"For God's sake, Sam," Derek remonstrated. "You're talking about vigilantes. We don't want none of that in Farnden."

"Exactly, Derek," Mrs. T-J said magisterially.

"I'd like to volunteer," Derek continued, "to tackle old Alf Smith."

"And I'll come with you," said Sam enthusiastically. "I reckon I could talk to him straight."

"Yes, well," Mrs. T-J said. "Perhaps we should take a vote on it. Anyone else like to volunteer? Two of us may be more than enough."

"I don't mind going with Derek," John Thornbull said. "After all, I've got a couple of dids working on my farm."

"You've *what?*" said Sam.

"I'm not sure whether that's a good idea, John," Mrs. T-J said. "After all, you are a councillor and we are discussing the possible eviction of the gypsies. It might be as well if you took a backseat for the moment."

"Rubbish!" said the parish clerk, not in the least overawed by his chairperson, as she insisted on being titled, sitting next to him. "If John went, we might get a balanced view. I vote for him."

"You don't have a vote," said Sam sharply. "You're not an elected member. So why don't you pipe down."

Derek could see the clerk's colour rising and butted in quickly. "If you agree, the rest of you, I think it'd be best if I went to see Alf on my own. He's not an easy man, an' he'd be bound to say he was being intimidated if two of us went."

"Good solution," said Mrs. T-J gratefully. "All in favour?"

All put up their hands, except Sam Stratford, who looked firmly at his boots.

After Mrs. T-J had gone back home to Farnden Hall, the others stayed chatting in the reading room. Sam looked around at the fresh paint and the framed portraits of Sir Henry and Lady Villiers, who had given the room to the village.

"My granddad used to play billiards here in the old days," Sam said. "All the lads played, and you could get a cup of tea for a penny. I remember him sayin' how they all hated it when the squire insisted on bringing a couple of tinker boys to play with them. They were good, too, Granddad said. No wonder, he said, with all that shootin' rabbits an' that. Got their eye in, didn't they?"

"He was like that, old Sir Henry. A man before his time, I reckon," John Thornbull said. "Anyway, Sam, tinkers trap rabbits, not shoot them, don't they? Sir Henry weren't against a bit of poaching now and then. Plenty for everybody, he used to say to my great-granddad. He was gamekeeper on the estate for years."

"A lot o' stupid ideas about lovin' your neighbour and that rubbish," Sam snapped. He turned away and called back to Derek, "Buy you a pint, mate?"

"You're on, boy," Derek replied, and the two old friends went off silently to the pub.

Alf Smith sat at the open door of Athalia Lee's caravan, contentedly smoking his pipe. He had been there for an hour or so, chatting, or just watching the others as they went about their business. They were used to him, grateful to him for allowing them to camp where their forefathers had stayed for as long as anyone could remember on their way to Appleby horse fair.

"Cup of tea, Alf?" Athalia said, coming to the door. She and Alf Smith had been friends for years, and Alf reckoned he had tinker blood. He remembered his grandmother talking about her mother, who had, before her marriage to a local farmer, travelled about. The men in her mother's family, grandma had said, were tinsmiths, making big tin cans for carrying all sorts of stuff from place to place. Alf had taken the trouble to learn quite a bit of the Romany language, and was accepted by them as a good friend.

The two sat drinking tea and watching a couple of baby rabbits playing in the undergrowth. "They'll be ready for the pot when we come back," Athalia said.

"If they're still around," Alf replied. "There's several in this village fond of rabbit pie."

"I expect we get blamed," Athalia said. "And now we're suspected of murdering an innocent walker in the night, so I hear. Is it safe for us here, Alf? Should we be on the move?"

Alf shook his head. "You'd just look guilty then. Runnin' away. The police'd be after you in no time. No, best stay here and answer their questions. Not all the village is against you."

Silence fell again. Then Athalia got to her feet. "Better be goin', Alf," she said. "George's gone to Tresham market, and he'll be back soon, rarin' hungry. And thanks for coming," she added, touching him lightly on the shoulder. "Oh, and by the way, who's that Missus Meade? Is she . . .?

Alf's face darkened. "Why?"

"She came here asking after a dog she nearly ran over. Had a cup of tea. Seemed nice enough."

"Have a care, Athalia. She's a snooper. Unpaid, so they say, but works with the cops. Known for it."

"Oh. Shame. I liked her. Still, thanks Alf. I'll watch it if she comes here again."

TWELVE

Derek had gone into Tresham to pick up some spares, and decided to call in on Alf Smith on his way back. He and Sam Stratford had had an argument about the gypsies last night in the pub. It had always been the custom to carry on important discussions away from the despotic chairmanship of Mrs. T-J. Nothing like a pint in the hand to sharpen the wits, Derek had said to Sam. But this time no agreement had been reached. Sam had been adamant. Gypsies were thieving vagrants, lawless and alien, and the sooner they were moved on the better. Derek had pointed out that they would be gone soon anyway. They were on their way to Appleby for the horse fair.

Now, as he pulled up slowly in Alf's farmyard, he remembered his gaffe. Sam had asked him how he knew they were going soon, and he had floundered about, not mentioning Lois and her old gypsy woman. He knew from Sam's face that he had been suspicious, though the conversation had been interrupted by the campaigning vicar and they had not returned to it.

He knocked at the back door, and Edwina Smith answered it. "Hello, Derek!" she said, surprised because Alf had not said an electrician was needed.

"No, I've not come on business," Derek said. "Is Alf about? I'd just like a word. Parish council stuff an' that."

Edwina's eyes narrowed. "Ah, then I know what it's about," she said. "You'll not get him to evict the gypsies, you know. He's practically one of 'em! Spends hours down there listenin' to their stories. They're on their way to Appleby this time. Alf's thinking of goin' with them again, but I don't reckon they'll want him."

"Right," said Derek. "Still, I'd like a word if he's around."

"Up in Junuddle," she said. "With the sheep."

Fortunately Derek knew that Junuddle was a field on the way to Waltonby. The origins of the name were lost in the mists of time. A historian who had lived in the village had been keen to research field names and had come across others for the village farmland. None of these were subsequently used by farmers or villagers, but they continued to talk about Junuddle without having the faintest idea what it meant.

Derek found Alf checking the water troughs, and was greeted warmly. "Good God, boy, it must be urgent for you to come trekking up here!" he said.

"Yeah, well, it is really," Derek said. He carefully avoided saying it was parish council business this time. "You got ten minutes for a chat?"

Alf frowned. "You don't fool me, Derek Meade," he said. "I know there was a parish council meeting last night, and I saw the agenda on the notice board outside the school. Item eight: illegal travellers."

"Clever bugger," Derek said, and they both laughed. "I drew the short straw and here I am to talk about it."

"Well, first of all, they're not them New Age travellers. They're gypsies, or tinkers. Second, they're not illegal, because they're on my land and I like them being here. And thirdly, what were these so-called complaints? They been coming through this village for generations, and haven't hurt a fly. Except maybe a few rabbits and hares, and they got my permission. So you can report that back to the old bag up at the hall. Now," he added, "why don't we go back to the house and try my missus's primrose wine, and forget all about my gypsies. Blimey, Derek, if you go back far enough, you'd be evicting me, too!"

They walked back to the house, and Derek tried to explain that the laws on eviction were not as simple as that. Health and safety could be involved. They had no clean water, no sanitary arrangements. And none of the children went to school.

Alf exploded. "Health and b-b-bloody safety!" he stuttered. "We're living in a police state, Derek boy. Those families in caravans are more healthy than we are. Fresh air, fresh food, hygienic in their own laws, that's why. Mind you, Athalia was telling me the new generation eat all kinds of ready-made rubbish from supermarkets. As for school, they learn all they need to know from the old ones."

Derek sighed. "You don't really believe that, Alf," he said. "Education is important. But on top of all that, there could be danger from some of the village people. You know as well as I do there's some as would take the law into their own hands."

"Let 'em try," Alf said, frowning, and he opened the door and called for his wife.

"Some of your primrose, me duck," he said. "There's a lad here as needs some lead in his pencil."

"Speak for y' self," said Derek, and sipped the wine that tasted like nectar. He knew he was defeated, and did not particularly care.

As Derek walked out to his van, he looked to one side into the scrubby wood. He could see long caravans clustered in a semicircle, with one small, dingy one off to one side, deeper into the wood. There were school-age children playing with a puppy on a string round the ashes of a fire in front of the caravans. He could see they were teasing it with a dead mouse, throwing it and then picking it up before the puppy could reach it. Derek smiled. The kids were having a good time, and the puppy was wagging its stumpy tail. Not a bad life, he thought, but then reconsidered. These kids would grow up ignorant and resentful, fearful and exiled from what was now reckoned to be a decent life.

On an impulse he walked along a path at the back of the caravans, listening and looking, and found himself approaching the one set apart. Two dark-faced men with caps pulled down over their eyes were sitting on the caravan steps, and one held a straining brindled bull terrier, all muscles and sharp teeth. It growled menacingly when it saw Derek.

One of the men stood up and glared. "What d'ya want? This is private land."

"But not yours," Derek said bravely. Perhaps he could have a conversation with these men and gain some insight into the situation. He was soon disabused of that idea.

"Bugger off, before I set this 'ere dog on ya!"

The other man stood up, and the menacing threesome began to walk towards Derek. No point in being a hero, Derek convinced himself rapidly. He turned around and walked rapidly back towards his vehicle, uncomfortably aware of loud mocking laughter as he went.

Gran and Lois were sitting at the kitchen table poring over the local paper. "Look at this," Lois said to Derek as he came in. "Somebody's been putting pressure on our brave boys in the constabulary."

Derek looked at the fuzzy photograph of a couple of lads with their faces shielded being escorted away from what looked very like Farnden playing field and bundled into a waiting police van. The headline, "Guilty of Highway Violence?" spread in large letters across the photograph, and the story beneath said that two young persons had been taken in for questioning in the case of Rob Wilkins, murdered on his way home to Long Farnden village.

"Cops wrong as usual, if you ask me," Gran said. "It's as clear as daylight them gypsies did it. It'll be difficult sorting out which one. They all stick together like fish glue. But it certainly wasn't those kids. One of them comes from a good home. His mother belongs to the WI."

"That clinches it then," said Lois acidly.

"Has Josie heard about this?" Derek said.

"We don't know. Only just seen the story," said Lois. "If she hasn't heard nothin', then it'll take some explaining." She gave Derek a kiss on the cheek. "Time I had a word with Cowgill," she said.

Derek sighed and Gran frowned, but Lois ignored them and went off into her office to make the call.

THIRTEEN

Hello, Lois!" Hunter Cowgill had a hard day, and he brightened when he heard Lois's voice. He motioned away the young police-woman who had just arrived in his office and signalled to her to shut the door as she went.

"I expect you'll be able to explain," said Lois without preliminaries.

"Explain what, my dear?"

"You know perfectly well. The story in the local. Two kids dragged away from the playing fields, suspected—"

"Not suspected of anything," interrupted Cowgill briskly. "Merely taken along to the police station for questioning. Their parents were, of course, with us."

"How come we didn't know?" Lois had checked with Josie before telephoning Cowgill, and discovered that the first her daughter had heard of it was when she opened the local paper on the counter in the shop.

Cowgill did some rapid thinking. This was only a very early stage in questioning, and the newspaper as usual had made a meal of it. He would like to know who had tipped off the photographer. At the same time, the last thing he wanted to do was alienate Lois, his Lois, and he prepared to eat humble pie.

"I do apologise, my dear," he said. "I should have had a reas-suring word with Josie. And you know, Lois, I tell you everything in due course."

There was silence from Lois. Cowgill was alarmed. He could not lose his contact with her, firstly from a professional point of view, and secondly, well, that as well.

"I'll meet you at the shop at eight o'clock." Lois said finally, looking at her watch. "You can clear up a few cases and still get there in time. Then you can fill us in with what's been happening. 'Bye."

She put down the phone, sadly aware that he had her over a barrel— in a manner of speaking. This crime had invaded her own family and there was no possibility of her giving up. Her usual weapon had lost its power this time. This time it was possible that she needed him more than he needed her. But nothing would induce her to admit it.

Josie saw her mother marching down the street, and opened the door to greet her, but Lois spoke first.

"Is he here? No, don't answer that question. I can see he's not. His car's not here."

"Well, actually, I am here," said Cowgill, appearing from the dilapidated car park round the back of the shop. "I thought it might be better to park away from prying eyes."

"No need for that!" Lois said sharply. "This is a purely official visit from a police detective to the victim of a family tragedy. Nothing else."

Josie stared at her mother. "Am I permitted to offer the officer a cup of coffee, then, Mum?" she said. Cowgill smiled. Young Josie was a chip off the old block.

"Of course you are," he said, "and I'd be very happy to accept. Shall we go in, Lois?"

It was on the tip of Lois's tongue to say her name was Mrs. Meade, and would he kindly not forget it. But then she realised she was being ridiculous, and meekly followed the other two into the shop. They climbed the stairs up to the tiny flat, and Lois said she would make the coffee while the other two chatted. She would be able to hear from the galley kitchen.

"And you can begin by explaining what's going on with those kids in the paper," she said to Cowgill.

Cowgill explained that there had been a complaint from Farnden about a gang of no-goods meeting every night at the back of the village hall on the playing fields. Substances had been mentioned. They had threatened the vicar, who had tried to clear them off the premises, and he had reported the incident to the police.

"So the newspaper put two and two together and made five, as is their custom," he said, patting Josie's hand. "Only possibly connected to the sad demise of your Rob," he added.

"If that was all it was," Lois said crossly, handing round mugs of coffee, "your lot wouldn't have moved in and bundled them off to the police station. A warning to them and their parents would have been a first step, surely. Are you keeping something from us, Hunter?" she added, using his name to annoy him. Well, if he could use hers. . . .

"A violent threat to an innocent citizen *is* a police matter, Lois," he answered.

"I think we'll have to accept that, Mum, for the moment," said Josie. "It is nice of you, Inspector, to come and explain. I did want to ask if you've had any other leads?" She smiled at him winningly, and Lois scowled. Surely Josie wasn't taken in by his switched-on charm?

Cowgill looked at Lois. "Well, yes," he said reluctantly. "There have been the usual anonymous messages to us in Tresham."

"Like this one?" Josie said, producing the creased note she had shown Hazel.

"What's that?" Lois said, taking it from her, reading it and then passing it on to Cowgill.

He sighed. "I am afraid we have had one or two like this. Looks like the same handwriting. Would you mind if I kept this, Josie?"

"No, of course not," Josie said.

At the same time, Lois chipped in firmly. "And we'd like a copy, please. Here," she added, taking it from Cowgill and giving it back to Josie. "Go and photocopy it on your machine." Josie obediently left the room, and Cowgill's face dropped the official expression.

"You look lovely when you're angry," he said, and Lois practically spat at him.

"Do you want my help or not?" she said.

He reached out and touched her shoulder. "What do *you* think, Lois?" he said, serious now. "I'll get the villain who murdered Rob if it's the last thing I do. And it may be exactly that," he added. "Don't think I underrate the possible dangers."

Lois shivered. The sight of Cowgill's calm, confident face smashed into a pulp flashed in front of her eyes, and she gulped. "Okay, then," she said. "Let's be friends, if only for Josie's sake."

"What's for my sake?" Josie said, returning with the letter and its copy.

"Everything we can possibly do to help," Cowgill said smoothly.

"Could we talk about the gypsies?" Lois said. "If all these anonymous notes are blaming that lot camped in Alf Smith's wood, I suppose you're going to do something about it?"

"Of course we must, Lois," he said. "But if you could give us any help on that, we'd be most grateful. Perhaps drop in and see Athalia Lee again? She's a good soul, and nothing that goes on in their encampment escapes her notice."

"What d'you mean, go and see her *again*?" Lois snapped.

Cowgill answered obliquely, annoying Lois even more. "I am good at my job, Lois, just as you are at yours. Now, I must be going." He turned to Josie. "I'll do my best to keep you up to date with how we are proceeding," he said. "And any help you can give your mother will also be most welcome."

He negotiated the narrow stairs with admirable agility, and was gone almost immediately.

"He's quite nice really, Mum," Josie said thoughtlessly.

FOURTEEN

Athalia Lee was washing clothes in a tub of rainwater at the back of her caravan. She was happiest without four walls around her, and along with the others preferred to sit outside round a fire, eating and drinking and telling stories. Skinning rabbits, plucking chickens, chopping vegetables, all were best done outside in the open air and the sun, or in the bender tent when it rained. She stuck to the old ways of housekeeping, washing and rinsing her clothes in rainwater collected for the purpose, never using tap water to wash the children's hair, or her own, and loving the silky shine of it when it dried in the sun. Not that there was any alternative in the old days, or even now. They had no available tap water, except on designated sites, which were much disliked by many true gypsies. Running streams and springs were good water, and the traditional camping places located accordingly.

Lois rounded the corner of the caravan and smiled. It was like a painting. Athalia with her hair screwed into a knot at the back of her head, her brown arms bare in the task of washing, scrubbing and squeezing. Her long skirt was splashed with water, and her old shoes muddy from the ground around the tub. Her eyes were bright when she saw Lois.

"So you come back, did ya? That's the girl. Come and help me lay out these clothes to dry and then we'll have a cup of tea. You liked my tea, I recall."

The clothes were spread out on bushes round the camp, and then Athalia and Lois sat in rickety chairs on the scrubby grass outside the caravan, holding mugs of steaming tea.

Lois was painfully aware of suspicious eyes on her from the gypsies who passed. A small group of children stood and stared, unashamed. Athalia clapped her hands and said something in their own language, and they flew away like startled sparrows.

"So you come to ask me some questions," Athalia said comfortably. "I reckon you didn't want my recipe for stew. It was your daughter's man who was killed, wasn't it." These were statements, not questions, and Lois nodded. This was a woman after her own heart. Straight to the point and no messing about.

"You know what they're saying in the village, then," she said, looking Athalia in the eye. "Them as don't like gypsies are blaming one of your lot. Meself, I'm not so sure. But I do know that nobody in Farnden is going to speak up for you if it comes out that it could've been one of your men."

"So why are *you* any different?"

"I'm not interested in whether the bloke what killed Rob was black, white or rainbow coloured. Nor whether he was a yobbo, an Irish traveller or a gypsy. All I want to know, and pretty damn quickly, is what coward attacked a man on a dark, lonely road for no reason."

"Might not have been a he," Athalia said, shooing away a skinny cat twining around her ankles. "Could've been a woman. An' there must've been a reason."

Lois stared at her. She'd not once thought of a woman. "Have to have been a strong woman," she said.

"Like yerself," said Athalia. She watched Lois's face and burst out into throaty laughter. "We get to be canny, Lois Meade," she said. "We been on the run for generations. No good believin' anybody. Go on, then," she added, "ask me a question."

Lois settled back in her chair, which lurched violently to one side. She had trouble righting it, and could not help smiling at the giggling children who were back on watch.

"How much do you know about this whole nasty business?" she asked, finally upright. "Any of your number got reason to have a go at Rob? What about those two working for Thornbulls? My Derek was in the pub when they came in asking for work, and he said they weren't exactly welcomed."

Athalia answered the questions with one of her own. "Who's that Sam Stratford? He don't live in Farnden, do he. Is he a friend of your man?"

"All the men in the pub are mates, more or less," Lois replied. "Except the vicar, maybe. He's a bit out of kilter in there, bless him, with his half a shandy and a packet of plain crisps."

Athalia laughed again. "At least we don't go a-lookin' for recruits," she said. "It ain't easy to get to be a gypsy, y' know. Very particular, we are. Some of us are Christians, o' course. But not his churchy kind."

"So they told you about the pub, did they, those two?"

"O' course. We know everything that goes on, Mrs. Meade. We have to. Now, don't look round, but there's a couple of our men as you must steer clear of. No good sending a posse of villagers down here to tackle them! Leave 'em well alone. Ask your Derek, an' he'll tell you I'm saying the truth."

"Derek?" said Lois. "But why . . ." At this moment the two men who had threatened Derek walked round the end of the caravans, the bull terrier tugging at the old rope restraining it. They stopped suddenly and muttered to each other, staring at Lois. The dog started towards her, and they pulled it back, wrenching its thick neck, which clearly felt nothing. Its growl was like something out of a horror movie. Athalia shouted sharply at the men, and they turned off in a different direction, calling back to her in angry words that Lois did not understand.

"Better be off now, Mrs. Meade," the gypsy woman said. "I reckon you got the answers to your questions. Come again, then, gel. And don't be scared of them two. People in this camp do what I tell 'em. You'll be all right. But I can't say as much for any others who come."

"Is that a gypsy's warning?" said Lois, getting to her feet. Athalia emptied the tea leaves on the ground and chuckled.

"You'll do," she said.

FIFTEEN

There's a quiz tonight at the pub," Derek said. He hesitated, not sure how to put what he was about to say.

"And you've got a vacancy on your team," said Lois flatly.

"Yep," he replied, relieved that she understood at once. "We shall miss our Rob. He was good on general knowledge, an' he knew quite a bit about art an' that."

"Well if you're going to ask me to take his place, you've got the wrong one! My general knowledge ain't good, and what I know about art an' that would fit on the back of a postage stamp."

Gran laughed. The three were standing by the kitchen window, watching the little dog Jeems chasing a chicken that had strayed into the garden from the neighbouring farm.

"Up she goes!" Lois said, as the chicken finally remembered it had wings and could get off the ground enough to clear the fence and escape into the field.

Gran went back to a saucepan bubbling on the Rayburn. "What about Sam's son for the team?" she said. "He's moved back to Waltonby with his wife, so Sheila's got all the family around her! Always was the mother hen type. Strong person, though. Didn't the son go off to university, Lois? Should be knowledgeable on all sorts of things."

Sheila Stratford, Sam's wife, was one of Lois's most reliable cleaners, and a proud mother of her clever son. He had married a girl of whom Sheila disapproved. "It wouldn't have mattered who she was, she'd not be good enough for your son," Sam had said to her.

Now Lois agreed that it was worth asking Alan Stratford. "He used to be a nice kid," she said. "Mind you," she added, "three years at Birmingham Uni could change a person."

"Possibly for the better," Derek said. "Good idea, Gran. I'll give Sam a ring right away."

The pub was crowded already at seven o'clock when Derek and Lois arrived. She had decided to come along and see how Alan got on with the questions. He had agreed with alacrity to join the team, and Derek noted that the lad had not even had to consult his new wife. Good for him, he'd thought. Start as you mean to go on. Derek reflected wryly that from the very beginning of his own marriage he had needed to consult Lois on everything, that is if he knew what was good for him.

Derek ordered drinks, and Lois saw Sheila beckoning from a corner table. "Good luck, then," she said, giving Derek a peck on the cheek. He joined his teammates and in due course the quiz began.

The pub quizzes had been taking place for some years, and were well organised by a couple who compiled the questions, set the rules and gave prizes. Since they were invited to a good number of pubs in the county, it was worth their while, and a nice little earner, as Sam said. Derek's team was one of eight, all teams having quirky names chosen for mysterious local knowledge reasons. His team was known as the Chargers, after a gang of playground heavies who had ruled the village school when three of its members were Mixed Infants.

"They haven't changed much, have they, Sheila?" Lois said now. "There's your Sam, Derek and young Alan, all been to the village school and still determined to be top dogs. Only difference is that now they're in the pub instead of the playground!"

Sheila agreed, and said that she could quite see them charging anybody who dared to challenge them. She laughed, but noticed that Lois did not join her. In fact, Lois was frowning and staring across the bar, where a couple of dark-faced men were standing.

"Are we ready now, teams?" said the question master, whose name was Ross. "Ross the Boss," he said, as he always said. "My decision on answers is final. Same for all, so quite fair. Now sirs," he added, looking across at the gypsy men, who had picked up their drinks and were making for a corner table. "Won't you join us? A couple more—how about you two ladies?—and we'll have another team."

"God, no!" whispered Sheila to Lois. "Sam would kill me," Lois remembered that when she started New Brooms she had thought Sam Stratford was a mild enough sort of man, but maybe he had his moments! Most men did, she thought philosophically.

The two men halted and looked around. A sly smile hovered round the mouth of the tall one, and he called across, "How about it, Mrs. Meade?" She saw it was the man who had taken her to see Athalia Lee and her dog.

Silence fell in the pub, an edgy, tense silence.

"Can't we get on?" Sam said in a loud voice. "We got enough teams without looking for rubbish." He said it as though he was cracking a joke, but the entire gathering knew what he meant, and did not laugh.

Lois stared at him. "Yeah, all right then," she said. "We'll have a go, won't we, Sheila?" She saw Derek frown and turn away.

All looked at Sam Stratford, who started towards his wife. Before he reached her, she stood up and said firmly, "Fine! We'll show 'em how, shall we, Lois?" She added to Lois in an undertone that it would be her fault if Sam belted her when they got home.

Before Lois could ask her whether she was serious, they were all called to order and the quiz started. The two gypsy men introduced themselves as George Price and Jal Boswell, and the questions began, on the usual range of subjects: general knowledge, sports, art, history, politics.

"Now, the Chargers are the number one team. General knowledge, first question: how many bones are there in the human face?"

Blank looks from the Chargers. "I know," whispered Lois to Sheila. "Fourteen! It was on one of them kids' yoghurt pots in the shop. . . ."

"No helpful hints, please!" said Ross, with a good-humoured laugh. He'd have to watch these two women, sensing at once a marital challenge of more importance than a few quiz questions.

The Chargers guessed a few wrong numbers, and had to give up. Ross said fourteen was the right answer and then moved on. Other questions were asked, and then it was the new recruits' turn. "Have you decided on a name for your team?" asked Ross. "It is not at all necessary, just a bit of fun."

There was a quick consultation, and then the tall gypsy, George, said firmly, "Yes. We are all agreed on the Didikye."

Sam stood up and spluttered, shocked beyond words.

"Very good," said Ross. This was the first time he had encountered this particular problem, but he prided himself on being able to handle all eventualities.

"Your question, then," he went on rapidly, not looking at Sam, or anyone else but the Didikye. "And I must stress that these questions are taken strictly in the order they are printed out in my list. Now, can you tell me the popular name given to the massacre of Jews . . ." he hesitated, and continued, "and others in concentration camps during World War II?"

The entire bar seemed to be holding its breath. Lois felt Sheila's hand slip into hers, and cleared her throat. "The Holocaust," she said, "and the others massacred were mentally ill or disabled people, and gypsies."

"Correct," said Ross, and, exchanging an agonised look with his wife, passed on to the next team.

No more embarrassing questions emerged, but the subsequent jollity of the evening was strained. In the end, the scoring was reasonably even. The big surprise, of course, was how many questions the gypsies were able to answer. The village, as represented by most of those in the pub, had quite decided that they would be without education or knowledge of the wider world. Some dreaded the humiliation for Lois and Sheila, and others looked forward to revealing just what scum the gypsy tribe would prove to be.

The evening proceeded slowly. Every time a question was directed at George or Jal, Sam would begin to cough or shuffle his feet. He was joined by a chorus of coughing, clearing of throats, surreptitious stamping.

"Rough music," whispered the vicar to his wife. Both had come in for the quiz and an evening of socialising with the locals. Father Keith had read books about village life, and knew all about stocks on the green, penitence stools, the burning of witches and summary eviction of undesirables by oaths and threats. He also knew about the banging of pots and pans outside their windows in the dead of night. "Rough music," he repeated.

"Not these days, Keith, for goodness sake!" Marjorie replied.

"Don't be too sure. It's in the village bones," he muttered, as the final round was announced.

Contrary to expectations, Lois, Sheila, George and Jal had not done so badly. They came sixth out of nine teams, largely owing to Lois's addiction to television, and Sheila knowing everything there was to know about football, farming and the contents of the *Reader's Digest* gardening book. Derek's team was beaten into second place by a quartet of incomers from Blackberry Gardens, and prizes were duly distributed.

"Thank you, Mrs. Meade," the tall gypsy said politely, and he and his friend returned to their corner seat. Lois and Sheila, flushed with relative success, subsided rapidly as they saw Sam, Alan and Derek bearing down on them.

"Home!" said Sam, and as Alan began to interrupt him, he grabbed Sheila's arm, picked up her coat, and marched her out of the pub.

All eyes watched them go, and then conversation resumed. Alan asked if he could buy Derek and the others in their team a drink, and Derek said certainly not. *He* would buy the drinks, and congratulated Alan on being a really useful member. "Hope you'll be a fixture with us, lad," he said, and went to order at the bar.

"Don't I get a drink?" Lois called after him.

Alan Stratford jumped up. "Please allow me to get this one," he said with elaborate courtesy. "A brave lady, if ever I saw one. Such a shame Mum had to leave, but then we all know Dad, don't we. What'll you have?"

The gypsy men left soon after, and the company relaxed. Now they could talk freely, and much was said that had been better left unsaid. Lois tried to monitor what she could overhear, and decided opinion was not really divided. The overall consensus was that it would be better if that dirty lot kept to their camping ground. Bad enough that they were there, making a mess and not controlling their wild dogs and wild children. Certainly nobody wanted them invading the hallowed ground of the public bar.

There were frequent glances at Lois, who was coolly drinking her glass of white wine. Whispers were passed around that somebody would have to have a word with Mrs. Meade, and probably Sam Stratford was the man to do it. As for Derek, he sat in a cloud of misery. He had no idea what he should think or do, but just wished the Almighty had sent him a bad dose of flu that had kept him at home, safe in bed with a hot toddy.

SIXTEEN

George and Jal walked in silence through the village, past the shop's security light and the telephone box with its small group of kids loafing about outside.

"Evenin' dids!" said one of the boys, and the others sniggered.

"Don't answer!" hissed Jal. "You got us into enough trouble tonight."

George didn't answer, but just kept on walking at an even pace. Under the one solitary streetlamp in the village, Jal could see that he was smiling.

They were out of the village, almost back at the encampment when the attack came. There were at least half a dozen, armed with sticks and uttering war cries. George turned to face them, pushing Jal behind him.

"Stop!" he shouted, and something in his voice caused the posse to hesitate. George could see they all had stupid masks or balaclava hats pulled down over their faces.

The leader stepped forward, without a mask or hat, and George could swear that it was Sam Stratford, though there was no helpful moonlight and he could not see clearly.

"Too frit to fight?" the leader said. "Yeller! You're not wanted in our village. We'll give you three days to get out. If you're not gone, we'll give you a helping hand!" His followers muttered agreement, and chanted "Get out! Get out!"

George began to laugh. It was the worst thing he could have done, and the gang moved forward. During the uneven struggle, he heard Sam—he was sure it was Sam—say, "For God's sake don't kill 'em! Enough now. Bugger off, all of you!"

Jal was crouching on the road, shivering and muttering, and George helped him up. "Anything serious?" he asked.

" N-n-no," stuttered Jal. "A f-f-f-ew bruises. Let's get back."

At the entrance to the encampment, a shadowy figure awaited them. "Athalia," said George. "Bit of bother back there." She said nothing, but held out her hand, then turned around and beckoned them to follow her. The door of her caravan banged shut, and at the same time all the lights in the site were extinguished. A heavy darkness hid them from sight, and there was no sound except the vicious barking of the bull terrier from the caravan in the wood.

SEVENTEEN
ᴣᴖ

Where have you been?" Sheila sat on a hard chair in her kitchen, a mug of tea in her hand. Opposite was her son Alan, looking nervous.

"No business of yours," Sam said. "Haven't you got no home to go to?" he continued, glaring at his son.

"I'm not leaving until we sort this out. Mum was in tears when I got here. It was only a bit of a lark, Dad. Mrs. Meade started it, and Mum just went along. What harm was there in it?"

Sam sighed, and subsided on to the third chair. "Got a cup of tea goin', gel," he said to Sheila, and touched her hand gently. She bit her lip, put her other hand over his, and said, "O' course there is. I'll boil up the kettle."

"Now, son," Sam said quietly, "there might be no harm in it, but on the other hand there might be. Them two gyppos are working for John Thornbull, and according to him they do a good job. I don't grudge them the work. But they're not like us. Ain't got the same morals, rules of hygiene, or food or mixin' in. Some don't speak our language. If it weren't for that Alf Smith they would have been moved on long ago. It's not a proper site, and if you go and see for yourself, you'll see they've made a real mess of it. The kids don't go to school much, an' their dogs are out of control and vicious."

"So if Alf lets them be, what can you do about it?" Sheila said.

"We can ignore them," said Sam. "If we all ignore them, like we have done in the pub, they'll stop coming in and move on eventually. Probably on the way to Appleby horse fair. They don't stay nowhere for long. That's part of their way of life. Not responsible for anything other than themselves. Don't pay no taxes, don't do anything for the villages they doss down in. You can see why folk don't like them."

"They fought in the war alongside the rest of us, didn't they?" Alan said. "Never recognised for that. An' thousands of 'em were exterminated by Hitler, nor none of the survivors got compensation like the rest. Ignored, as you recommend, Dad."

Alan looked at his father, who was now shaking his head sadly. Time to give him a bit of support. "But they're not saints, Mum," he said. "They poach and thieve and set their dogs on anybody who goes near them. As it happens, I did go past there and thought I'd walk along the old footpath round the back of their camp. A couple of very nasty-looking characters advanced out of a decrepit old caravan, with a snarling bull terrier on a piece of rope."

"What did they say?" Sam said, suddenly alert.

"It was what they did, not what they said," Alan said. "They let that dog go, didn't they. I ran for me life, and I could hear them laughing. Just as the brute was snapping at my heels, one of them whistled and it stopped dead. I kept running. That's your saintly gypsies for you, Mum," he added. He got up and put on his jacket. "Better get back," he said, and waved to both as he left.

In the quiet kitchen Sam and Sheila sat in silence. Then Sheila took Sam's hand again. "I'm sorry," she said. "I know you mean it for the best."

He nodded. "Time for bed," he said. "Not the best evening we've ever had in the pub."

"Sorry," repeated Sheila, and watched his retreating back.

"Oh," she called after him, "and Sam, where *did* you go after we got home?"

Gran was waiting for Derek and Lois to come home, wanting to know the result of the quiz. The moment they walked in she knew something was up. It was doubtful whether they would tell her, so she asked how the quiz went.

"The Chargers came second," Lois said. "Derek was very good, answered a lot of questions. It was interesting."

"Good. And how did Alan Stratford get on?"

"Useful," said Derek.

"Nice chap now," Lois added.

"Right," said Gran. "Thanks for a really full description of quiz night in the village pub. I might as well be off to bed. There's coffee in the pot on the Rayburn. Good night both."

"Hey, wait a minute, Mum," Lois said, sitting down heavily at the table. "You might as well hear it from us, as get a garbled version from the gossips."

"Hear what?" Gran said.

"About the new team on the block," Derek said, taking over. "The Didikye, they call themselves."

"What!" Gran said.

"Team captain, Mrs. Lois Meade."

"That's enough, Derek," Lois said, and gave her mother a fair and accurate account of what happened. She did not spare herself, and said she felt awful about Sheila getting into trouble with Sam.

"But I'm not sorry I agreed to do it," she said. "Them gypsies are a lot better behaved than some of the kids I could name. They keep themselves to themselves."

"I reckon it's the tall one is the stirrer," Derek said. "The little 'un hardly ever speaks. But the tall one looks as if he'd not mind a challenge. Knew a lot, too, Gran. Maybe not a true gypsy."

"Do you reckon it's too late to ring Sheila?" Lois said. "Sam looked as if he might teach her a lesson when they got home."

"He'd not hurt her, Lois," said Gran. "Not Sam Stratford. He may have a sharp tongue, but he's never hurt a fly. Never would."

"Leave it 'til morning, me duck," Derek said. "It'll all look different in the morning."

EIGHTEEN
ॐ

We should be going," Athalia said to George, when they were inside. "I feel it. Surely y' know in your bones when you should move on, when you're not wanted?"

"We're not wanted anywhere," George said. "But at least Alf

Smith doesn't mind us being here. He likes us around, he says."

"Don't be a fool," Athalia replied. "He has this fancy idea that he is a gypsy way back. Likes to think he's one of us."

"Maybe he is," said George. "After all, he wouldn't be the first one to claim Romany ancestry. We're a mixed up lot, aren't we?"

Athalia shook her head. "Only a few of us have married outside," she said. "You of all people should know that. It's not easy once you've done that. Your father found out the hard way."

George drew himself up to his full height and banged his head on the caravan ceiling. This made Athalia laugh, and the tension dispersed. "Yeah, I know," he said, "but we survived. Anyway, we weren't talking about me, we was talking about Alf Smith. He's a good bloke. Wants to come to Appleby with us again. What d'you reckon?"

Athalia shook her head. "He could go by himself this time, but not try to be one of us. You know what the others are like, us being blamed for that murder. Appleby could be a foreign country in fair week. Romany families from all over the world, exchanging news. Appleby folk lock their doors and batten down the hatches. Shops shut, and hotels turn us away. Mind you, I blame us for a lot of it. There's always the bad 'uns. And none of us try to mix in. I remember bein' with my daughter and her dog, crossing the bridge. An elderly woman came by and said something nice about the dog. My girl glared at her and walked on, pulling the dog behind her. Now that wasn't doin' us any good, was it?"

George shook his head. "But about tonight," he began, and gave Athalia a brief account of what happened. "They were waiting for us. Me and Jal going along at our own pace, minding our own business. We'd joined in the quiz in the pub, and caused a lot o' barracking. Then on the way home, kids outside the phone box called out after us, but we kept going. Jal was pulling me along, scared I'd have a go at them! Then there they were, this gang of big kids, waving sticks and shouting."

"Who were they? Did you get a look at them?"

"It was very dark, but I reckon I know the ringleader."

"Who?"

"Can't tell you. Not until I'm sure. Then we'll know what to do."

Athalia shook her head. "We should be moving on," she repeated. "I don't like it at all. Bad things will happen. Listen to what I say, George, and trust an old gypsy woman."

He smiled at her. "We'll go, Athalia," he said, "but not until we're ready."

In a comfortable modern house in Blackberry Gardens, Nancy and Joe Brown turned down the sound on their television and listened. There were unmistakable sounds of their seventeen-year-old son stumbling his drunken way into the kitchen in the dark. Joe turned the sound up again and stared at the screen without taking anything in. His wife, Nancy, got up from her chair. "Shall I go to him?" she said in an anxious voice.

"No. Let him get on with it. I'll sort him out in the morning."

"But he might—"

"Might what? Throw up? Break a leg going upstairs? Whatever happens he deserves it. Leave him alone to suffer. Maybe he'll learn that way."

Nancy said nothing, but sat down again, her hands clenched. She wished for the hundredth time that they had not moved out to this small village. If they'd stayed in Tresham there would have been youth clubs, bowling alleys, all sorts to keep teenagers off the streets. It had been Joe who was keen on the move, just because his ancestors had lived in Long Farnden. They'd been farmers until the family line came to an end. A bad end, as it happened, when his great uncle had gone bust and the farm had been sold. Joe didn't want to farm—he was doing nicely in the property business—but he said he felt the call of the land. Call of the land, indeed! It was as much as Nancy could do to get him to cut the lawns.

To their surprise, the sitting room door opened and a grinning Mark stood there, holding out a pair of muddy boots.

"Get these clean for me, Mum, there's a love," he said. "Got to go for that interview tomorrow, early. Hi, Dad. Dad? Anyone at home?" he added to his father, who had not bothered to look at him.

"Bugger off! And clean your own boots!" Joe said. He turned off the television and stood up. "No, wait a minute," he said. "Where've you been all this time? In the pub, from the look of you. You know what the police said. If you and that no-good friend of yours should catch their eye again you'll be in trouble."

"God, I'm so scared!" Mark said mockingly. "And you'll be pleased to hear me and the rest have been out in the fresh air. Training for the local marathon we are. Your son is fit and strong, just like you wanted." He swayed a little, and put out a hand to steady himself on the door post. "Ready for anything, we are now. We'll show you," he giggled, and until his father slapped him around the face, he was unable to stop.

NINETEEN

Morning, Hazel. You're early?" Lois was still in her dressing gown. It was a slinky satin number that Derek had given her last Christmas, entirely inappropriate, she said, for a working woman running a cleaning business. But she loved it, loved the smooth, slithery feel of it. If only she hadn't gone to the pub last night, if only she'd had a long, scented bath and waited until Derek came home, full of bonhomie and love. . . .

She sighed, and dragged her mind back to Hazel, who was saying she was phoning from home and was very sorry she'd not be able to go to the office, as she had a stomach bug that had now resulted in the trots.

"Sorry, Mrs. M—both ends! I'll let you know how it goes and be in touch later—ooh! Here we go again—'bye!"

Gran was downstairs already, and Lois was drawn towards the kitchen by the irresistible smell of frying bacon. "Morning, Mum," she said. "Looks like I have to go into the Tresham office today. Hazel's poorly. Just as well I haven't got any appointments."

Gran handed her a mug of hot coffee, and a plate of sizzling bacon. "Better get this down you then," she said, "I don't suppose you'll have time for lunch. Oh, yes, and by the way, I lay awake last night for a long time, thinking about Rob and Josie an' that. Nothing much seems to be happening on that front. Have you heard anything from your cop friend?"

"No," Lois said shortly. "But I reckon the village has made up its mind who dunnit."

"Gypsies?"

"Right first time. If the police don't move soon, I reckon there's going to be trouble. Really nasty stuff, Mum."

"What about them roughs from behind the village hall? What happened about them?"

"Nothing, 'sfar as I know. That was a nonstarter, anyway. Knee-jerk reaction from Cowgill, probably." She mopped up delicious bacon fat from the plate with a piece of fried bread and stood up. "Derek's shaving," she said. "I'll go and sort some papers, then I'll be off. Thanks for a healthy breakfast. Yum."

"I'll be seeing Mrs. Pickering this afternoon," Gran called after her. "Might get some useful gossip." What a mess, she thought to herself. And Lois getting in deeper, as usual. "Derek!" she shouted up the stairs. "Breakfast's ready!"

"Hello? Is that you, Elsie?"

"Yes, it's me," said Gran. "Are you poorly?"

"No," Mrs. Pickering said. "You're coming over this afternoon, aren't you? Well, I thought of asking my neighbour in for a cuppa. Would you mind? She's not a bad sort, and has a pig of a husband."

"O' course not," Gran said. "What's her name? I might have met her in the shop."

"Nancy, Nancy Brown. Right then, I'll see you about half past three. Oh, and could you pop into the shop on your way and bring me a packet of those oatie biscuits Josie's got in stock?"

At half past three exactly, Gran rang Pickerings' doorbell. "Come on in, Elsie," Joan Pickering said. "Come and meet Nancy."

Gran's first impression was of a neatly dressed woman, greying hair and a wary look that seemed familiar to Gran.

"Hello, Mrs. Weedon," Nancy said. "You won't know me, but I know you from the shop. I think you were in the stockroom one day when I came in. It's your granddaughter, isn't it, who runs the shop?"

Gran nodded.

"I must say how sorry I was about her—um—partner. What a dreadful thing that was. Are they any nearer to solving . . ." Her voice petered out, and at that moment Gran remembered her. On the front page of the local newspaper, she was standing with her husband behind a couple of youths who had been hauled in for questioning shortly after Rob's death.

"Not that I know," Gran answered. Should she mention the yobs or not? She took a cup of tea from Joan Pickering and accepted an oatie biscuit. Well, as her husband used to say, nothing ventured, nothing gained.

"I've remembered where I saw you before," she said pleasantly, with a big smile, and explained. "I expect one of the lads was yours?"

Joan immediately chipped in with an offer of more tea and a very obvious change of subject. "I've been trying to persuade Nancy to join the WI," she said. "It's good fun, isn't it, Elsie. Back me up. Not jam and Jerusalem anymore."

Nancy looked gratefully at Joan, but turned back to Gran. "To answer your question, yes, one of the lads is mine. Mark. The one with spiky hair and a row of rings through his ear. Thank God the police let them go with a warning. The man who complained wasn't very happy, but I think they got a good scare from the police."

"Is he your only?" Gran asked.

"Yes, more's the pity. We tried and tried, but no luck. So Mark was always very precious. Still is, even though . . ." Her voice trailed away again.

"Is he still at school?" persisted Gran. "Looks older than school, from the picture."

"He's left. Trying to get a job, but who's going to give him one? They take one look and that's it. Don't ring us, we'll ring you. And none of 'em bother to take a look at his CV and see that he did well at school. Very well. Got good results in GCSEs, and then mixed in with a bad lot in the sixth form. I don't mind telling you, Mrs. Weedon, his father and me are pretty desperate."

This is not what Joan Pickering had planned, but she realised quickly that her neighbour needed to talk, and Gran was the perfect listener. At half past four, she began to stack the cups on the tray, and the other two rose to their feet.

"That was very nice, thank you," Nancy said to Joan. "And really nice to meet you, Mrs. Weedon," she added. "Perhaps you'd like to come and have tea with me one afternoon?"

Gran said that would be very nice, and of course Nancy must come up to Meades' house for a coffee or tea soon. "My daughter would like to meet you, I'm sure," she said. "She's got two sons," she added. "Might give you some tips." She smiled kindly, and waved goodbye as Nancy left.

"Well, that was in at the deep end, Elsie," Joan Pickering said.

"I was hoping we could cheer up the poor woman, not remind her of her troubles. We could've talked about gardening, or knitting, or what books we'd been reading."

"Oh, sorry," said Gran, who was not in the least sorry. "Still, I think she got some stuff off her chest. Sounds like a bit of a problem there. What's the father like?"

Joan Pickering shrugged. "Don't know much about him," she said. "I've seen him over the garden fence several times, I suppose. And I've heard him shouting once or twice. Probably at that Mark. Sounds like he deserves a clip round the ear."

"Bet you never clipped your Floss round the ear."

"No, well, but she's a girl, isn't she? And as for her father, well, Floss's dad has never been violent, but he's done a good deal of shouting over the years. I reckon the Browns will sort themselves out. Anyway," she added, "how much do I owe you for the biscuits?"

Lois, meanwhile, was bored. She'd been sitting in the shop all day, and apart from three or four potential clients, she had seen nobody, and nothing was going on in Sebastopol Street outside. She looked at her watch. Another hour to go. Hazel was so efficient there was no filing or paperwork to do. Maybe she would ring up somebody. Gran? Out to tea. Derek? Busy at work. Josie? Ah yes, it would be useful to talk to Josie. She seemed pretty stable at the moment, but Lois was not sure what was going on inside.

"Hello? Long Farnden village shop. Can I help you?" Josie's light, attractive voice was full of friendliness and efficiency. No wonder the shop was doing so well.

"It's Mum. I'm stuck in Sebastopol and have run out of jobs. So I'm ringing to bother you and find out how you are. Just say if the shop's full. Customers come first."

"No, I can spare a minute or two," Josie said. "Not like you, Mum, to have time to spare. Anyway, I'm glad you rang. I've just had Gran in on her way back from tea with Mrs. Pickering. Apparently another Blackberry resident was there. Mrs. Brown, from number seven. Seems she and Gran had a good old chin-wag. Gran was full of it. Poor woman is the fond mama of one of those louts who lurk behind the village hall. She and her unsympathetic husband are at their wits' end, apparently. Their precious Mark is, according to her, a reluctant dropout with all the nasty habits to match."

"Was he one of those taken in by Cowgill?" Lois said immediately.

"Yep, seems so. Of course they were released without charge, weren't they? But I reckon we could do with a bit of ferretin' into the squalid lives of those charming delinquents."

"Right. Glad I rang, Josie. We'll have to get Gran to invite her new friend to tea and a spot of interrogation."

"Already done," said Josie, and her light laugh gladdened Lois's heart. "Next Tuesday afternoon, three thirty, with a promise of chocolate cake. You're invited, Mum."

Twenty

Monday, and the New Brooms team was gathering for their weekly meeting. Cleaning schedules were fixed, and updates were included on Andrew's work with interior décor clients. His assignments were increasing, and he was beginning to wonder if perhaps soon he would need an assistant.

"How's Josie?" he asked, when they were all settled in their seats, facing Lois and waiting for her to begin.

"She's doing very well, thanks, Andrew. Doesn't talk much about Rob, but I suppose that's normal. She has a demanding job to do, and seems to have decided it's best to get on with it."

"I think she will," said Hazel. "Talk about Rob, I mean. She's been in the office on the point of saying *something*, then rushed out again. Must be difficult for her, poor lamb."

"Any news on who did it?" Sheila Stratford asked bluntly. Her Sam had clammed up on any conversation about Rob's murder, except to say he couldn't believe those bloody gypsies were still in the village.

"Time to get on with the meeting," Lois said briskly. "Now then, shall we go through the schedules?"

Everything seemed to be going like clockwork, and Lois thanked her lucky stars that at least there were no problems with the business. As they were getting to their feet and preparing to leave, the doorbell rang, and Lois heard Gran going to answer it. "No thank you, not today," she heard Gran say. "We don't need more pegs these days, what with the drier an' that."

Lois rushed out in time to call Athalia back from halfway down the drive. "Please come in a minute, will you?" she called.

Athalia hesitated. "You're busy, Mrs. Meade."

"We're finished. Please, come in for a minute."

"I'll go round to the kitchen door," Athalia answered, and Lois heard Gran muttering that she wasn't having dirty feet in her kitchen.

When Lois had seen off the team, she went through and found Athalia standing outside the kitchen door, with Gran at the sink looking mutinous.

"Please come in," Lois said firmly, and to Gran's very obvious disapproval, escorted Athalia into her office and shut the door.

"Sit down, please. I've been wanting to talk to you again, and I'm sure you didn't come here to sell pegs."

Athalia nodded. "Quite right," she said. "I want you to tell me something about that rumpus the other night. When George and Jal were set upon by a gang and roughed up."

"What makes you think I know anything about it?"

"Because George is sure Samuel Stratford was the leader, and his woman works for you. We have to know, Mrs. Meade, because next time it could be much worse."

Lois did some quick thinking. How much should she tell Athalia? That Sam Stratford was a bigoted racist of the kind that unfortunately still held some influence in the locality? Or that Sam Stratford was a nice bloke, good worker, kindhearted to his neighbours and friends? A pillar of society and a loyal parish councillor? All were true. She decided to ask a question instead.

"Did they tell you about the quiz?" she said.

Athalia nodded. "A mistake, Mrs. Meade. It is always best for us to keep ourselves private, stick with our kind and not try to mix in. I believe it was you agreed to join with George and Jal in the quiz? Well, I ask you not to do that kind of thing again. It ain't no help, whatever you might think. Now, are you going to answer my question about Samuel Stratford?"

"If you will answer one or two of mine."

"Let's hear them, then."

Lois asked for more information about the two gypsies with the bull terrier. "Young Alan Stratford saw them and received the same grim greeting as I did. Is it possible they could be really violent?"

"If you mean did they attack your Rob, I don't know. I can't think why they should bring down trouble on themselves without anything to gain. Poaching, yes. Trespass, yes. Thieving, even. But not murder. I could almost stake my life on that."

"Almost?"

"Nothing absolutely certain in this life, Mrs. Meade. My mother used to tell fortunes, and she would always say that. Mind you, people never listen. They believe what they want to believe, and I know opinion is against us. I have told George we should move on, but he won't. We may have to leave him behind. Appleby fair is getting closer. So what about Samuel Stratford."

"Why do you call him Samuel?"

"Because that's his given name. I happen to know that."

"Right, well, a bargain's a bargain," said Lois, and gave Athalia as fair and balanced account as she could of the Sam Stratford she knew.

"We had a visitor this morning," Gran said to Derek at supper time.

Lois glared at her. Really, Gran was getting more uppity every day. Perhaps she should have a word with her. Lois looked at the steaming steak and kidney pie on the table, the gleaming saucepans hanging over the Rayburn, the quarry tiles polished to a warm red glow, and knew that she could not do anything of the sort. Her mother shared this home with them equally now, and she certainly earned her keep. She was entitled to say anything she liked, within reason.

"Who was that, then, me duck?" Derek said, looking suspiciously at Lois. He knew at once that whoever the visitor had been, Gran had disapproved.

"It was a gypsy, selling pegs," Lois said innocently. "Gran told her we didn't need any."

To her surprise, Gran said nothing more. Derek said only that he reckoned washing pegged on a line in the garden was much fresher than in a tumble drier.

"Douglas stopped and talked to me this morning," he said, changing the subject. "He was on his way to a client, and saw the van. We had a half in the pub in Waltonby. Seems him and Susie are close to setting a date for the wedding. In the autumn, they reckon, probably end of September. There'll be a lot for you to do, me duck, so you'd better leave your spare time clear. Once Cowgill has pulled his finger out and found Rob's killer, best not to do any more ferretin'."

Lois bridled. "It'll be Susie's Mum doing the organising," she said. "We shall help, of course, but the main job is done by the bride's parents. We could offer to pay for the drink, maybe. I don't think they've got many pennies to spare."

The telephone rang, and Gran looked at the clock. "Who's that at this hour?" she said.

"It's not late, Mum," Lois said, getting up to answer it. "We don't batten down the hatches at eight o'clock, do we?"

"Hello? Who's that?" Lois's mouth was full of pie, and Cowgill was not sure at first that he had the right number.

"May I speak to Mrs. Meade, please?" he said.

"It's me, of course," said Lois. "What do you want? We're in the middle of supper."

"Ah, I'm sorry, Lois, but this is urgent."

Not again! Lois's heart lurched and she grabbed the back of chair. "Tell me!" she said.

"There's a fire, a big one. Thought you might want to know. Down at the gypsy camp. I'm going down there now. If you're not interested, forget it." He was gone, and Lois turned to the others.

"Fire," she said. "Somebody's set the gypsies on fire. Come on, Derek. We might be able to help."

"Lois!" Gran said. But she was wasting her breath. Lois had her coat on and was out of the front door, reluctantly followed by Derek. As soon as they got to the end of the High Street they could see the red light and smoke and sparks rising into the twilit sky. When they reached the edge of the encampment, a police barrier prevented them from going further.

"Derek!" Lois gasped, out of breath from running. "It's Athalia's caravan! Oh my God, the whole place is exploding!" Children, dogs and horses were fleeing into the wood, and fire engines were still arriving. Lois's ears were assailed by screams, barking, sirens wailing, men shouting, and over everything the roar of the fire.

She hid her face in Derek's jacket, and he put his arms around her. "Bloody hell!" he said. "Whatever bugger did this?"

TWENTY-ONE

By midnight, the fires were out, and groups of gypsies stood around staring at the remains of their homes. Lois had established that both Athalia and George were safe, and had been told to make herself scarce. "Anything could happen tonight, Mrs. Meade," Athalia had said. "There's a time bomb ticking in this village. Go home to your family. We can look after ourselves."

Derek finally managed to persuade Lois to leave, and they met Alf Smith as they walked away.

"A bad business, Alf," Derek said. "I reckon you should have moved them on sooner. You've done 'em no favours, boy."

Gran was waiting up for them. "So?" she said to Lois.

"So what?"

"So what did you say to that gypsy woman you took into your office this morning?"

Derek glared at Lois. "What's this? I thought she was just selling pegs?" he said.

Lois sighed. She was exhausted, and very depressed by what Athalia had said. They didn't want help, or integration with what they saw as a hostile world. She couldn't change things single-handedly.

"Lois?" Derek looked at her coldly.

"Well, the gypsy woman is called Athalia, and she seems a good woman. We've talked before, and she told me how they live, or how they want to live, if people would leave them alone."

Derek sat down heavily on a kitchen chair. "You fool, Lois," he said. "Gypsies are not some persecuted romantic race of honest folk. They've earned their reputation of bein' lawless thieves. They're everything people say they are. And before you interrupt, I *know* they're not all the same. Some, like your Athalia, are no doubt good people wanting to keep an old way of goin' on. And some are like those two with the bull terrier, villains to the life, who hate us, and wouldn't think twice about doin' us harm."

This was a very long speech for Derek, and Lois listened carefully.

"And what about the upright and honest characters who set fire to men, women and children tonight?" she asked. "What are they up to? What old way of going on are they trying to preserve? The old witch hunts? Rough music to get rid of outsiders who don't want to fit in?'

"Don't be ridiculous, Lois," said Gran. "Derek is quite right. And don't forget the proper sites being made for them now. Running water, respectable places, where they can settle down and send their children to schools and clean themselves up."

Lois thought of the things that Athalia had told her about their own rules of hygiene, marriage, and teaching their children how to survive. And overall the tradition of generations who need to be travelling. But she was tired out with trying to think it straight.

"I'm off to bed now," she said. "It'll be a bad day tomorrow, if I'm not mistaken."

As she reached the bottom of the stairs, Derek called out to her.

"Hey, Lois, love," he said. "There was something I meant to tell you. Did you see that hooded wonder pass us by as we left? No? Well, I caught a glimpse of his face, and I could swear it was the one in the paper. Son of those new people in the village," he added.

"Well, it couldn't have been him what done it," Gran said stoutly. "If it *had* been him, he'd've scarpered by then, for sure."

Derek walked out of the kitchen and took Lois's hand. "We only want you safe, me duck. Tomorrow's another day."

They went upstairs hand in hand, and Gran shrugged her shoulders. How *nice* of them to have offered to do the locking up and putting the cat out! How considerate to send her off to bed first, after what must have been a worrying evening for her, too. Huh! She went round the house, banging doors and turning keys, shouting loudly at the cat and Jeems, and coughed her way upstairs when she hadn't even the smallest tickle.

TWENTY-TWO

Next morning, against the advice of Derek and Gran, Lois took Jeems, and keeping her on the lead, walked down to the campsite. Although it was only ten o'clock, she saw that the gypsies had been at work, probably all night. Everything was tidy, with the wrecks of caravans still hot to the touch, and against each one a bender tent constructed from bent saplings securely anchored and covered with tarpaulin.

Inside the half circle, a fire was leaping and smoking, and most of the gypsy families sat around it. A black pot simmered, and Lois caught the scent of rabbit stew. They were silent, except for the children, who ran around as usual, and when they saw her, pointed and shouted, and not in a friendly fashion.

Athalia saw her, too, and walked over to where she stood. "I thought I told you to stay away!" she said crossly. "There's a lot of sad and angry people here this morning. We shall be moving on shortly, and then you can forget about us. The police have been here, and given us twenty-four hours to be gone."

"But can you get your caravans on the road by then? Looks like the fire did a lot of damage." Lois thought how great it would be if a group of the village men came down to help. But she knew this was pie in the sky. Nobody but Alf Smith would help these people.

"We've sent for help from our own. Now go away and don't come back." She turned, but looked back at Lois and said, "No hard feelings, Mrs. Meade. Not your fault. People don't change, neither them nor us."

"Can't I help at all?" Lois asked sadly.

"Yes," Athalia said, and Lois brightened. "You can find the man who killed your Rob, and stop them hounding us for a crime we had nowt to do with."

"Lois! Lois!" It was Derek, running towards her. "For God's sake get back home," he said. "That Cowgill's on the phone and won't go away until he's talked to you."

"Goodbye, Athalia," Lois said. "And good luck. Maybe we'll meet again someday."

"I doubt it," said Athalia, and disappeared into her tent.

"Well? What d'you want?" Lois felt supremely tired and depressed. And, worst of all, she felt ashamed of living in a village that had done this to an almost certainly innocent group of outsiders.

"I need to talk to you. Can you come down to the station? It is perfectly legit. About the fire in the gypsy encampment."

"No," Lois said. "I had nothing to do with it. I'm not on the parish council, nor neighbourhood watch, nor any other of the do-gooding lot who stood by last night and did nothing. If you want to talk to me, you'll have to come here, with a very good reason. *And*," she added, "an explanation of why people whose homes have been destroyed have got to move on in twenty-four hours, or else."

"Eleven o'clock," Cowgill said. "I'll be with you at eleven o'clock."

On the last stroke of the church clock, Cowgill knocked at the door. Gran opened it and, as instructed, showed him into Lois's office. Lois was sitting behind her desk and motioned him into a chair opposite her. Now she felt in the driving seat, and in control of the conversation.

"The first question is mine," she said. He nodded.

"Why do they have to get out of this village in such a short time? What did they do wrong? Aren't they the victims of this bloody awful crime?"

"That's three questions, Lois," Cowgill replied, attempting a smile. Lois immediately wiped it off his face.

"I warn you, Cowgill," she said. "If you want my help, just get on with it and don't try your winning ways on me."

"Right," he said. "In answer to your question, we have given them notice to move on, and there's no 'or else' about it."

"You're evicting them," Lois said angrily. "No need to mince words."

"As I said, we have given them instructions to move on for their own safety, and they are well aware of this. Feeling must be running high in Farnden for someone to do such an efficient job of setting the whole encampment ablaze. And anyway, Lois, they were going soon to get to Appleby for the fair."

"And how are they supposed to get there now?"

"They are apparently getting help from their own contacts. Now, the second question. We have no reason at the moment to suspect them of any crime. As you know perfectly well, there have been anonymous letters and phone calls implicating them in Rob's death.

We have no evidence of this, but are still investigating."

"Wasting time," said Lois. "Meanwhile, the real murderer is probably a hundred miles away."

Cowgill ignored this, and continued. "And as for the third question, yes, of course they are victims. In any other circumstances we would be suggesting victim support. But they refuse all offers of help from anyone but their own contacts."

"Can you blame them?" Lois asked. "Wouldn't you, if you'd been hounded from pillar to post for generations, and—"

At this point, the door opened and Derek came in. He sat down and stared at Cowgill. "Finished?" he said. "Like to ask me some questions? I was there, too, you know."

Cowgill sighed. "Very kind of you to offer," he said. "Did you see anything that caused you to suspect who might have been responsible for this horrendous crime? Any strangers you didn't recognise?"

Derek wondered for a couple of seconds if the hooded lad he thought he'd recognized would count as a suspicious stranger, and decided quickly not to mention it. Now was not the time for the plods to go tramping into the Browns' home. He would discuss it with Lois first.

He shook his head. "Not really," he said. "The whole place was well lit up by the fire, but I only saw gawpers from the village, firemen and the dids, of course, and a few kids rushing around. Gypsy kids, runnin' and screamin', horses goin' mad with fear. That kind of thing."

Cowgill got to his feet. "Very well. Thank you both for your help. If you think of anything that would help us find out who did it, please give me a ring."

Lois was well aware that they had given him nothing to thank them for. But she was too full of anger and pain to care, and showed him out of the house without a word.

TWENTY-THREE

Lois's day was not going well. The interview with Cowgill had left her feeling unsettled and regretful. Not that she cared about his feelings, she told herself, but she had momentarily forgotten how much she needed him for information and advice on the hunt for Rob's killer.

Then she had had a complaint about Sheila's work for a new client in Fletching. "She takes too much on herself," the woman had said. "I asked her to clean out a cupboard in the kitchen, and when I checked it—long after she'd gone, of course—I found half the stuff had been thrown away! And today is bin-men day, so I had no chance of reclaiming it. Really, Mrs. Meade, it is too much. Please see that it doesn't happen again, or I must look elsewhere for a cleaner." Lois had assured her she would have a word with Sheila. When she did, Sheila protested that half the tins were rusty, and the jams were growing mould.

Then came a call from Josie in tears. "Mum, I can't cope. It's suddenly got me. I'm not going to see Rob anymore, am I? And the last things I said to him were angry and horrible." Lois said she would send Floss round at once to take over, and Josie must come home and stay for the rest of the day with Gran and herself.

And then, worst of all, there was a knock at the door and Douglas's Susie stood there. As soon as she was settled in the kitchen with a coffee in front of her, she, too, burst into tears. It seemed she and Douglas had had a row, and she had told him she wouldn't marry him if he was the last man left on earth. She had given him back his ring, and now she was heartbroken.

"I didn't mean any of it! What am I going to do?"

"If he was the last man on earth, there'd be nobody to do the ceremony anyway, would there?" said Lois, having difficulty keeping a straight face. "Don't worry, love. It's just cold feet. Had them myself, didn't I, Mum?"

Gran said she remembered it well. "There she was," she confided, "all ready and dressed for church, an' suddenly she went bright red and came out in a rash. Yelled that she didn't want to marry him, and flung herself down on the bed in floods of tears." ·

"What?" Susie said, staring at Lois. "You did that? I can't imagine you doing that, honestly, Mrs. Meade."

"Time you started calling me Lois. And yes, even I can lose it," Lois said, smiling broadly now. "Douglas is probably biting his nails and waiting for you to ring. So you might as well do it now."

"What, right now?"

"Yes, right now." Lois got up and led Susie into her office, sat her down and left the room, shutting the door firmly behind her.

Back in the kitchen, she told Gran that Josie would be coming round. Floss was free, and would be taking over the shop as soon as she could get there.

"Perhaps we should get Josie and Susie together," Gran said dryly. "Shut 'em up in the sitting room with a big box of tissues and see what happens." Then she retracted, and said that Josie's grief was a lot more serious than Susie's, and she'd better start making a chocolate cake for her favourite granddaughter.

"You've only got one granddaughter," Lois said.

"Exactly," said Gran, and began to assemble her baking things. After a good half hour, Susie emerged from Lois's office.

"Problem solved?" Lois said. She need not have asked. Susie was all smiles.

"I think we love each other more than ever," said Susie, in a soppy voice.

Lois and Gran exchanged glances, and then Lois said she was very pleased, and was sure that Susie would want to be off now, back to work. She suggested a meal out somewhere for the two of them this evening.

"Douglas has already booked at the Vine House. Isn't he wonderful?" Susie said softly. She gave Lois a peck on the cheek, and then another for Gran, and disappeared with her head in the air.

"Next," said Lois. "Or is that three? No, four. Cowgill, new client, Josie and Susie. Should be quiet for a bit, then. Ah, there's Josie," she added, seeing her passing the kitchen window. "If only we could work the same magic for *her*, Mum."

Gran nodded, and beat the cake mixture with extra fury.

Cowgill stood in his office, staring out of the window at the traffic and passing shoppers on Tresham's main street. He had returned from talking to Lois and Derek with his heart in his boots. He had never seen her so set against him. They had such a good relationship—he the patient, adoring policeman, she the feisty cleaning woman, independent and cheeky—no, insulting would be a better word—but always with an affectionate good humour behind it. Or so he hoped.

His telephone rang, and he snatched it up. It was one of his team, asking what he considered was a totally unnecessary question. "For God's sake, man!" he answered. "You don't need me to tell you that. If you can't deal with that, you're in the wrong job!" And he cut the man off midsentence.

His attention was drawn to a gang of youths standing outside the boarded-up Woolworths shop on the opposite side of the street. Grey hooded sweaters, heads down and causing a block on the pavement so that shoppers had to step into the street to walk around them.

"Right outside the station!" he shouted. He lifted his internal phone and barked instructions into it, then returned to the window to watch. In seconds, a constable was there, but not fast enough. All but one disappeared into the crowd, but the one left was frog-marched back into the station, out of Cowgill's sight. His phone rang. "Well?" he said.

"Usual, sir. Swapping downers and uppers and God knows what else. Got one of them down here. Shall we carry on, sir?"

Cowgill was about to agree, but then hesitated. Time to do a spot of proper policing, he decided, and said he'd be down in ten minutes. "Be nice to him," he added. "Don't want irate parents on our doorstep too soon."

Before he went in to see the boy, his assistant handed him details. Mark Brown, he read. Blackberry Gardens, Long Farnden.

"Very nice development, sir. Executive dwellings, luxury interiors, all that."

"Makes no difference, does it?" Cowgill replied. "Sometimes I think they're the worst. Done all the preliminaries?" He walked slowly into the room where the unattractive teenager sat, biting his nails.

TWENTY-FOUR

Alf Smith was still asleep and snoring. His wife Edwina had been awake since half past five, worrying about the gypsies. She was, as always, angry with Alf for allowing them to stay. When did it start, this silly obsession with his ancestors being gypsies? Just because Smith was a common tinker name from the time when they were tinsmiths. Not all people called Smith were gypsies, for God's sake. If only she and Alf had had children, he'd have something else to think about.

She was stiff now from trying not to move restlessly and wake Alf. Early mornings were not his best time of day. She reached for her watch on the bedside table and saw that it was still only half past six. Maybe if she slid out of bed quietly, she could grab some clothes and go out to the chickens without disturbing him. The cockerel was crowing, so they were ready to be out and about.

Alf did not wake, and Edwina crept through the house and out by the back door without a sound. She walked up to the chicken run and stood stock still, horrified at what she saw. Carcases everywhere, half-eaten and strewn about the run. Fox! Edwina had kept chickens for years and knew the signs. The fox would kill for the pleasure of it, and then take one or two back to his hungry family. It was like a madness that got into them. Like those college kids who ran amok with a gun, spraying bullets without caring who got them. Enjoying it. And then shooting themselves as they came to their senses. But the fox had no such conscience. He was all instinct, and now would be gone to his earth.

But how had he got into the chicken house? Easy enough for him to dig through to the run, Edwina knew that. But she was absolutely sure she shut up the house itself last night. So somebody came after her. She forced back tears. Should know better than that, she told herself. You've been a farmer's wife for long enough.

Turning her face from the carnage, she walked out of the run and up the track that led to Junuddle. It had begun to drizzle, and she had no coat. But she walked on, oblivious of the wet grass soaking her slippers and the mist that shrouded the hilltops.

She came out of Junuddle and took the path towards the copse where the gypsies were encamped. Why, she had no idea, except perhaps some vague desire for revenge. Of course, it had been them. Alf had been absent during the fire, dealing with a difficult calving in the cowshed, and they'd have noticed, blaming him for not helping. Oh yes, their friendship was quickly dissolved. In any case, they knew she did not share Alf's ridiculous notions, and they were her chickens.

She stopped at the edge of the copse and stared through the sparse trees. They'd gone. Nothing at all remained, except for a heap of bulging black plastic sacks left neatly near the roadside. The ashes of the fire had been raked, and, but for the flattened, scorched grass, they might not have been there at all.

As she stood, her thoughts whirling, she heard footsteps behind her, and turned in alarm. It was Sam Stratford, and he stood beside her in silence. After a minute or two, he took her hand.

"That's all right then," he said, and they turned back, walking side by side until they were in sight of the farmhouse.

When he had gone on his way, Sam thought about Edwina. They had been at the village school together. He'd been there three years when she started, and on her first day she had been brave and refused to cry when she dropped milk down her new dress. He had been told to take care of her, and she was his first love. They had been partners for country dancing, practised in the playground to old Miss Truscot's creaky gramophone, and then performed at local fetes. Gathering Peascods, Strip the Willow: he could still remember the steps. Edwina had been a skinny, lively little thing, and could dance rings around the rest of the small elephants in the infant class. He smiled, remembering how he had raided his mother's garden for a paper bag full of green gooseberries, which he had presented to Edwina with a proposal of marriage when they were grown up. When he went on to the next school, the romance had come to an inevitable end.

She was still an attractive woman, he thought, and chuckled as he climbed on to the quad bike, which was his preferred mode of transport round the villages. What had she seen in old Alf Smith? Land? A family farm to inherit? It couldn't have been Alf's physical charms. He was an ugly, boring old bugger, with his ridiculous obsession with gypsies.

Ah, well, his precious tinks were gone now, and it had not been all that difficult to get rid of them.

"Breakfast ready?" he said to Sheila, as he opened the kitchen door. A good smell of frying bacon answered his question. Sheila said nothing. She did not even turn to look at him.

"Still sulking?" he said crossly.

"Did you have anything to do with it?" she asked, at last looking him straight in the eye.

"O' course not," he said. "What d'you think I am? Some bloody vigilante? I won't say I didn't want to see the back of them. I did. But I know the right way to go about it. I've not been on the parish council for years without learning a trick or two, you know."

"Mm. Well, better get on with your breakfast. I have to be over at Fletching by half past, so you'll have to stack the dishes. Are you home for dinner?"

"Don't know," muttered Sam. "I can get me own, anyway." He washed his hands at the sink and sat down in front of a plateful of eggs, bacon, fried bread and black pudding. As he watched her retreating back, he thought that maybe he hadn't done so badly in marrying her. After all, Edwina hadn't had no kids, and it's not a real family without kids.

Sam and Edwina had not, as they thought, been unobserved. Deep into the thicket, the battered old caravan had remained. The two brothers and their bull terrier, now muzzled to keep him quiet, had holed up without appearing for the duration of the fire. They'd kept out of sight while tents were erected, and distant gypsies arrived in assorted lorries to help move Farnden's encampment on to pastures new.

They had emerged to see the tail end of the procession as it departed quietly. Harry brooded on the rotten sods who had gone without a word to the brothers. Nobody said "See you at Appleby." And nobody wished them luck, which was no surprise to either of them. Their faces were black with dirt and rough weather, and their hearts were black with anger, resentment and hate.

They had not really belonged to the rest. Old Athalia Lee had allowed them to pitch on the edge of her circle, but they knew it was a fragile thing. That bloody wimp from the village shop getting done over had been the beginning of the end, they knew. The minute they heard about it, they knew they would be blamed. In fact, each blamed the other. They had gone off in different directions that night, and neither of them knew where the other had been. Conversation was always sparse between them, and limited to essentials. The only thing they loved, and they were agreed on this, was the dog. Buster, they called him, and he was everything to them.

Now they sat in silence on the caravan steps, idly teasing Buster with a rabbit skin rolled into a ball.

"Gone, then," Harry said. His brother nodded. "What shall we do?" Harry continued.

"Stay here," answered Sid. "We got to think. Keep out o' sight for a bit."

"We could use what we just saw. Them two havin' a smooch," Harry said.

Sid stared at him. Always the clever bugger, Harry, he thought.

"Alf might like to know about his missus holdin' hands with Stratford. We could 'ave a word with 'er. What d'yer think?"

"I don't. You do the thinking," said Sid.

TWENTY-FIVE

Soon after Lois settled in her office at home to catch up on neglected paperwork, she heard the front door knocker and the bell at the same time. Somebody in a hurry! She sighed. Then she heard Gran's steps coming up the hall and knew she could rely on her to open the door, find out who was there and what they wanted. For once, Lois hoped Gran would keep all comers at bay.

But no. There was a tap at Lois's door and Gran said Mrs. Brown was wanting to see her urgently. "She's in a terrible state, Lois," she added persuasively.

"Hello, how are you?" Lois said, hoping to cool off the poor woman, who had obviously run all the way from Blackberry Gardens. She was out of breath, and her face was scarlet.

"I'm so worried, Mrs. Meade," she said, finally finding her voice. "It's our Mark. You know, our only son. He's in big trouble this time."

Lois stood up and went to the door. "Mum! Coffee wanted. Thanks." She returned to her desk and sat down. "Now, how's about starting at the beginning. Mark was at the fire, wasn't he. Me and Derek saw him. Is it to do with that?"

Nancy Brown nodded mutely and burst into tears.

Oh, Lord, Lois said to herself. This is going to take all morning at this rate. Gran came in with coffee and when Nancy was calm again, Lois took a different tack.

"I saw his picture in the paper. He hangs out with that lot at the back of the village hall, doesn't he?"

"Yes, unfortunately." Nancy's voice was stronger now. "He got hauled into the police station after your Rob was killed. This is nothing to do with that, o' course. But then he was seen in Tresham— right opposite the cop shop!—exchanging pills with his mates. Inspector Cowgill saw them from his window, and that was that. Back in the police station and a call to us to be there. His father was furious, and started on him the minute we got there."

"So he was questioned?"

"Yes. Hadn't got a leg to stand on. It'll be a court case this time."

"Not nice, but not a great surprise to you, is it? Not needing urgent help from me?"

"That's not all. While we were all in there, Cowgill came in and began asking questions about the fire at the gypsy camp. Seems they'd had a report that Mark had been seen hanging around there. . . ." She looked accusingly at Lois.

"Well, it wasn't me or Derek!" Lois said sharply. "But the whole village was there, enjoying the show. Anyone could have reported him. One of his so-called mates, for a start. He'd be well shot of that lot."

"Sorry." Nancy wiped a hand across her face wearily. "Mark was so stupid. He said he'd been with a bunch of his friends, spying on the gypsies. Collecting evidence, he said, so's they could be evicted. He said someone in the village had asked for the gang's help, but he wouldn't say who. Said they were the first ones to spot the fire under one of the trailers. Used his mobile phone to dial 999, he said, and flew into a paddy with Cowgill, saying he got blamed for everything and they'd just done a good turn."

"What did Cowgill say to that?"

"Nothing much. Just told us all to wait, and stalked off out of the door. And that's it, really. Mark knows the form about the drugs. He's been through all that before we moved here. But the fact that he was at the camp before the fire started is really bad. His father won't speak to him, Mrs. Meade, and I'm desperate."

"What do you want me to do?" Lois said, still not sure why the woman had come to her.

"We've heard you help with things like this. Finding out things. We hoped you could find out who started the fire. You know all the people in this village, and your cleaners get around. The gypsies talk to you. I've heard that from several people. If the police knew who started the fire, it would let Mark off the hook, and we could face the rest."

"But Mark knows, doesn't he? All gangs have leaders. Surely you could persuade him to tell you who's giving the orders? Wouldn't he tell his father, if not the police?"

"You're joking," Nancy answered miserably. "They're not speaking. None of us are speaking. The house is like a morgue. I wish we'd got a dog. At least I could talk to a dog. And Mark loves dogs. Maybe if Joe had let him have a dog. . . ."

Her voice tailed off, and she seemed to retreat into herself, staring down at her hands.

"Drink your coffee while it's hot," Lois said. "I'll think about it, and if there's anything I can do I'll give you a ring." Then as an afterthought she added, "Would Mark talk to me?"

Nancy brightened. "I'll try," she said, and stood up. "Thanks a lot for listening. I'll let you know what he says."

Sam Stratford had called in at the farm where he worked before he retired, asking if they needed any help this morning. As a casual worker, he was invaluable to them. And it kept his mind off grave-yards, he thought, as he headed for home. Now, who was it used to say that? His granddad, that's who. Morbid old sod, he'd been. He had been an elder or something like that in the village chapel, and disapproved of everything jolly and of everybody who thought being jolly was intended by God.

The kitchen was neat and tidy, and empty. Sheila must have been back and gone out again. Although the extra money from her cleaning was even more welcome now, he still wished she'd give it up. There was quite enough for her to do round the house and in the garden. She could be a bit more like Edwina, who helped Alf on the farm a lot, and had her chickens. Sold eggs regularly to the WI market. Poor Edwina. She'd been upset about the fox getting into her henhouse. Must have been the tinks. Though why they should get at the Smiths was a mystery. Alf Smith was their only friend, the silly fool.

The telephone rang, and Sam heard his son's voice. "Dad? Just thought I'd warn you. We've had the police here. Just gone. They say they're talking to everyone who might help them. Asked what time they'd be likely to find you at home. Be prepared, as the Boy Scouts used to say."

The police knocked on Sam's door ten minutes later. He sat them down in the sitting room and offered them a drink, which they refused.

"Just a few questions, Mr. Stratford, about the fire at the gypsy site," the older of the two said.

"Fire away," said Sam, and the policeman raised his eyebrows. "Oops—sorry!"

"Right. First of all, when did you first know about the fire?"

Sam answered all their questions with disarming honesty. He had no need to lie. It was the questions they didn't ask that would have given him a moment's pause. But they seemed to accept what he said, made a few notes, and thanked him for his help. They spent exactly a quarter of an hour with Sam, and then left.

TWENTY-SIX

At the estuary of the River Lour, where a network of deep channels ran down to the sea, a small village led a precarious existence on patches of dry land. Every so often a flood tide would invade the village and wash away anything that was in its path. When it retreated, it left inches of mud and rubbish, which the villagers once more cleaned up, vowing they would sell up and move. But who would buy? They were miles from anywhere, with the only facility being the village pub.

It was here, opposite the pub and on a scrubby piece of ground that seemed to belong to nobody, that Athalia and her band of gypsies came to rest. The village was so accustomed to seeing them on their way to and fro Appleby that they hardly noticed them. Their horses were tethered, the dogs on lengths of rope tied to trailer wheels, and the children bothered nobody. The channels were their playground, and they came home like mudlarks, chirping and filthy.

It was a cloudless, sunny day, and Athalia and George perched on rickety kitchen chairs on the grass outside the trailer. They sat in silence for a while, and then George said, "What about them other two, then?"

"No good thinking about them," Athalia said. "We're well rid of them. They're like them pariahs—living on the fringe, scrapin' a living from thieving and begging and never shy about using their fists. Well rid of them," she repeated.

"Isn't that what *we* do?" said George. "Ain't you just described us lot—thieving, begging and handy with a sharp stick?"

Athalia turned on him. "Rubbish!" she said. "Poaching is not thieving. More like borrowing from nature. And nobody here has been begging. Door-to-door selling, yes. But we always got somethin' to sell in return for money. Lace, pegs, them lovely flowers made of shaved wood. Do you remember your Dad making those? Took such pains, and they looked alive when he'd finished. Chrysanths was his favourite. And even if today the lace comes from machines an' the pegs are plastic, we're still not beggin' are we?"

George smiled. "Just kiddin', Athalia," he said. "But I'd still like to know what those two are up to. D'you think they stayed behind, or took another route? Were they going to Appleby, anyway? That ole horse of theirs wouldn't hardly get them as far as that."

"They had a truck. Terrible old thing. I never knew nothing about them. Just said they could pitch down along of us. Are you thinking what I'm thinking?"

"Most likely," said George. "You first."

"D'you reckon one—or both—of them did for that Rob bloke?"

"Yeah, that's what I was thinking."

They stared out across the estuary, where a V-shaped skein of geese crossed the clear sky. "But why?" Athalia said.

"Good question," George said. "If I knew that I'd go straight to the cops. We owe those two nothin' at all."

Edwina Smith took her egg basket and looked out of the kitchen window. Beautiful day, and here she was, stuck with old Alf, when she could be out walking with Sam, talking about happy days when she was top of the class and Sam's best girl.

"I'm just going out to check the hens," she said over her shoulder to Alf, who sat at the table with the local paper spread out before him.

"Says here one of those kids from round the back of the village hall is in hospital. Drug overdose. Apparently she's some relation of Mrs. T-J from the Hall. That's one up the hooter for the old girl. Just because she's a Justice of the Peace, she thinks she can preach to everybody who don't tread the same blameless path as she does. Huh!"

Edwina turned back and looked at the paper. "Poor kid. What else does it say?"

"Seems she was staying with her great aunt up at the hall. Don't suppose that's much fun for a young kid. Probably went into the village looking for more cheerful company and found that grubby lot. Still, Mrs. T-J will buy her out of trouble. No doubt of that. Money talks."

Edwina walked through the vegetable garden, noted that the lettuces were going to seed, and went out through a small gate into the field. The new hens were across the far side, and she walked slowly, feeling the warm wind on her face and thinking about the poor girl in hospital. She'd wanted a daughter, but at least she and Alf had not had the problems that children bring. Alf could have done with a son to help on the farm, but now they didn't talk about it.

As she neared the chickens, she was startled to see a figure approaching. But surely they had all gone? This was definitely one of them, slouching along with a waddling bull terrier at his heels. Should she turn around and run back to Alf? Oh, for God's sake, she told herself. Pull yourself together, woman.

"Mornin' missus," the man said.

"This is private land," Edwina said, holding her egg basket in front of her like a shield.

"Never mind about that," the man said, his voice changing. "Just wanted you to know me and my brother saw you this morning, holdin' hands with that Sam Stratford. Oh, yes, we know all about him and you."

Edwina stared at him, and said nothing.

"So I come to bargain."

"Get off our land!" said Edwina, taking a step forward. The dog growled and showed its teeth. She stopped, her heart racing.

"Here's the bargain," said the man. "You leave us a small donation tomorrow morning. Under this stone will do. Here, by the corner of the run. And we'll keep our mouths shut."

"You'll find nothin' but the police waiting for you," said Edwina.

The man laughed. "I don't think so, missus. Old Alf can be a terror when he's angry. We know that, me and my brother. No, you do what I said, and he'll never know nothing about it."

Edwina bit her lip. "What do you call a small donation? A fiver?"

This time Harry—it was, of course, Harry, the clever one— laughed louder. "Make it fifty, an' that'll bc cheap at the price," he said. "Half a dozen eggs'd be useful, too," he added, and went off rasping out guffaws of laughter, and dragging the dog behind him.

TWENTY-SEVEN
⁊

Lois had driven into Tresham with Gran to do some shopping, and decided to come home via Waltonby, where she could call on Sheila Stratford and see if she was feeling better. She had been off sick yesterday, and had sounded rough on the telephone. It was not like Sheila to give in to ailments, but this time she could hardly speak to Lois.

"Well, you can go in if you want to, but I'll stay in the van," Gran said. "She's bound to be full of germs. Why couldn't you just phone her?"

"Personal touch, Mum. I'll probably just shout through the letter box, if that would suit you better."

But when nobody answered the door, Lois walked round to the back and peered through the window. Sheila was standing at the sink, filling the kettle. She was wrapped in a man's dressing gown, and had pink fluffy slippers on her feet. When Lois tapped on the door, she turned swiftly, her face pale except for a red tip to her nose.

"Did you ring the bell at the front?" she said apologetically, beckoning Lois inside. "It's been broken for a couple of days. Sam's going to fix a new one as soon as he can get into Tresham. Sorry about this cold, Mrs. M, but as you can see, I'd not be welcome in clients' homes!"

Lois said she was on no account to come back to work for a week. "You'd best go back to bed at once. Here, let me fill that hot water bottle. Shall I make you a cup of tea? I suppose Sam will be back at lunchtime? Have you got food, or shall I fetch you something from the shop?"

To Lois's amazement, Sheila handed her the hot water bottle and burst into tears. Gasping that she was sorry, and it was just that she felt so lousy, she mopped her streaming eyes and nose with a handful of tissues.

"Is that really all?" Lois was suspicious. Sheila was not one for weeping.

"Sort of," Sheila replied.

"What else, then? Something to do with Sam?"

Sheila subsided into a chair and nodded. "We've had row after row ever since we did that quiz with the gypsies that night in the pub. And he's been acting strange. Going out without saying where he's going, and then when I asked him yesterday he said he'd been at Alan's. But Alan phoned later and said no, Dad had not been round."

Lois's heart sank. It was all her fault for persuading Sheila to do the quiz. "What did he say about the fire?" she asked.

"That's another thing," Sheila said. "I was really worried about that, in case he was mixed up in it. He's been so angry about the gypsies, and threatening all kinds of ways of getting rid of them. Said he was going to tackle Alf Smith and force him to give them the push. Alf and Sam never got on, not for years, and I was worried there'd be trouble there." She stopped to sneeze violently, and Lois nervously backed away. She thought of Gran getting restless in the van.

"Then I asked him outright if he'd had anything to do with it, and he turned on me. Denied it, and accused me of being a suspicious woman, not fit to be his wife."

Another burst of tears caused Lois to look at her watch. "Listen, Sheila," she said. "The first thing you do is get better. Then we'll see about you and Sam. Derek always says you can't interfere between man and wife, so I'll be careful! Anyway, when he sees what a state you're in, it'll probably all come right. He's a kind man, really, isn't he? Something's wrong, I can see that. But let's leave it until you've shaken off this cold. I must go now. Mum's waiting in the van, and you know what she is! I'll give you a ring tomorrow, see how you are."

Gran was fuming. "I'll never understand you, Lois Meade!" she said. "With a business to run, and everybody relying on you, and you go and poke your head into a houseful of germs!" She shrank away from Lois, saying she was sure she was already catching this dreadful cold. "So dreadful that it's keeping Sheila Stratford off work, and she's not one to swing the lead," she continued.

"She was upset, as well as full of cold," Lois said. "Mostly about Sam. They haven't been getting on too well lately."

"And I know why," Gran said. "Sam Stratford always had strong opinions. And for some reason gypsies get him going more'n anything. Folk say he and Alf Smith have nearly come to blows in the pub many a time, arguing over gypsies. And blacks. Sam's not over fond of blacks."

"Oh, my God!" Lois exploded. "And him a church warden and parish councillor! If that's what being a Christian means, I'm glad I'm not one of that lot."

They were driving up to the house now, and Gran began to laugh. "There's Christians and Christians, Lois. Just so long as you don't dress up in saffron robes and chant up and down the High Street in Tresham."

"What I believe is my own affair," answered Lois sniffily, and they came to stop in the drive. "Anyway, we'd better get out now so's you can spray disinfectant all round the house."

Mrs. Tollervey-Jones, chair of the parish council, privately shared many of Sam Stratford's views. She had taken charge of all the things necessary for the council to handle the aftermath of the fire, and made the right noises about persecution and violence not being the way to tackle a problem. She was co-operating with the police, of course, and had twice answered questions from that chilly policeman, Inspector Cowgill. He could have been a little more respectful, she considered. He had been verging on arrogance in her opinion, and she was near reporting him to the commissioner, who was a friend of hers. She sighed. It was not like the old days, when a position in society meant something.

She moved away from the long windows looking out over the park, and walked across the drawing room to the door, her sensible shoes clacking on the parquet flooring. Rugs were scattered sparsely, and she liked the authoritative sound of her heels on the wood blocks. At the foot of the curving staircase, she looked up and shouted at the top of her voice, "Sally! Sally! Are you coming down for lunch? Ready in five minutes. Don't be late." Her voice was kind. Sally was a worry to her at the moment.

Up in her room, Sally Tollervey-Jones, aged sixteen, looked at herself in the mirror and frowned. She saw a pale face with dark circles under the eyes, long stringy blonde hair darkening at the roots, and thin lips tightly clenched. It was this place getting her down, she told herself, excusing her spell in hospital from taking too much stuff. How could she get out of here?

Her great-aunt was the most unpleasant person she had ever met. A real bully. Sally had had enough of being bullied. She had been a victim right from the start, she believed. A hard-hearted nanny, then a nursery school where she'd been pushed around because her parents never came to see the teachers, followed by a series of boarding schools. She knew in her heart that the frequent exclusions had been her fault, but blamed it all on other people. Her parents, teachers, bigger girls, anyone but herself. She had been a little comforted to hear that another member of the T-J family, Annabel, had felt exactly the same, and been sent to stay with Mrs. T-J in the hope that she could work a miracle. Family history repeating itself. Fat chance of being directed on a cheerful straight and narrow path in this mausoleum!

Since she had been in Long Farnden her life *had* changed, but not for the better, her aunt would say. No, it was because she had been warmly welcomed by the gang behind the village hall. She was not stupid, and knew they thought she would have ready money for what they traded. But she did not care. Mark Brown was, like her, new to the gang, and he had taken charge of her, protecting her against those who mocked her accent and were nervous in case she would prove disloyal.

She fancied Mark Brown, and the feeling seemed to be mutual. The drugs they shared drove away the miseries, if only for a while. She had been careless in ending up in hospital, but now began to feel better, and looked forward to seeing him again and finding a way of escape.

"Coming!" she shouted, and descended the stairs two at a time.

Mark Brown, unused to being the subject of adoration, lay stretched out on his bed listening to rap and thinking about Sally. It was comforting to talk to someone who had had a worse time with parents than he had. At least his Mum and Dad had been *around* being nasty to him. Sally had told him about her absentee parents. She was never quite sure where they were, her father being a diplomat and her mother a mouse who followed him about when it was permitted, and vanished down her mouse hole when left alone.

"Mark, Mark!" His mother's voice just about penetrated the music, and he sat up.

"What?"

"A visitor for you!" She sounded nervous. Oh, God, not another policeman. Why couldn't they leave him alone? He ran his fingers through his hair, put on his glasses to be more studious and serious-looking, and went slowly downstairs.

"Ah, there you are, son," said his mother. "This is Mrs. Meade. She's Elsie Weedon's daughter, and her Josie runs the shop."

"I know who she is," Mark said shortly. "Hi."

Lois supposed this was as polite as he could manage, and felt a little encouraged. Not a bad start, anyway.

"Mrs. Meade wanted to have a chat," Nancy Brown said. "She might be able to help us with the police, and so on. I'll get you both some coffee." She scuttled out of the room, looking nervously at Mark.

"I thought you were a cleaner?" Mark began, looking casually out of the window.

"I run a cleaning business, yes. And I'm not at all sure I can help. Your mum is a bit optimistic. Still, she reckons if we could find the maniac who started that fire it would let you off the hook for that, though there's nothing I can do about the drugs."

"Not your business," Mark said flatly. "As for the fire, I've told them already. I don't know nuthin' about who started it." He began to go towards the door, and Lois snapped back at him.

"Sit down. I'm not here for fun. I've got plenty of work to do, so I'll thank you to sit down and listen. I don't care a damn what you do to yourself, but I'll help your mother if I can."

"I notice you don't include my dad," Mark said, subsiding into a chair.

Lois ignored that, and glared at him so that he had to pay attention. "No doubt you know about my daughter's partner, Rob, who was beaten up as he walked home, not troubling anybody. The cops still haven't found out who murdered him, and now there's been a fire in the gypsy camp that could have killed the lot. Children, their mums and dads, dogs and horses. The whole lot. What do you think about all that?"

To Lois's horror, he grinned. "I think," he said slowly, "that this is a bloody rotten village to live in. Take your life in y' hands every time you walk down the street."

Lois stared at him, appalled. "So that's what you think, is it?" she said. "Then there's no point in my being here." She stood up and called to Mrs. Brown that she wouldn't have any coffee, thanks, and had to be going. "I've got better things to do with my time than talk to this . . . this . . ." She thought of Nancy's feelings; he was her boy, after all. ". . . your son. He's not in the mood, I'm afraid."

As she walked to the front door, she sensed Mark coming up behind her.

"Sorry," he said. "I do have a thing or two to say. Might help. An' if I tell you my side of it, will you listen?"

TWENTY-EIGHT

Lois is late," Derek said. He had come back from Fletching after finishing a rewiring job on an old house that had just changed hands. Townies had bought it for an extraordinary price that Derek wouldn't even have considered for a crumbling cottage in the High Street. It was in a bad state, with a tiny muddy yard, an outside lavatory, and—he could hardly believe it—a tin bath in the shed. The new owners were prepared to spend thousands on it, of course, but it would never be more than a two-up, two-down workman's cottage that had belonged to the Tollervey-Jones estate. The old duck must be running short of money if she was selling off her inheritance, thought Derek.

Gran told him Lois had popped in to see Mark's mother and would be back shortly. She had to admit that time was getting on, and was beginning to feel guilty at having asked Lois. Perhaps there'd been a row, and she had stormed off somewhere else before coming home.

Derek chatted on about the old house, and Gran said she was sure she'd heard tell of the old man who lived there for years on his own. "Squalid, people said it was, and told him so, but he said he changed his underpants once a year, so what were they on about?"

Derek choked on his cup of tea, and reached for the dishcloth to mop up the spillage. Just then Lois passed by the window and came into the kitchen like a whirlwind.

"You're back, then," said Derek mildly.

This unleashed a stream of words from Lois, mostly directed at Gran, about people who shouldn't have children if they didn't know how to bring them up, and the modern generation who had no respect, no morals and no ambition to make anything of their lives.

"Why don't you sit down, me duck, an' have a cup of tea. Gran's made a batch of scones." Derek smiled and took her hand. "Tell us all about it," he said.

"I can't," Lois said. "All I can tell you is I've had a conversation, if you can call it that, with Mark Brown. At Gran's suggestion. Supposed to be helping Mrs. Brown cope with her wayward son. Some hopes, Mum! He's a selfish little sod. Tried to persuade me it was all his Dad's fault. He's an only child, and all his old man's ambitions rest on him. His school results were never good enough for his father, so he says. When he suggested going off for a year round the world, there was an explosion that lasted for days. Oh dear," Lois sighed. "I've probably told you more than I should've, but how often have you heard all that before?"

"I suppose it's the first time for the Browns," Derek said calmly. "Only son, an' all that."

Lois sat down heavily. "You're right as always," she said. "Well, I stuck it out. At least he told me *his* side of that gloomy family.

But the crux of it was that Mrs. Brown reckons if we find out who killed Rob and who started the gypsy fire, that'll let Mark off the hook of them particular crimes. I'm not even sure that he is suspected of being involved, anyway. Drugs yes, possibly mixed up with the gypsy fire, but I've heard nothing since that story in the paper about the gang being involved in Rob's death."

"Ring your cop, Mum," Josie said. Lois had not seen her coming into the kitchen where she perched quietly on a stool by the door. "Who knows, a miracle might have happened? They might have got one whole step forward in the hunt for Rob's killer."

"How about *your* cop?" Lois countered, and immediately regretted it. Josie's face closed up, and she said nothing more. Lois knew that Matthew Vickers had been around regularly, ostensibly checking to see if she had remembered anything new, but actually because he just wanted to see her. She had recognized him outside the shop that evening. Josie obviously did not mind this at all, but was aware that people would talk. Probably did already.

Lois changed the subject, saying that she must sort out a replacement for Sheila Stratford. "She'll be off for a week, poor thing," she said.

"Is Sam coping?" Gran said. Lois looked at her. There was something in her mother's voice that suggested the question was more than an idle enquiry.

"Good heavens, yes," Lois said. "Now he's retired he should have all the time in the world. Surely even Sam's heard of ready meals from Tesco, with plenty of fresh orange juice?"

"More likely that wife of Alan's will do the looking after," Gran said with a shrug. "Sam Stratford was never one for housework. He used to say he didn't keep a dog to bark himself."

"Charming," said Lois.

"We got a parish council meeting this evening," Derek said. "I can have a word, see if he needs any help." Derek was beginning to feel outnumbered by hostile females.

Lois disappeared into her office, Josie went back to the shop, and Derek and Gran were left once more by themselves.

"What d'you reckon, Derek?" said Gran. "Did that Brown boy tell Lois the truth, or is he a liar like the rest of that lot behind the village hall?"

Derek shook his head. "Don't ask me," he said. "Our boys must've been through bad patches, but I don't remember anything like this."

"That's because you were a good father," Gran said. "From what Mrs. Brown has told me, young Mark might have been exaggerating to Lois, but not much."

After Lois had gone, Mark went straight up to his room and put on his headphones. He listened to the familiar music for five minutes or so, then took them off again. His thoughts were whirling. Had he told the Meade woman enough to satisfy her? It had been nothing more than the truth, he reassured himself, if not exactly the whole truth. He slid off his bed and looked at himself in the mirror. Could be worse, he told himself. At least, Sally T-J seemed to approve. Maybe he'd slip out quietly and cycle up to the hall. He could throw stones at her window, or something stupid like that. He couldn't imagine the old bat welcoming him in through the grand front door. . . .

TWENTY-NINE

Derek was a newish member of the parish council. A vacancy had come up, and he had been co-opted between elections. He was reluctant to agree, but Lois had persuaded him, saying, "Think how useful it would be to know what's going on in the village!" He had answered that he was sure it would all be very confidential, even between husbands and wives, and in any case, he'd added, the idea was to serve the community, not snoop into its private affairs. In the end, as always, Lois had persuaded him, and he had to admit that, once he'd accepted that the wheels of the local authority turn slowly, it was much more interesting than he had expected.

He arrived at the village hall early. Only Mrs. Tollervey-Jones was there before him. She made a point of being there first so that the others would feel suitably chastened for being late. He greeted her politely, and she answered absentmindedly, unlike her usual brisk self. Derek sat down and said nothing more, allowing her to arrange her papers.

"Um, Mr. Meade," she said finally. "Could I ask you for advice? You have a daughter, haven't you? Josie in the shop?" Derek nodded, and said he'd be pleased to help if he could.

"Well, I have my great-niece staying with me. Sally. She's sixteen, and has not had what I consider a suitable upbringing. Her parents have been away a lot and left her to her own devices, and I am afraid she is a very unhappy girl. Lately she has found unsuitable friends. Here in the village. You are probably aware of the gathering behind the village hall. On the whole, they have been left alone, except for the complaint followed up by the police in their heavy-handed way."

Derek nodded encouragingly. He had no idea how he could help, but well remembered Mrs. T-J's granddaughter Annabel, who had led his smitten son Jamie a dance for a while. They lived in a different world, these kids of rich-bug families.

"The truth is, Derek," Mrs. T-J continued, "I feel generations too old to tackle Sally's problems. And her parents are useless. Always were. She has just had a spell in hospital—overdose—that sort of thing. Of course, as a magistrate I am aware of that scene, and managed to keep the police out of it. But when it's in the family . . . different. I am sure you, as a family man, appreciate that. I thought perhaps you or your wife would be able to . . . You know?"

Ah, thought Derek, so that's it. She means Lois, not me. He had a good idea what Lois's suggestion might be. Send the girl to a state school, give her a smaller allowance and make sure every spare minute was filled with some useful activity. And a curfew if necessary. Still, he wouldn't preempt Lois's advice, and promised he would mention it to his wife. "I always left our Josie for Lois to deal with," he said.

"Most grateful," said Mrs. T-J, as other members began to arrive, including Sam Stratford, who sat down next to Derek. "Evenin' mate," he said.

"How's Sheila? Need any help?" Derek whispered, as Mrs. T-J rustled her papers and stood up.

"Poorly. But no, we're fine. Alan's wife is helping. Tell you more later," he added. Mrs. T-J glared at him and said that if everyone was ready, she would open the meeting.

Lois sat in her office and stared at the telephone. She did not want to ring Cowgill, but knew it was the only way of finding out what was happening in Rob's murder investigation. She could also pump him for information on Mark Brown, and what they had in store for him. She sighed. It was a good opportunity, with Derek at the parish council meeting and Gran off with Mrs. Pickering.

She dialled his personal number. It rang for a long time, and she was about to disconnect when his voice said, "Hunter Cowgill here."

"Sorry to bother you out of hours," Lois said briskly, setting a suitable tone. "I need to have an update on Rob's case, as Josie has made it clear she thinks I have given up."

"Lois! How nice to hear from you. I was half asleep in a chilly room, with only television for company. Now, let me switch it off and collect my thoughts."

Lois had a vision of him sitting in a darkening, cold and tidy room, lonely and sad. She softened her tone, and said that she'd also something to tell him that might help.

His next words revised her vision.

"Give me a minute," he said. "I got back from a triumphant round of golf, celebrated à little too lavishly in the nineteenth hole, and dozed off."

"Bully for you," she said. "Are you sober? Clearheaded enough to understand what I'm saying? I must say I hope there are no riots on the streets of Tresham tonight. You'd not be much good, would you?"

"Off duty, Lois," he said, sharply now. "Even I am allowed a few hours off duty."

"So what's new in Rob's case?" she repeated.

"You will not approve, Lois," he began, "but evidence is hardening against the gypsies. We have located them, of course, and the local branch has them under surveillance."

"You mean a bobby walks by once in a while?"

"I am not at liberty to tell you more on that, Lois, as you very well know. To continue, witnesses have come forward with information on another disturbance in the same area on the same evening. An hour or so before Rob was attacked, a young woman was menaced by a dog outside the entrance to a pub garden in Waltonby. We checked with pub customers, but nobody saw it. The woman described it as a bulldog sort of terrier, and said that it was dragged away from her by a gypsy-looking man before it could do more than scare her out of her wits. He disappeared so quickly she had no chance to speak to him. Unfortunately, nobody was around to witness this. There were no customers in the garden. All watching the match on the pub telly. A passing motorist saw something, but did not stop. He rang in later to report what he had seen. A big man and a dog, he said, but could give us no further description."

"So what have you done about that?" Lois said, her heart sinking as she recalled the ugly pair with a bull terrier in the gypsy encampment.

"Pursuing our enquiries, my dear, as always. Now, what have you to tell me?"

"Probably not much more helpful than your titbit for me," Lois said sourly. "It's just that I had a conversation with Mark Brown. Him of the uppers and downers and presence at the gypsy fire. Mother and father live in Blackberry Gardens, and asked me to talk to him."

"I'm with you, Lois. All ears."

"He's a spoilt, selfish little sod," Lois said, "but possibly with mitigating circumstances, as you lot would say. Claims his father is an unloving bully, and his mother too scared to challenge him. Only child, loaded down with parents' ambitions and never able to live up to them. Or just determined not to. Denies having anything to do with Rob's case, but owns up to being around on the night of the fire. He's one of the village hall gang, and hinted at a mastermind who gives them orders. Harassing gypsies is one of their fun activities, but denies starting the fire, and claims he was the first to alert the fire station. For some God-knows-what reason, I believed him."

"A mastermind?" Cowgill pounced on the nugget of important information at once. "Who is it? Did he tell you?"

"Of course not! He's not a fool, that boy. Given a new direction, he'd probably be quite useful to somebody. Blimey," she added, "I sound like a social worker. Better take that last bit unsaid. I have to go now, anyway. I can hear Derek back from the parish council meeting."

"Thanks, Lois," Cowgill said hurriedly. "You are the light of my life." He heard Lois disconnect and smiled. She knew that, of course.

THIRTY

When Edwina Smith went out to release the chickens next morning, she checked the stone at the corner of the run. The envelope containing fifty pounds and the box of six eggs had gone. She breathed a sigh of relief, and set about opening the chicken house and topping up the feed trough. The sun came out from behind a high mist, and her spirits rose. Turning to walk back to the house, she froze.

"Morning missus," said a gruff voice behind her. She turned around and saw the same rough-looking man who had accosted her before.

"What do you want?" she said as sharply as she could manage. "You've taken the money and the eggs. Now bugger off!"

"Not s'fast, lady," Harry said. "I think you must'a misheard me. I said seventy-five pounds would put things right for you. Make sure the extra's here tomorrer. Same stone. An' another dozen eggs. Me brother's very fond of eggs. Don't forget, now. Alf's a wicked man when he's roused. We know that from the past, don't we?"

Edwina was speechless. What did people say about blackmail? Never give in to it. And she foolishly had done so. Now she was trapped. She couldn't call the police, or tell Alf—or Sam, even. He would be so angry with her at involving him and getting herself into this mess in the first place. She turned away from the gypsy and half ran back towards the house. As she ran, she heard growling and snuffling behind her and knew that the bull terrier was following her. She stopped, knowing it was the best thing to do with a chasing dog, and heard the man laughing hoarsely as he pulled it back on its long rope lead.

Safely back in the kitchen, she heard Alf's heavy footsteps coming downstairs. "All right, gel?" he said. "You look puffed out. What made you run?"

Edwina took deep breaths and subsided onto a chair. "Oh, you know me. Thought I'd see how far and fast I could run now. The village marathon is next month, and I had this silly idea I might take part. Not sure now!"

Alf laughed and patted her arm. "We're none of us as young as we used to be," he said. "I'll make you a cuppa, me duck. You sit there an' get your breath back."

The gypsy's words came back to Edwina as she sat quietly while the kettle boiled. "Alf's a wicked man when he's roused." She could not remember a time in the whole of their marriage when Alf had been harsh or unkind to her. What had that man meant? Ah, well, she had a lot of thinking to do, and her garden was the place to do it. She would dig over that rough patch this morning. Something mindless to do that would give her time to think.

"Soon be time we was movin' on," Harry said to Sid, as he put the eggs in a bag, ready for Sid to take to market in Tresham. The two of them had a stall just round the corner from the regular market, where they sold anything they had managed to acquire during the week. They kept this going by moving around the county in a radius within reach of Tresham. Their stock consisted of odd items of garden tools, plastic chairs from people's sheds, and stuff that Sid had persuaded old ladies to give him for "valuation." They kept a sharp eye open for cops inspecting the stalls, and could pack up and vanish faster than any stallholder on the legitimate market.

"Known for a bargain, we are," Harry told Sid as he took boxes of junk out to their lorry. Eggs were a new line for them. Harry had written a card saying: "New layed eggs—cheapest in town." He intended to vary the price according to the look of the customer. He knew that food had special regulations, but reckoned he could conceal a few dozen eggs from official eyes. There had always been an unwritten agreement in the market that one stallholder would not shop another, but Harry was not too sure now. Smart, foreign-looking men had taken up stalls lately, and he didn't trust them.

"When shall we go, then?" Sid said. "And where?" Sometimes he thought sadly how nice it must be to have a proper home, with kids and a wife and a garden. But he and Harry had never had a proper home, and he wasn't really sure how you managed one. You couldn't just hitch up the van and go when things got a bit warm, that was for sure. Now he helped Harry load up, and suggested they go to that scrubby old yard behind an old barn in Fletching. "Nobody ever goes there," he said. The barn's not used and the old farmer's past carin'. An' the track's so rutted nobody but us would take a vehicle down there." He thought privately that their van would one day fall to pieces being shook up on their travels, but he said nothing about that. Harry could get very annoyed.

"I'll think on it," Harry said. "Next week'd be soon enough, I reckon. One more present from Alf's missus would be useful, and then we'll go. You can't trust wimmin, Sid. She'll probably get help against us sooner or later."

Sid thought the trick Harry was playing on Mrs. Smith was stupid. It went against all Harry had taught him over the years. Too much out in the open, being seen. Talking to people who would recognise you again. Harry was being greedy, and that always came to grief.

When they were ready to go, Harry locked up the van with the bull terrier chained to one of the wheels. "Do yer job," he said to the dog. "Anybody comes round here snooping, let 'em have it."

As he turned towards the lorry, he caught sight of a figure coming towards them through the trees. It was Alf Smith. Harry scowled and began to climb into the lorry, but Alf called out. "Wait! I want a word with you." Sid was already inside the cab, and he shrank into his seat with fear.

Harry stood his ground, stocky legs planted wide and hands in his pockets. "Yeah?" he said.

"You know who I am," Alf said. "I'll make it short and sweet. I want you off this land by tomorrow morning. You never asked permission, and I wouldn't have given it. Athalia Lee had no right to let you stay here, and I'm ordering you to go."

Did he know already about Sam Stratford and his wife? Harry could not be sure, but he answered as politely as he could. "We're going today," he said. "When we come back from market, we'll pack up and be off in the morning. You'll never know we've bin here, Mr. Smith."

"One more word," said Alf. "I'd advise you to get rid of that dog. They're illegal now, and I've had complaints."

"Who from?" said Harry sharply.

"None of your business, but it's enough for you to know he wears a uniform and drives a car with a siren. With me?"

Harry nodded. He knew now that Alf's missus had not told. Yet. "Must go now," he said. "The best business is done early. Don't you worry, Mr. Smith, we'll be gone."

"And don't turn up here again," Alf said, a parting shot as the lorry moved forward and out on to the Tresham road.

THIRTY-ONE

Sheila Stratford was feeling better. The fever had gone, though she wobbled a little as she got out of bed. She decided to have a shower, get dressed and do a few small jobs around the house. She could hear in her head her mother's voice saying, "Get up, gel. You'll feel better when you're properly dressed."

Alan's wife had been in and tidied round, but Sheila did not think much of her housewifely skills, and reckoned there'd be a lot to do downstairs. As she thought, there were heaps of newspapers, Sam's clothes, bags of shopping not unpacked, and ashes six inches deep in the fireplace. Was she being unfair to her daughter-in-law? The heaps were quite tidy, and the ashes had been swept into a mound. But no, the girl was hopeless. Not brought up to run a house and family, that was for sure.

When Sam came in at lunchtime, his face brightened as he saw the table had been set and Sheila at the cooker stirring soup.

"Feeling better, me duck?" he said. "Now don't you go doing too much at first. You had a nasty fluey cold, and that takes it out of you."

"I'm better doing something," Sheila said. "Lying up there thinking stupid thoughts is no good to man nor beast—nor woman."

"What stupid thoughts?" Sam frowned. What was she on about now? He had decided to make a big effort and forget about that quiz night. Time things got back to normal, and that included no more clandestine meetings with Edwina in the woods. The pair of them were old enough to know better.

"Never mind that now," Sheila said. "Let's have this soup while it's hot. Are you going by the Farnden shop this afternoon? We need supplies. Josie has some chicken breasts that'll do us nicely for tea. She gets 'em from the farm, so they're really fresh."

"Yeah, sure. I can do that. An' I thought I'd call on old Alf and see if Edwina's got any eggs to spare. They're different from shop-bought as chalk from cheese. Might make me a bit late, but you'll be all right, won't you?" Oops! So much for good resolutions, he told himself.

Alarm bells rang in Sheila's head at his words. They always did these days when he said he'd be a bit late. Still, if he was just going to Alf's, that would be fine. And Edwina's eggs were certainly good.

"I might try a little walk in the fresh air this afternoon," she said. "Perhaps up Junuddle and around a bit. Not too far. Now, d'you want some more?"

Sam said quickly, "Not as far as the farm, Sheila. Not on your first day out of bed. Don't want a relapse, do we?"

Mark Brown and Sally T-J had also decided to enjoy the fresh air. They had discovered a tumble-down shelter in the corner of Junuddle. It had once been a solid, brick-built shed, protection for the sheep when March winds brought strong torrents of sleet, or on baking summer days when the sun seemed dangerously close to the fields, parching the grass and drying up ditches and streams.

Slowly the shelter had fallen into disrepair, with loose red bricks crumbling in heaps and slates fallen from the roof. Enough of it was still shielded from view, however, for Sally and Mark to settle down and have a smoke. Up to this afternoon, tha... is all that had happened.

But now, when Sheila Stratford strolled along, taking deep, healing breaths, she was curious about glad shouts coming from the shelter. She stood irresolutely, listening until things had quietened down. After all, whoever they were, they were trespassing, and she supposed Alf Smith would want her to see them off his land. She coughed. Total silence, so she coughed again and walked towards the entrance. Peering into the dim interior, she could see two frightened faces in the gloom. She did not immediately recognise either of them, but walked in and said, "What d'you think you're doing? This is private land."

"Nothing," the girl said. "We're not doing anything. Just talking and getting away from the world." The boy giggled.

Mmm, thought Sheila, and sniffed. Obviously not an innocent ciggy, then. Well, what they were up to was none of her business, but trespass was, and she told them briskly to get themselves together and be off as quickly as they could, before Mr. Smith came after them with a pitchfork.

This time it was the girl who laughed. "Nobody uses pitchforks now! Anyway, Mrs. um—" Her posh accent reminded Sheila of someone. Oh, yes, now she guessed at the girl's identity. Well, better confirm it.

"I'm Mrs. Stratford," said Sheila. "And what're your names?

No, on second thoughts don't tell me. If I don't know who you are I shan't be tempted to tell your parents. Now get going, both of you." She remembered what Sam had said about not going too far, and started on her way back home, thinking nostalgically of the sweet-smelling haystacks where she and Sam had done their courting on balmy summer evenings.

Mark and Sally straightened their clothes in silence. "Have you done this before?" Sally said.

Mark shook his head. "Not all the way," he said, his voice muffled in embarrassment.

"Nor me. D'you think I'll get pregnant?"

"For God's sake! Don't even mention it! That would really be the end for me. I'd be turned out, all my belongings in a red spotted kerchief, and told to go as far away as possible, never to return."

Sally laughed, peals of teenage laughter. "I expect they'd make me get rid of it."

"Costs a lot," said Mark. "At least, I think it does."

"Money's no object," said Sally. "They think money can fix everything. Well, they'd be wrong this time. If I'm pregnant, I shall go through with it. I fancy the idea of being a teenage mum. And if it bothers you," she added, suddenly angry, "I won't say who dunnit. I'm used to managing on my own. I'm off, anyway. See you around."

Mark followed slowly. He watched until she vanished round a spinney at the corner of the field. Perhaps his reaction had been a bit selfish? Oh, God, if only he could think clearly. At the moment, his head was full of the swirling effects of the shared smoke. And, he admitted to himself, of his first go at the real thing, better than he had ever rehearsed.

"Hi, Sam," Edwina said. He was standing by the kitchen door, watching her approach from her vegetable garden.

"Alf about?" he said. "I've knocked and shouted, but no answer."

Edwina shook her head. "He's gone to see his sister over the other side of Tresham," she said. "Won't be back for a couple hours. She's a bit poorly. How's Sheila?"

"Much better, thanks," he said. He moved towards her, but she sidestepped him and went into the kitchen.

"My hands are covered in dirt," she said, "but come on in. We can't be too careful, can we, Sam. We've had one or two trespassers here lately." She shivered at the thought of the man with the dog.

"Where?" Sam said. "What were they after? There's been some barn thefts locally."

Edwina smiled. "Not exactly barn theft," she said slowly. "Anyway, they soon scarpered when they saw Alf." She dried her hands, and Sam moved towards her. She felt the old, dangerous, spreading warmth as he put his arms around her.

"Two hours, me duckie," he whispered in her ear, and led her towards the stairs.

THIRTY-TWO

Josie was busy in the storeroom when Sam came in. He called her name, and she yelled "Hello, Sam. Just coming."

She had known Sam Stratford ever since Mum and Dad had moved to Farnden.

"How're you, me duck?" Sam said, as she appeared, smiling her usual welcome. There were times when she felt very far from smiling, but she always managed. A warm welcome to all comers had paid off. The village shop was doing well, when all around were closing down. Josie enjoyed being the hub of the village, and she was the recipient of many secrets and private thoughts. "You won't tell anyone, will you, Josie," yet another confidante would say, and Josie promised. What is more, she kept her word.

"A dozen eggs, please," Sam said. "And Sheila says a couple of those fresh chicken breasts you get from the farm."

He had remembered the eggs on his way home. What with this and that, and Edwina being on edge in case Alf came home early, he'd forgotten to ask for eggs. Never mind, Sheila wouldn't know the difference. Josie sometimes took Edwina's surplus.

"How is Sheila?" Josie asked. She knew from Mum that Sam's

wife had been ill. "On the mend, I hope?" Sam said yes, she'd be back at work in a day or two. He looked around and took a box of Milk Tray chocolates from a shelf. "Dragon food," he said.

"What?" said Josie. "What did you call them?"

"Dragon food. A German student working on the farm told me. He said that's what they call presents bought by husbands who are late getting home. Roses from the roadside, an' that. Dragon food. Food to appease the dragon!"

Josie laughed and wondered privately why Sam needed to appease Sheila. Being late home wasn't anything unusual in the farming community. If a job needed finishing, the worker stayed until it was done.

The doorbell jangled behind Sam, and he turned. It was Alf Smith.

"Thanks, Josie," Sam said, picking up his purchases. "Cheerio, gel."

Alf Smith stood in the doorway, not moving.

"'Scuse me, Alf," Sam said.

"Not so fast," Alf said. "I want a word with you."

"You're not so late as I expected," Sheila said approvingly. "Did you get the chicken breasts? And the eggs from Edwina?"

"Yep," Sam said, dumping them on the kitchen table. His face was pale, and his expression grim. "By the time I'd finished helping with the pigs it was too late to go to the Smiths, so I got the eggs from the shop. Josie said she gets them from Edwina, anyway." He had decided to make all his stories hang together, but oh, what a tangled web we weave. Echoes of the past! His Dad had been forever using the old adage to young Sam when as a boy he had been poaching, or chasing the vicar's daughter.

"Well, thanks anyway," Sheila said. "I went for a little walk, not too far, and I feel a whole lot better. I'll ring Lois and tell her I can start work tomorrow. It's my old lady down the road, just a couple of hours, so I'm sure I can manage that. She relies on me to tell her what's going on in the village, an' that."

Sam grunted, and went through to the hall. "You all right?" Sheila shouted after him. "You look a bit ropey. Hope you've not got my bug!"

"I'm okay," he said. "Bit tired, that's all." And serve you right, at your age, he told himself silently as he trudged upstairs to change his shoes, Alf's harsh words still ringing in his ears.

Lois sat staring at a blank computer screen, thinking about Rob. She realized that the urgency had gone out of the family resolve to find his killer. Well, in a way, that was natural. Other problems came to the fore, needing urgent attention.

When Lois last spoke to Cowgill, the case against the gypsies seemed to be hardening. But which gypsies? The whole lot hadn't formed an avenging posse and ambushed Rob as he came home, drunk and helpless, she was sure of that. The most likely of them was the pair in the ratty old caravan, with the killer dog. But if that was so, why hadn't the police got them in custody, or in for questioning, or some other ruse for preventing them from disappearing from sight? They were, so Cowgill had said, liaising with the local force where the gypsies had gone.

In a belated blinding flash, Lois saw the answer. The brothers and their dog had not gone with the rest. They had obviously been outsiders hanging on to the coattails of the others while they were in Farnden, and by now could be anywhere in the country. Time for a word with friend Hunter.

Lois looked at her watch. He should still be around, and she dialled his direct number.

"Hello, Lois! How's my girl today?" He sounded uncharacteristically bouncy.

"No, you've got the wrong person. This is Lois Meade, and I'm nobody's girl."

"All right, Lois. I am suitably humbled."

What was he talking about? Had he finally flipped, poor old thing? Lois got down to business.

"It's about Rob's killer. You said it was looking like the gypsies were involved. I've been thinking. Which of the gypsies did you speak to?"

"All of them," Cowgill said, his voice now brisk and professional.

"Including the two with the bull terrier? The *illegal* pit bull terrier?"

There was a pause, and then Cowgill said he did not have the necessary papers in front of him, but he would check and get back to her.

"Which means, I suppose, no, you didn't even *see* the two men with the *illegal* pit bull?"

"If they were on the site of the fire, we talked to them. I'll call you back, Lois. Five minutes."

Lois felt better at having done something, moved the whole thing on a step or two. From all her experience of working with Cowgill, she reckoned that you cannot leave it safely to the local police, at least not if you want a swift answer.

"Lois!" It was Gran, shouting from the kitchen. "Have you finished with the phone?" she continued, coming into the office. "I promised Joan Pickering I'd call her. She's got this idea for a Farnden market in the village hall. Maybe once a month. People take stalls and sell things, and the WI makes a profit from renting out the stalls."

All this came tumbling out, and Gran's eyes were bright with enthusiasm. "What a good idea," Lois said, thinking how useful it would be for Gran to be involved. It would take her mind off family problems, especially Josie's tragedy. It had really knocked Gran sideways, tough as she was. And it would be a good place for Gran to keep her eyes and ears open.

"Five minutes, Mum," Lois added, "then I'm done."

The phone rang on cue. "Lois? Apparently our men questioned everyone at the gypsy camp immediately after the fire was put out, but they don't remember seeing the two with the pit bull terrier. They reckon they must have scarpered quickly, before they could be questioned. Can you describe them again? It might be important to follow them up."

Lois was furious. Of all the gypsies at the camp, the two with the dog were the most likely to have attacked Rob. And now they'd gone—probably where nobody could find them. She described what she remembered of them, and said she'd ask Derek, because he saw them, too.

There was one more thing she could do. She would tackle Alf Smith, and see if he could help. Sam Stratford had been known to call him "gypsy lover" in the pub, but Lois reckoned she could coax a few facts out of him.

THIRTY-THREE

Next morning, Matthew Vickers drove slowly on his way to Long Farnden. He was thinking about Josie Meade, and wondering how he could ask her tactfully if she'd like to see the new comedy film in Tresham. He'd checked out that it was a nonviolent family film, and colleagues at work had confirmed with a sly smile that it was a laugh a minute.

His eye was caught by a pile of dirty, wilted flowers by the road-side. Another accident, he thought sadly. Then he remembered. Of course, it was where Rob had been beaten up and left to die. He drew into a gateway, got out of his car, and walked back. The least he could do was take them away. If Josie drove by—although she probably avoided that route into town—it would be a dreary reminder. He gathered them up, not noticing one separate from the rest, propped up against the fence a few yards away.

He placed the pile in the boot of his car, and turned his car around. He would dump the flowers back at the station, but remove the cards and take them to Josie. A perfect reason to go and see her later.

Lois had decided to see Alf Smith as soon as possible, and as Derek and Gran were both out early, she took her jacket and made for the door. Then the phone began to ring and she reluctantly picked it up. It was a man's voice, saying he had some information about Rob's accident. He described the house he lived in, on the road where it happened. Would she like to meet him there straight away?

Lois stiffened. "Not unless you tell me who you are," she said. But the caller had gone, and she sat for a few minutes, wondering what to do. She could alert the police, but dismissed that idea. Whoever it was might be useful. She could go that way round to Alf Smith. That would be best.

The phone rang again, and this time it was Josie. She was feeling low, and wondered if Lois could go shopping in Tresham with her. Was Gran free to take over the shop?

"No, but I can get hold of Floss. She's not cleaning anywhere at the moment. I'll ring back." She did not tell Josie about the anonymous caller. She would mention it in the car, and judge what to do by her reaction. The visit to Alf would have to wait.

Fifteen minutes later, with Floss behind the counter, Lois collected Josie and they set off. "Thanks, Mum," Josie said. Lois said that she had been going out anyway, but nowhere important.

"Going where, Mum?" Josie asked, feeling guilty.

"Just down the farm on the off chance I could see Alf Smith."

"I should stay clear of him! When Edwina brought some eggs in, she said he's in a bad mood at the moment, an' he had a real set-to in the shop with Sam Stratford. I nearly had to push 'em out. Putting off the customers, they were."

Lois asked what the row had been about, but at that point Josie pointed at the roadside and said loudly, "They've gone! Rob's flowers—they've all gone!"

Lois slowed down the car and said she supposed there were rules about leaving them by the road for too long. The council had probably taken them away.

"Hey, there's one left! Over by the fence. Can you pull up, and I'll get it."

Lois stopped and got out quickly. It would be better if she collected the bunch. Josie was quite composed at the moment, but the slightest thing could change that. She stooped to pick them up, and noticed immediately that the flowers were fresh, and the card crisp and clear. She looked at the message and gulped. Oh God, what now? In black capitals, the message was blunt: IN MEMORIAM—LOIS MEADE, SUPER-SNOOP. REST IN HELL.

Her first reaction was to screw up the card and lose it. Then she knew this wouldn't fool Josie. The scarlet flowers were newly placed there, not at all wilted, and there was no reason why the card should have been lost so soon. She got back into the car and silently handed the bunch to Josie, who read the card and turned on her mother, fear making her sharp and accusatory. Lois calmed her down, said it was probably a hoax, and decided to tell her about the anonymous caller.

Lois said they should really get on into Tresham, but Josie insisted on continuing to look for the man who'd called. She was intrigued, and said they couldn't afford to ignore any leads that might help. And, she added, there were two of them, and both were big strong gels! They drove up and down the stretch of road where the house was supposed to be, but found nothing except a ruined cottage, with boarded-up windows and a pile of bricks in front of the door. Finally they gave up, did their shopping in Tresham and returned to Farnden, where Lois suggested they have a cup of tea before Josie returned to the shop.

"What d'you think's going on, Mum?" Josie said when they were settled. Lois did not reply at first, and the sound of the shelf clock ticking filled the room.

"Not sure," she said at last. "But one thing's clear. I was set up. Whoever it was guessed I would drive up and down looking for the house, and almost certainly see the one remaining bunch of fresh, bright red flowers by the fence. He was gambling on my stopping to look at it, and succeeded."

"You'll tell the police, Mum, won't you? You could be in danger."

"Doubt it," said Lois. "More likely it was a black joke. But yes, I'll tell the police. And I'll find out where the rest of the flowers went." Then she reconsidered. Perhaps she would leave reporting it until later, after she had had a chance to speak to Alf Smith.

As it happened, Josie was the first to find out about the flowers. Next morning early, Matthew Vickers walked briskly into the shop and said he'd got something for her. "It's about those tribute bunches of flowers at the roadside. I took them away so's you didn't have to see them wilted and dying. I've saved the cards and brought them in for you."

"That was thoughtful," Josie said, and wondered whether to mention the bunch she and Lois found. She decided against it. It was Mum's concern, really. Although she suspected her mother would not report it, Josie reckoned she should give her the opportunity.

Matthew said it was the least he could do. Then he took advantage of being in favour, and asked her about the film. When she said she just had to check her diary, he left the shop walking on air, and nearly collided with Mark Brown, who was sidling in. He had seen the police car, and tossed up whether to go into the shop or keep walking. He'd decided to go in. After all, he was not exactly wanted by Interpol. He had a couple of job applications to send off urgently, and needed stamps.

"Now, Mark, what can I do for you?" Josie said.

"Two first-class stamps, please," he said. He liked Josie. She always treated him like a responsible adult and looked him straight in the eye. Pity about her mother. After his session with Lois he had brooded on her attitude to him and put her at the top of his list of most hated people. And next came all those villagers who either looked away when he passed, or sent him looks of such venom that he felt like running home for sanctuary. Home to what, though? he thought to himself. Equally venomous looks from his father?

"I'll take those letters, shall I?" Josie said. "They can go straight in the bag for collection."

"Thanks," Mark said. "And a packet of Rizlas, please."

"Sold out. Sorry."

Mark could see a box with several packets of cigarette rolling papers clearly visible. But he turned tail and left the shop with his head down. Everything and everybody conspired against him.

Josie picked up the letters and was about to put them in the postman's bag, when Mark's handwriting caught her eye. She had seen it before, very recently, but not on an envelope. That curly *R* and looped *L* were unmistakable. She picked up the phone and dialed her mother.

"Mum? Have you still got that horrible card? Can you bring it down straight away? I've got something to show you."

THIRTY-FOUR

It was Saturday, Derek's day for the garden and football. Tresham United were playing away up north, and although a pub group were going in a minibus, Derek had decided not to join them. His son Douglas had asked him to go over to Gordon Street and help fix a new television aerial, and Lois said she would go, too, and do some shopping. She had, as always, an ulterior motive, and was hoping to spot Mark Brown with his unsavory mates.

"He's a good liar, Mum," Josie had said. "If I were you, I'd start from a position of not believing a word he says."

Gran had decided to stay at home, and when she had stacked the dishes after lunch, she put her feet up in the sitting room and turned on the television. She was asleep in minutes, and as the sunshine poured through the windows, and a mindless quiz game chuntered on, Gran in her dream walked beside the river with her late husband, planning with him an uneventful retirement.

She was awoken by an insistent tapping sound. Fearful at once of burglars or violent tinkers, she sprang up and stared at the window. A stranger stood outside, smiling and beckoning to her. She was certain she had never seen him before, and wondered what to do.

"Mrs. Weedon!" he shouted. "Let me in!"

So he knew her name. But that didn't mean anything. She walked to the front door and saw with relief that the chain was on. With great care she opened the door a crack and saw the man already standing there.

"Who are you and what do you want?" she said fiercely.

"I'm Greg, Rob's brother. Can I come in?"

"How do I know you're Rob's brother?" Gran said. "He never said nothing about a brother."

"Well, we didn't get on all that well, and I've been in Australia for a long time. Please let me in. I didn't know he'd died until I decided to look him up while I was over here. I went to the vicarage first, and the reverend told me."

"Well, I don't know," Gran said. "I promised my daughter I'd not let anyone into the house. We have to be so careful these days. But they'll be back about six this evening. You could try again then." She shut the door firmly, and waited until she heard the footsteps retreating down the drive. Then she rushed to the back door and locked it quickly.

Josie! She took up the telephone and dialled the shop. Josie answered, and said she'd be wary of a stranger looking nothing like Rob but claiming to be his brother. She agreed with Gran that it sounded suspiciously dodgy. But by the end of the afternoon, no such stranger had come in, and Josie relaxed. Maybe somebody playing a joke on poor old Gran. She remembered the threatening tag on the flowers, and thought bitterly that if it, too, was a vicious joke, then Mark Brown was even more dangerously disturbed than they had thought. But the stranger could not have been Mark. Gran would have recognised him immediately.

She locked up the shop and feeling unsettled, she went upstairs to the flat and turned on the television. The news bulletin was full of catastrophe as usual, and she turned it off again. Perhaps it would be a good idea to walk up and see Gran. Maybe Mum and Dad would be back by now.

Father Keith watched from his window as his wife drove in. She had been over to Fletching to recruit another market stall-holder—hand-thrown pottery this time—and came in looking triumphant.

"She's keen," Marjorie said. "Nice stuff, too. Look—I bought a little bowl from her."

She handed him a grey blue bowl, not quite perfectly circular, and he said should he hand throw it now, or leave it until later?

" Ha-ha," Marjorie said. Sometimes she could strangle him. "Anyway, how was your afternoon? Any messages? Visitors?"

"No messages. One visitor."

"Interesting?"

"Not sure," Father Keith said, his face serious now. "A youngish man came to the door claiming to be Rob Wilkins's long lost brother from Australia. Said he was looking for Rob, so of course I had to tell him he'd been killed in an accident. I didn't elaborate, and when he asked who he could see who might talk to him, I sent him up to Meades' house. I was rather anxious that he shouldn't catch Josie alone in the shop. He obviously knew nothing about her, but had been told somewhere that Rob lived in Long Farnden."

Marjorie put down the bowl and slowly took off her jacket. "Mm," she said thoughtfully. "Maybe we should mention it to Josie?"

Father Keith shook his head. "I think I've done all that is necessary," he said. "I'm sure Mrs. Meade will get to the bottom of it."

"Hi, Josie!" Derek said. He and Lois had returned from Tresham, where he had done a good job for Douglas. He was now looking forward to Gran's newly baked jam sponge and a cup of Sergeant-Major's tea. Susie's brew was, not to put too fine a point on it, like cat's pee.

Gran was unsmiling and as soon as she had the tea on the table, said, "Sit down, all of you," she said. "I want some advice."

"*You* want some advice?" said Derek, laughing heartily.

"It's not funny, Derek," Gran said. She told them about the man who said he was Rob's brother returned from Australia, and added that she had not let him in. "I said he could come back around now," she added, looking up at the clock.

"You did exactly the right thing," Lois said.

"And Gran told me about him, too," Josie said. Lois nodded approvingly.

"Right!" Derek said. "Just as well I didn't go with the other blokes to the football. If he comes back, you can leave him to me."

"It just might be true," Josie said mildly.

"Maybe so," Lois agreed. "But we'll need proof of some sort. Anybody could come claiming to be Rob's brother, probably hoping for any money that might be going begging. We all thought he was an orphan with no relatives, didn't we?"

"He never mentioned a brother to me," Josie said. "Still, families do have feuds and cut off from each other for ever." She was thinking it might be rather comforting if the man really was Rob's brother. Something left of him, in a funny sort of way. On the other hand, she was fully aware that it might be trouble in the making.

"More cake?" Gran said to Derek, and as he was holding out his plate, they all heard the front doorbell ring.

"Ah," Lois said. "Are you going, Derek?"

He looked longingly at the slice of cake held out towards him, but stood up and said that of course he, as head of the family, should go and tackle the likely impostor.

He went to the door, and the others listened.

"That's him!" Gran said. "I recognise the voice. Oh, Lord, I hope Derek doesn't ask him in."

Josie said nothing, but stared at the door and continued to listen. When she heard two sets of footsteps coming down the tiled hallway, she retreated to the other side of the table, next to her mother.

"Sorry to interrupt," the stranger said. "Mrs. Weedon said to come back, and I am really grateful to Mr. Meade for asking me in. I won't take up too much of your time, but I am pretty desperate to find out what happened to my brother. My name is Greg, by the way."

"You weren't that desperate to find him up to now," Josie said in an icy voice.

He turned and stared at her. "You must be Josie," he said.

THIRTY-FIVE

It was early evening by the time Lois set off for Alf's farm. She had Jeems on a lead, and the little dog pulled from sniff to sniff, slowing up progress and giving time for Lois to decide exactly what she wanted to know from Alf.

So far, the new things to think about were the appearance of Rob's possible brother, the likelihood of Mark Brown's handwriting on the threatening card, and the identity of the caller who had lured her to a nonexistent rendezvous on the Tresham road. Was there a connection here? But for now, her reason for talking to Alf was to find out about the gypsies. She really needed to know where most of them had gone and what had happened to the two men and their dog.

Edwina opened the door and looked pleased to see Lois. From what she had heard from Sam, Lois was a good employer and a hard worker. Edwina knew folk said she did a bit of snooping on the side, but this was only gossip.

"Come in, Lois," she said. "Can I offer you a glass of something? Your Derek is very fond of my primrose wine!"

"Thanks," Lois said. "I really came to have a word with Alf. Is he around?"

"You're in luck. He's just come in, an'll be down in a minute. Cleaning up a bit! I reckon when you have beasts on the farm you never really get rid of the smell. Good job I'm used to it!" She thought of Sam, and how he never had Alf's aura of muck. A nice piney smell, that was Sam. Then the thought struck her that it was probably Sheila who kept him clean and fresh. Oh God, what a muddle.

Alf came in, smiling and saying how nice to see Lois. "It's usually your Derek who comes to call on parish council business," he said. "Still, my gypsies have gone now, so that's sorted."

"I'm afraid it *is* the gypsies I came to see you about," Lois said apologetically.

"What's happened, then," Alf said.

"Come and sit down, Lois," Edwina said. "We can have a chat, if you've got time. Here, would you like one of my scones?

Made this afternoon. Get the raspberry jam out, Alf."

Edwina was curious. She was sure Lois would not want to see Alf about Sam—if she had discovered something about them, surely she wouldn't go straight to Alf? And certainly not when they all sat companionably round the kitchen table. No, Lois had said it was the gypsies. She'd come about the gypsies. In that case, there were several things Edwina would like to say on the subject, though she had decided to keep that blackmailing one to herself. Those two had gone, thank God, and taken their killer dog with them. She hoped that was the last she would see of them.

"Nothing's happened, s'far as I know," Lois said. "I just wondered if I could ask you a few questions. We're no nearer finding out who attacked Josie's Rob, and the police are still pointing the finger at the gypsies."

"Bloody idiots!" Alf said fiercely. "They can't see further than their noses. Them gypsies have been coming here for years and years, generations of 'em. There's never been any trouble, an' I would trust them a lot more'n I'd trust several so-called respectable people in this village. Anyway," he continued, calming down, "what did you want to know?"

"Where they went. I talked to Athalia and George while they were here, and they were so nice. I thought if I could get in touch with them and maybe have another chat, they might remember something useful."

"O' course I know where they went," Alf said. "But if I tell you, the police'll be on to them at once. All I can tell you is that they're on their way to the Appleby horse fair. Might be going up meself."

"When is it?" Edwina said quickly. The thought of having the house to herself was exciting.

"Early June," Alf said. "Though even if you went, you'd be hard put to find them. Hundreds and hundreds of gypsies and horses turn up, and it'd be like looking for a needle in a haystack."

"But *you'd* know where to look?" Lois said.

"Might do," Alf said. "What else did you want to know?"

Lois could feel him clamming up. He would know about her contact with Cowgill and be suspicious.

"There were a couple of them. They looked like brothers, with a pit bull terrier," she said. Might as well come straight to the point. "I saw them, and so did Derek. So did Sam Stratford's son, Alan, when he was out for a walk. But nobody's seen them since the fire, and they weren't with the other lot when they left. To be honest, Alf, they were not how you described your friends.

They threatened violence, kept an illegal dog, and camped in the thicket in an ancient old van away from the others. What d'you know about them?"

Alf was silent, and Edwina stared fixedly at him. Her heart beat faster, and she wondered what was coming out now. Should she tell all? It would probably be a good time, when Lois was here to soften Alf's anger with her.

Alf cleared his throat. "Yeah, well," he began, "I never saw them two before. I asked Athalia about them, and she said they'd just tagged along. They weren't travelling with the rest. Just turned up and asked if they could stop here. I didn't like it, and told them to go." He didn't mention that they had still been hidden in the thicket after the fire. The police might think he had withheld evidence, or whatever it was they called it.

"So where did they go?" Lois said.

Alf shook his head. "Don't know, me duck," he said. "They're the sort that give the Roma people a bad name. Somebody said they'd seen them selling things in Tresham market. Fly-b'nights, they are. Picking up a living in any way that comes handy, and not all of it the right side of the law. You want to keep well clear of them."

Lois took a deep breath. "D'you reckon they were the ones who attacked Rob?" she said.

"I doubt it," Alf said. "A couple of cowards, both of 'em. That sort always are. They let that dog do their fighting. Unless, o' course, they were drunk. Like your Rob. Anything could've happened then, couldn't it?"

Lois was silent. She realised that Alf had not told her anything she did not know already. She finished her tea and began to get up.

"Just a minute, Lois," Edwina said. "I can tell you a bit more about them two."

Alf stared at her. "What d'you mean, gel?" he said. "Did they threaten you?"

Edwina slowly stuttered out the story of the money paid over to keep them quiet. She did not mention Sam, the reason for their blackmail. She said she had caught them stealing chickens, and they had said they'd set the dog on her if she said anything to Alf.

"I was scared," she said. "I know I should've told you, but he was really scary. Anyway, it was only the twice. Then they were gone."

Lois and Alf stared at her. "You poor thing," Lois said. But Alf said nothing. He frowned, looked down at his clenched hands, and

got up from his seat, shoving the chair back behind him so that it
fell over with a crash.

"Alf!" Edwina said. "Where're you going?"

"Out!" Alf said in a hoarse voice, and he was gone, banging the
kitchen door behind him.

Edwina was pale, and turned to Lois. Her hands were shaking.
"What shall I do?" she said.

"You'd better tell me the real reason he blackmailed you," Lois
said. "Then we might know better what's to be done."

But Edwina shook her head and composed herself. "Best leave it
to me," she said. "Alf'll calm down. He always does. He'll be fine
when he comes back. Sorry he went out like that, Lois, but it's his
way of dealing with it. Better than losing his temper with me, anyway."

Lois shrugged. If she did not want to tell her the truth, that was
her affair. But she was sure Edwina was hiding something, and guessed
the blackmail was about something much worse than stealing chickens.

THIRTY-SIX

Have you told the police about your bunch of flowers, Mum?" Josie
faced her mother over the shop counter next morning. There were
no other customers and Josie meant to persist. Lois had evaded the
question once before and now said nothing.

"Mum?"

"Well, no, not yet," Lois finally admitted. "I was waiting until
I'd seen Alf."

"*Why* Alf Smith? What's he got to do with Mark Brown?"

"Nothing, really. But one of the gypsies—one of the ones who
did the pub quiz that night—was set on by a gang of lads as they
went home. Alf was a real friend to the gypsies, and I wondered if
he'd heard anything more from George. That was the one who did
the quiz."

"Like if Mark Brown was one of the lads?"

"Yep. Exactly."

"And?"

"Alf was a bit suspicious of me," Lois said. "I asked him about the two roughnecks with the pit bull terrier, and he told me a bit about them. But something Edwina said upset him and he stormed out."

"So now you'll tell your friend Cowgill. Promise, Mum. That message on the flowers was very nasty."

"Could be teenage spite, trying to frighten me off," said Lois. "It don't necessarily mean I'm in danger."

"Mum!"

"All right, Josie. I'll have a word with Cowgill. But you know what the cops are like. They'll want to take the card, analyse the writing, drag Mark Brown into the cop shop again, an' that'll be more trouble for his parents."

"And a good thing, too!" Josie was fast becoming angry with her mother, and decided to play a last card. "Perhaps I should tell Dad," she said. "Maybe he could do something."

"Good try, m'love," Lois said, and, picking up her groceries, she left the shop.

When she had gone, Josie turned over in her mind what had been said. Something lurked in the back of her mind, something that she hadn't taken up with her mother. Oh, yes, it was something about Edwina upsetting Alf. What had she said? Josie remembered the spat between Alf and Sam Stratford in the shop, and frowned. Edwina, Alf . . . and *Sam*? Could it have been? No, that was quite ridiculous. They were too old for that sort of thing.

The shop door opened and Josie was surprised to see her brother Douglas arrive. He was carrying an empty gas cylinder and looked thunderous.

"Hi, Doug!" Josie said. "What on earth are you doing with that?"

"We've had some power cuts in Tresham," he said shortly. "And last night was the last straw. This is empty, as always when you need it. The evenings are chilly, an' Susie complains. She's a chilly mortal, bless her."

"There must be gas cylinders in Tresham? Did you try the garages?"

"No, I wanted to see you anyway. How are you feeling now? We wondered if you were up to coming to a movie with us? We could have a pizza first, and make an evening of it."

Josie smiled. Douglas had always been her favourite brother. She considered Susie was lucky to get him. There was such a difference in their ages, and Josie hoped that the impending marriage was a good idea.

"Thanks, thanks a lot, both of you," she said. "Actually, I've just accepted an invitation to see the film. Maybe when there's a new programme?"

"Who're you going with, then?" Douglas said, surprised. Maybe with Mum and Dad, that was most likely.

"Never you mind," Josie said. "He's just a friend, and couldn't be more respectable."

Douglas raised his eyebrows. "Right," he said. "Fine."

"So you'll ask me again, won't you," Josie said.

After she'd exchanged the gas cylinders and they'd had a chat about nothing much, Douglas left. Josie looked at the telephone for a couple of seconds, and then dialled Matthew Vickers.

Cowgill was in his office, standing at his favourite place by the window, looking down on the street. He was puzzled. This Rob Wilkins case was taking much longer to clear up than he had anticipated. He had to tread carefully when speaking to Lois, or to Josie, for that matter. Lois's daughter was becoming wonderfully like her mother.

But Cowgill had thought right from the beginning that Rob had been a weak sort of man, easily swayed, and he had not been at all surprised to see from the records that he had been given a warning after causing an affray in Tresham late one night some time ago. Drunk, he'd been. How had this apparently meek and mild man kept his other self from Josie? Ah well, he wouldn't be the first to play Jekyll and Hyde.

He turned around as there was a knock at the door. "Come!" he said.

Matthew Vickers put his head around the door. "Can you spare a moment, sir?"

Cowgill nodded. He was very punctilious about not allowing Matthew to deviate in any way from the routine and regulations of the police station, just because he was his nephew.

Matthew came in and shut the door. "It's about the Rob Wilkins case," he said. "Anything new? I'm hoping to take Josie Meade to a movie and it would be nice to be up to date on where we are. Sir."

Cowgill shook his head. "I'm still certain it is connected with those gypsies in some way. There *is* something you probably don't know, and had better keep to yourself."

"Of course, sir. I am not a junior recruit."

It appeared that he had not heard much about the other side of Rob's character, and Cowgill decided not to make too much of it. He was not at all sure he approved of Matthew's date with Josie. Still, as far as he could gather, she hadn't agreed to go. "Just be very careful," he began, and then Matthew's mobile rang.

Cowgill watched as a broad smile spread over his nephew's face. "That's great," Matthew said. "I'll pick you up around six thirty. Best bib and tucker! See you then. 'Bye, Josie."

"She's agreed to come with you, I gather?"

"Yeah—that's really good. I was hoping I'd be able to help her face her bereavement, but worried that it might be too soon."

Not to mention hoping to lure her to your lonely cottage in the middle of nowhere, Cowgill thought. The lad might have more luck with Josie than he, Cowgill, had had with her mother. But enough of that. He felt quite cheered up, wished his nephew a jolly evening, and dismissed him.

THIRTY-SEVEN

Acouple of days later, Derek was on his way home when he came upon a cyclist whizzing along in the middle of the road. He slowed down and waited for him to get to the side of the road. The fool must have heard the van coming up behind him, but he remained in the middle of the road and Derek hooted crossly at him. To his annoyance the cyclist kept going as before.

Finally, at the turning to Farnden Hall, he swerved off to the left and disappeared. For two pins Derek would have followed and given him a piece of his mind, but he was tired and hungry and anxious to get home. He thought the man looked familiar, but with all that Lycra and an all-concealing helmet, it was difficult to be sure.

Mark Brown continued at speed and circled round to the stable yard at the back of the hall. He looked up at the windows along the first floor, and was rewarded by the sight of Sally waving and smiling. Hooray, she was in a good mood! He parked his bike out of sight behind the end of the stables, and waited. After a few minutes, the back door of the house opened, and Sally beckoned him in.

"She's off magistrating," she said.

"She's what? Thought you did that in the privacy of your own bedroom," he said.

Sally laughed long and loud. Her laugh was very loud, and sometimes irritated Mark. But all the girls of her kind laughed like that.

"Come into my parlour, said the spider to the fly," Sally said in a silly voice.

"Huh?"

"Never mind," she replied. "Just come on in quickly. We can go to my room and listen to some music. By the way," she added. "That shiny getup is very sexy—all is revealed!" Her laughter pealed out into the yard and Mark looked around nervously. He scuttled into the kitchen and she shut the door, patting his bottom as he passed her.

She led the way across the lofty entrance hall, with its chessboard of black and white floor tiles, carefully washed every Friday by Sheila from New Brooms. He followed her up the wide stairway, which became a T-junction at the top, with a long corridor stretching to right and left. Sally turned right, and halfway along she opened the door to her room and beckoned him inside, her finger to her lips. "There's other people in the house," she whispered. "Including ghosts . . ."

Mark's eyes widened. "You're not serious?" he whispered back. He had been determined not to feel overawed by the grand house with its myriad of passages and doors firmly shut, but the oppressive atmosphere made him shiver. A sudden deep barking startled him even more. Blimey, it was the Hound of the Baskervilles! Well, he was no Sherlock Holmes, and he sat down on the edge of Sally's bed trying to conceal his shaking hands.

She appeared not to notice, and switched on her player. Loud music filled the room, and she laughed. "Now we can shout if we like," she said. "They're used to me making 'that awful noise,' as the old girl says."

"You mean Mrs. Tollervey-Jones? Who else is there here?"

"A deliciously handsome young man—no, not you—who comes

to garden a couple of days a week. Doesn't do much digging and that sort of thing. Likes riding round on motor mowers and Aunt's latest toy. He persuaded her to buy a quad bike thing, like farmers whiz around on. He can wind her round his little finger."

"Don't like the sound of him at all," Mark said. "Who else? He's not much in the house, presumably?"

"Oh, cleaning women come and go. And Aunt's committee friends. You know the sort." She opened a drawer in her dressing table and pulled out a small bottle. "Need a little encouragement?" she said, and shook the pills inside.

Two men walked silently through the spinney of poplars that grew along the kitchen garden at the rear of the hall.

"Are you sure she'll be out?" Sid walked a couple of paces behind Harry, relying on him to know the way. If Sid had had his way, they would be miles away from Long Farnden by now. But Harry insisted that there were still rich pickings to be had locally, and they were happily settled where they were by the old barn. "S'long as you keep yer stupid head down!" he had warned Sid. "An' let me do all the talking."

Harry had crept all round the hall one night, and said the stables were not locked and except for one, where there was a rusty old nag, they were used as storerooms for all sorts of promising goodies. Now they had a couple of big rucksacks and if surprised by the old girl, planned to say they were walkers hoping for a drink of water to see them on their way. "We can say we're lost, Sid," Harry said. "An' you can put on that innocent look o' yours that always works with old ladies."

"Supposing she asks to see inside the bags?" Sid seldom questioned Harry, but this job looked to him fraught with danger.

"We scarper. Quick as we can," Harry answered. They came into the neatly planted kitchen garden, through a small gate and into the stable yard. Harry was about to make for the nearest stable when Sid stopped. "Listen!" he said. "What's that music?"

Harry looked up at the back of the hall. "It's only that chit of a girl," he said. "Look—her curtains are drawn across. Stoned out of her mind, you bet. Probably got one of her mates up there. They'll not notice us. Specially if you don't make no noise, you idiot!" Sid had walked straight into an old bucket standing beside the stable door.

Harry was right on all counts. They filled their rucksacks with all kinds of saleable loot, from old books to ancient umbrellas and rusty garden tools that would shine up a treat. Sally's curtains remained drawn, and they had the yard to themselves. Until the horse suddenly began to neigh, a loud, frightening sound.

"That's enough, innit?" Sid said, anxious to be gone.

"No hurry. There's another cupboard here," Harry said. "You're used to horses, for God's sake! It's hungry, I daresay. Gi' it a mint. You always got a packet in yer pocket, ain't yer?"

This time, Harry was wrong. The horse was snickering now because it knew the sound of its owner's car coming up the long drive to the house and Mrs. T-J always greeted her old friend before going into the house.

"Christ!" said Harry, as he heard the engine noise, and looked around for Sid. But Sid had gone, fast as a greyhound, through the kitchen garden, the spinney and across the field, leaving Harry, who was not so quick on his feet, to lumber along behind.

Mark, prone beside a snoring Sally, also heard the car. He flew across to the window and peered from behind the curtain. "Sally!" he said. "Wake up! Your aunt's back!"

She didn't move. Out for the count, thought Mark, and took another look into the yard. To his surprise he saw Mrs. T-J hop nimbly out of the car and take off round the back of the stables, followed closely by the Hound of the Baskervilles, which had cleared its compound fence with ease and was running beside her.

Mark saw his chance, and, cursing his tight-fitting cycling gear, he stumbled out of Sally's room, down the wide stairway and out of the kitchen door. He'd hidden his bike as usual, and retrieved it quickly. Before there was any sign of Mrs. T-J returning, he pedalled for his life down the drive towards home and safety.

"Where've you been?" his mother said, as he banged into the house and collapsed on a chair in the kitchen. "You look as if the devil was behind you!"

"That wouldn't surprise me," said his father. He looked scornfully at his son, and vanished out into the garden.

"So what's happened? I thought you were going into town on your bike?"

Mark shook his head. "Got a flat tyre," he said. "Had to mend it on the side of the road. No bugger stopped to help."

"Don't swear," Nancy Brown said automatically. She didn't believe her son. From long and wearying experience she knew he was lying. She also knew that it was useless to try and get the truth out of him.

Mark stood up. "I've got some work to do in my room," he said. "See you later," he added, and clumped upstairs. There was a short silence, and then the familiar unmusical thud-thud filtered through the house. Nancy sighed and rubbed her eyes.

I wish I could get away from the two of them, she thought, not for the first time.

THIRTY-EIGHT

The next day dawned slowly. By eight o'clock it was barely light, with heavy grey skies and rain sheeting across Lois's garden, blown almost horizontally by a strong gale-force wind.

"And I'm supposed to be fixing an array of security lights outside that new mansion. Y' know, that monstrosity that's gone up where Boreham's old farmhouse used to be," Derek said, standing by the window.

"Not in this downpour!" Lois said. "Elec and water don't mix. I won't have you brought home shrivelled and scorched," she said. "I smell breakfast," she added. "Let's see what it's like when we've eaten Gran's special."

She was halfway down the stairs when the telephone rang.

"Hello? Is that Mrs. Meade?" For a moment, Lois could not place the voice. "It's Mark Brown here."

There was a silence, and Lois waited for him to say more. In the end, she said, "What can I do for you, Mark?"

He coughed, and then in a hoarse whisper said, "Can you spare me a few minutes this morning? Got something to tell you. Could be important."

Lois looked at the clock. "Come at half nine," she said. "I've got a client to see, but not until eleven. See you then." She hoped it *was* important, and not just another rant about the evils of his father.

"Lois! Breakfast is getting cold on the table!" shouted Gran.

Mark rang the doorbell punctually at half past nine. Gran was there to let him in, and said, "Hello, boy, come on in." She had no idea what he wanted with Lois, but, from a motherly point of view, saw in front of her a young and vulnerable lad.

"Hi, Mark," Lois said. She came out of her office, and added to Gran, "No coffee at the moment, thanks, Mum, We've only just had breakfast." She waved Mark into her office and shut the door firmly. Gran shrugged huffily and went back to the kitchen.

"Sit down, Mark," Lois said. She had decided to let him know straight away that she was well aware of his record of lies and drugs, and added, "Now, you know I have to take everything you say with a pinch of salt, so don't waste my time. Tell me the truth, whatever it is you've got to say."

"Wow!" he replied. "Here I am, come up here to help, and you give me the bum's rush before I get started! Okay, okay, I swear on the Bible—"

"That's enough of that," Lois snapped. "Just get on with it."

Mark had rather liked the idea of telling his story to Mrs. Meade. He could spin it out and show he was one up on her, at least.

"Well, I was going to the police," he said, "but they ain't likely to listen to me, so—"

"So I am the next best thing," said Lois. "For God's sake, what is it you come for?"

Mark stood up, offended. This wasn't what he had expected at all. "Perhaps I'd better be going, then," he said, trying a new tack.

Lois slapped her desk with the flat of her hand. "Off you go, then!" she said, and began to shuffle her papers.

Mark sat down again. "It was yesterday," he said. "I biked up to the hall to see Sally. She'd said her aunt would be out, and we could listen to music in her room."

"Listen to music? That's a new one."

"Well, we'd been up there a while, and we had the curtains drawn. Then I heard a noise outside in the yard. It was that horse, making a row enough to wake the dead. I went to the window, and saw these two men. One was sort of keeping watch, and the other was inside a stable, filling up a rucksack sort of bag with all sorts of stuff. Apparently Mrs. T-J keeps all kinds of rubbish that should've been taken to the dump ages ago."

He paused, and said he knew his mother was like that. Never threw anything away. He smiled at Lois, but she did not smile back. "Get on with it," she said.

He sniffed, and continued. "I tried to wake Sally, but couldn't, an' I was just wondering what to do when the lookout suddenly shot off round the back of the stables, and the other one followed. Then, to my horror, I saw a car pull up in the yard, and I recognised it." He paused dramatically, but met with stony silence from Lois.

"It was Auntie, of course," he said, sighing. "She got out, and to my surprise, she immediately legged it out of the yard after the men. She must've seen them as she drove in. Then along came the Hound of the Baskervilles—"

"Who?" said Lois angrily. How much of this was true? He seemed to be making it up as he went along.

"Her bloody great dog," Mark said. "You know, Sherlock Holmes—"

"I know, thanks," Lois interrupted. "So then?"

"I saw my chance to get away, and took it," he said.

"Leaving Sally to face the music?"

"Nobody else knew I'd been there," Mark said defensively.

"Did you recognise either of them?"

"Well, I did think I'd seen them before. I'd need to have a better look, really. But I was in Tresham on market day last week, and saw a stall run by a couple of dids. They were rubbish. They weren't in the marketplace proper, but just round the corner, by the Crown. It was mostly junk on the stall, but they'd got a queue waiting."

"Just the once, then?"

Mark paused, weighing up whether to tell Lois the rest, or keep it to himself. It might incriminate him in the fire investigation. He decided to tell. "I reckon I might've seen them on the night of the fire on the gypsy site. Saw the back of two similar, yanking their dog along towards that spinney. They disappeared fast, and I never thought any more about it. But these two at the market had a similar sort of bull terrier chained to the leg of the stall."

Lois leaned forward towards him, and he saw he had caught her attention now, good and proper. Oh God, he thought. I've said too much now. He got up quickly and made for the door. "I should've kept it to myself," he muttered.

"No, you did the right thing," Lois said. "Could be really helpful. And Mark," she added, as she saw him out of the house, "just be careful with Sally. She's reckoned to be a right handful."

"Spoilt brat?" he said, and ran down the drive.

Cowgill arrived in his office and almost immediately the telephone began to ring. He picked it up, frowned, and held it a good six inches from his ear.

"Morning, Mrs. Tollervey-Jones," he said. "Could you just hold on a moment. Can't hear you very well." Another blast issued from the phone, quite audible to his assistant, who had followed him in.

Cowgill sat down, made signs of drinking and desperation, and his assistant nodded. "Coffee," she said, and disappeared.

After listening for a few minutes, he nodded. "Of course, madam," he said. "We shall be investigating this immediately, you can be sure of that. Yes, I shall keep you informed on progress. Right away. Good morning, madam."

He sighed deeply, looked at his watch, and dialled.

"Hello," said Lois impatiently. "Oh, it's you. What d'you want? I've wasted enough time this morning."

"Sorry about that, Lois. You might be interested in what I've just heard." He began to tell her the substance of Mrs. Tollervey-Jones's call, but she interrupted him.

"I know all about that," she said. "Tell me something new. Like who killed Rob."

His voice changed, and he said sharply, "You know very well we have just about every man in the station working on that. This theft might even mean something. Do you know any more than I do about the men?"

She told him what Mark had said he knew of them, including recognising them from the gypsy site.

"So what we need to know," she said, "is where they are holed up now. Must be somewhere around here. Shouldn't be beyond the best detective in the county to find out."

"I only wish I thought you were serious, Lois," he said.

"I am serious," she replied.

THIRTY-NINE

Athalia Lee sat on the steps of her trailer, soaking up the sun. She looked across the scrubby patch of ground at the old railway track that had run beside the main channel of the river. It had been built in an attempt to popularise the village and the surrounding countryside as a tourist attraction, but the muddy banks and treacherous marshland had not appealed to day trippers. The railway had fallen victim in the nineteen-sixties to Dr. Beeching, then Chairman of British Rail, who closed down thousands of miles of track in a misguided plan to improve railway efficiency. It had deteriorated sadly over the years, but lately had become the Loare Pathway, equipped with bird-watching hides and warnings about the danger of deep mud, which could entrap the unwary.

She watched idly as an inoffensive-looking man walked slowly past the Black Duck Inn and five minutes later returned. He had walked up and down four times. Athalia had counted, and knew for certain he was a plainclothes cop, checking up on them. He looked across at the gypsies, and then disappeared into the pub. Well, he could check all he liked. He would find nothing wrong.

Then she saw George coming back from the small field where they were allowed to graze their horses, leading his small black and white mare. The field was poor land, not useful for anything much, and gypsies had been using it for generations. Like most of the others, George had no need of a horse. Gypsies had become motorised, but horses were in their blood. Appleby horse fair proved that, and he and the others would soon be moving on there.

"Where's Jal?" George frowned, and Athalia saw that he was upset.

"What's happened?" she said.

"I got to see Jal. Have you seen him?"

"Yeah—he's over there, splittin' wood. Is something up?"

George did not answer, but went quickly over to Jal. Athalia saw them talking, heads close together, and then Jal put down his axe and followed George back the way he had come.

Athalia stood up and smoothed down her skirt. She walked at a steady pace, taking the same path as the two men, but keeping her distance from them. It was not easy going through the tough, reedy grass and tussocks of moss and lichen, and several times she stumbled. But she was lucky. Neither of them looked back, seemingly intent on finding whatever it was as quickly as possible.

Finally the men slowed down and came to a halt at the edge of the channel. The tide was out, and banks of glistening mud lined each side. Birds were feeding, and a rat scampered away from the carcase of a dead swan. Athalia came up quietly, and looking down from the bank, saw that the swan was not the only dead thing caught in the mud. At first she thought it must be a badger that had fallen into the water and drowned. Then she saw the body was smooth and shiny, and obviously bloated. Her gorge rose. She retched, and the men swung round and saw her.

"Athalia! Get out of here. Now! Get back and say nothing! Not a bloody word!"

George walked towards her and, putting his hand on her shoulder, turned her around and gave her a gentle push. "I'll talk to you later," he said.

"I'm a romani rye, I'm an old didikye," Athalia sang softly, as twilight deepened over the estuary of the Loare. Cars were rolling up now, parking in the small yard, and men and wives, some with small children, made their way into the pub. There was a strong smell of frying, and Athalia wrinkled her nose. Ugh! Burgers and chips, no doubt. She disapproved, and had occupied her time since being sent packing by George by preparing and cooking a meat pudding. The old way took time. She made the pastry dough and rolled it out, then tossed the diced beef in flour and piled it on to the pastry. An Oxo cube and a little water, and then the whole lot tied up in a floured cloth and suspended in boiling water, where it simmered for at least two or three hours. She went to her trailer door and looked out. "I live in a trailer beneath the blue sky," she sang, "I don't pay any rent, I'd rather live in a tent, that's why they call me a romani rye." She chuckled to herself. Songs learned in childhood came back word perfect. One of the consolations of old age, she said to herself. Then she noticed a shadow emerging from George's trailer. It was him, and he was heading towards her.

Now perhaps he'll explain, Athalia muttered, and withdrew inside.

"Mmm! That smells good," he said, sniffing hungrily.

"Not ready for a long time yet. Then you shall eat your fill."

George nodded his thanks and sat down. He lived alone now, his wife having run off with a television camera man who came to make a film with a party of university students. He hated the idea of being on show, and had refused to take part, but Bonnie had loved it. Two days after the filming, she vanished. He had received one post card from outside Buckingham Palace, and her message had been brief. "Dear George. The man I'm with is rich. He treats me well. Goodbye. Bonnie."

Now he sat without speaking, staring into space.

"So tell me what it were all about this morning," Athalia said.

"Nothing much," George said.

"Don't give me that," she said. "I wasn't born yesterday." She laughed. "Nor the day before, neither!"

"It was just an old dog. Must've stumbled and ended up in the river. Been there some time from the look of it."

"Dogs can swim."

"Perhaps it were drunk," he replied.

"George," Athalia said, banging her fork on the table. "Are you going to tell me the truth, or shall I turn you out with no supper?" She was fond of him, of course, and had never understood why that stupid wife of his had left him. And she a true gypsy on top of it all.

"It *was* a dog," he said again. "But it weren't just any old dog. Jal and me recognised it at once. Not many of them dogs around now. Know what I mean?"

There was silence for a minute, and then Athalia sighed. "I see," she said. "So what are we going to do about that?"

"Nothing. At least, not yet. We'll wait and see what turns up. Anyway, we'll be gone by the end of the week."

"Followed by the cops, no doubt," said Athalia, getting up to look in the saucepan.

He looked at her, frowning. "Cops?" he said.

"They're keeping an eye on us here," she answered. "It takes more than a plain grey suit to disguise the polis." She told him about the perambulating policeman, and said that if he was keeping an eye on them, she had certainly got *him* under observation and would know him again anywhere, anytime.

FORTY

Another week, thought Lois, and no nearer finding out who attacked Rob. It was not often Lois felt low, but so little progress was taking its toll on her natural optimism. She shook herself and managed a small smile, thinking of barmy old Mrs. T-J up at the hall, who had once said to a group of clinically depressed patients come to enjoy a strawberry tea in her gardens, "Now, I want you all to pull yourselves together!"

Feeling cheered up, Lois remembered her dad's advice. Write it down, me duck, and you'll think more clearly. She picked up a pen. A list of names first.

Josie and Rob: Been together for several years. Josie fed up with him? Rob too mild and blind to his good luck in finding Josie? And now, hints that there had been another side to him. Drunk and belligerent. Enemies? Long lost brother? Ah, yes, that one. They'd heard no more of him. More ferreting needed there.

Cowgill and Matthew Vickers: Policemen. 'Nuff said.

Sheila and Sam: Something wrong between them. Sam's hatred of gypsies. Small barney between Sam and Alf in the shop, as reported by Josie.

Alf and Edwina: Happily married? No children. Alf's love of gypsies—Edwina not agreeing. Why should Sam and Alf disagree so violently? Money and women—those were the usuals. More thinking needed.

Mark Brown: Lying little git. Was it his handwriting on the label? And now, of course, she remembered the phone call that took her along that road where she would be sure to see the flowers. It *was* him, Mark Brown. Clever, but risky. And now a twosome with Sally Tollervey-Jones. Sally: another unreliable character, but moneyed and protected by family position. More info on the village hall gang needed.

So who is the gang's mastermind? One likely person, known for his unrelenting prejudice against gypsies and blacks, occurred to Lois, but she dismissed the idea at once, not wanting it to be true.

Last but not least, the gypsies, tinkers or travellers. No good thinking of them as like us. Different way of life, rules and regs and values. Athalia a good woman, but where would her loyalties lie? The two quiz men? George and Jal, she remembered. George was nice, knowledgeable . . . fanciable! More information needed. Or would she just like to see him again? Lois laughed, feeling much brighter.

And then the two nasties with a pit bull and a market stall. Definitely more ferreting needed there.

"Lois!" It was Gran, calling from the kitchen.

"What?"

"On the wireless! It's all about the Appleby horse fair! Come quickly!"

Lois looked down at her notes with some satisfaction, and went swiftly out to the kitchen. It was a series of programmes that Gran loved. A pleasant-voiced girl went around the country finding interesting things to talk about. *Our Britain*, it was called, and Gran never missed an episode if she could help it.

Lois sat down at the table and listened carefully. The Appleby horse fair in Cumbria had been taking place for hundreds of years. Every so often somebody tried to close it down, but it was still going, stronger than ever. The woman on the radio said the whole town is taken over by huge numbers of gypsy travellers, their vans, trailers and horses. Horses change hands for bundles of cash undeclared to the Inland Revenue, and the horses are paraded and shown off in trotting races prior to deals. The Romani language is universally spoken, and some say it is as well to stay clear after a certain time in the evening.

As she listened, Lois began to think she would really like to go and see for herself. Maybe catch up with Athalia, George and Jal. It would be no good asking Derek to go with her. She knew what he'd say without asking him. But she could go alone, or maybe take Josie for a bit of a break. The idea began to grow, and she resolved to make some arrangements. Gran and Floss could help with the shop for a few days.

"You wouldn't catch me going anywhere near Appleby that week!" said Gran, reading Lois's thoughts. She's an old witch, my mum, Lois said to herself. How does she do it?

"Nobody's asking you to go, Mum," she said. "Still, it must be a wonderful sight to see, with them old caravans all painted up, and the horses at their best. Exciting, too, with that wildness in them all."

Gran looked dismayed. "Don't even think of it, Lois Meade," she said.

Lois not only thought of it, she went down to the shop to sound out Josie. There were no customers, and Josie listened with interest. "How long would we be away?" she said. "You know Gran is apt to make an intelligent guess at pricing and totalling up."

"I reckoned about three or four days," Lois said. "I could arrange for Floss to take over the shop, anyway. We'll ask Andrew Young if he has time to fill in. Depends on his décor jobs, but he might be glad of the extra cleaning—or even behind the counter? I think the difficult thing will be to find somewhere to stay in Appleby. Thousands of people come and go during that week, apparently."

"D'you want me to do some phoning around?" Josie offered. They fixed dates and times, and Lois went away feeling quite restored. All she had to do now was break the news to Derek and Gran. Her optimism took a small dive, but she was up again by the time she had called on Floss and received an enthusiastic response from her.

"I reckon Andrew will be keen, too," Floss said. "Ben met him in town, and he was just finishing that décor job in Waltonby. We shall be fine, Mrs. M. Go and enjoy yourselves, but don't get taken off by the raggle-taggle gypsies!"

Lois waited until they were sitting round the kitchen table at teatime. Derek was cheerful, having had a winner at Lingfield races. "Came in first, miles ahead of the others," he said.

"Was it that Tony what gave you the tip?" Gran said suspiciously.

"Never you mind," Derek said. "All you need to know is that it won."

"D'you reckon he tells us about the ones that lose?" Lois said to her mother. They laughed together, and Lois judged the atmosphere was about right for breaking the Appleby news. Inevitably, she was wrong.

"Definitely not," said Derek, immediately sober. "I'm not havin' any wife of mine goin' to that gypsy fair. Hundreds of 'em! You'll not be safe for one minute. And what about Josie? Young girl like her? How could you even consider it, Lois?"

Gran said, "You must be mad. And who's going to run the shop? I have other things to do, you know, besides standing in for Josie selling groceries."

"And newspapers," Lois said.

"Lois! Be serious," Derek said.

"Right. I'm being serious. So here's what we'll do. Josie and me will stay in a reputable hotel or B & B, and not be out late. There's loads of police around. It's been happening for hundreds of years, so they know all the dodges. Now, Floss will take over the shop, and the Post Office will supply a temporary. Andrew will take over Floss's cleaning, and the whole thing will run like clockwork."

"So you don't want me to do the shop at all?" Gran said, now feeling left out.

"Wouldn't dream of asking, Mum," Lois said. "I know what a busy woman you are."

Derek sat in silence, frowning. At last he said, "Why didn't you ask me to come with you?"

Lois took a deep breath, crossed her fingers under the table, and said that she would love him to come, but thought he wouldn't be interested.

More silence. Gran got up from the table, taking dirty crocks and putting them into the sink.

"Derek?" Lois said.

"Lois."

"Well?"

"Well what? Are you asking my permission?"

Lois shook her head. "But I'd like to know if you've changed your mind at all," she said gently.

Derek sighed. "It's no good, Lois," he said. "You know you'll do exactly what you want, whatever I say." He paused, and she said nothing. "Well," he continued, "I suppose there's safety in numbers. You and Josie must stick together. Don't let her out of your sight. And ring me every evening. I can't say I'm happy for you to go, but if that's what you want. . . ."

Lois stood up and put her arms round Derek's shoulders. She kissed him on top of his head, and said he was the best husband in the world. Gran clattered dishes in the washing-up bowl, and said crossly, "Lois Weedon, I don't know where your father and me went wrong. And that's all I'm saying."

Lois knew that when her mother lapsed into using her maiden name, she was truly in disgrace. "It'll be fine, Mum," she said. "I'll bring you a nice little horse back from the fair."

After that, she judged it wise to shut herself in her office for half an hour while they chewed it over between them.

She had just sat down and switched on her computer, when the phone rang. She answered it at once, and heard a voice that was faintly familiar. "Mrs. Meade? Lois? This is Greg . . . here. Rob's brother. I have something very interesting to share with you. Would it be possible for me to pop round in about an hour?"

"Fine," said Lois. "You know where we are. In an hour, then. Derek and Gran are here, and I'm sure they'll be pleased to see you again."

She put down the phone and smiled. Things were definitely looking up.

FORTY-ONE

Four of the gang had gathered behind the village hall, and were lazily discussing films they had seen on television. Not all four lived in Long Farnden. Two of them had cycled over from Fletching, without the proper helmets, of course, but with hoods up and eyes down.

"Hey, did you know they're advertising crash-proof hoodies' gear?"

The others laughed, doubting his word. Sally T-J came sprinting round the corner, and asked if Mark Brown had been there. The others shook their heads. She subsided in a crouch on the tarmac, and lit a cigarette. "Right," she said, "I'll wait. He'll probably turn up."

"Somethin' to tell him?"

"Mind your own business," Sally said, and they all laughed knowingly. They said that if it was what they thought it was, Mark Brown would do well to stay away.

Five minutes passed, and the four said they were off to Waltonby. A new source had moved into that village, and they were keen to try it out. Sally didn't move. Her head was sunk into her shoulders, and she drew on the cigarette in some desperation. What should she do if Mark didn't turn up? Twenty minutes went by.

"Sally?" It was him. "Where's the others? I thought we were meeting them here tonight?"

"They've gone over to Waltonby. New contact. I waited for you. Wanted to see you specially," she added, and looked up at him appealingly. Then she stood up and put her arms round his neck. "Do you love me, Markie?"

"You know I do," he said warily. This wasn't the bright, casual Sally he was used to. Still, a few declarations of love wouldn't come amiss just at this time. He wasn't sure how much more contempt he could take in his own home, from his own parents.

He kissed her, and she rested her head on his shoulder. "This is different, isn't it, you and me. I've not felt like this about anyone else," she said.

Mark began to hear alarm bells. "Nor've I," he said. "But we're young yet, as they're always telling us. You'll probably be fed up with me after another couple of months. Move on to somebody rich and aristocratic."

Sally shook her head, her face still buried in his jacket. "Nope, it's because you're who you are. Not rich and not aristocratic. That's why I love you, 'cos you're real."

Oh, God, thought Mark. She's not telling me all this because she's . . . oh, no, not that.

Her next words interrupted his thought, confirming it before he'd had time to ask. "So I hope you'll be pleased, Markie, to hear that I'm up the duff. We are going to have a baby."

"We?"

She looked closely into his eyes so that he couldn't do his usual trick of turning away and avoiding anything he did not want to hear.

"Yep. It takes two. You and me have made a baby. The beginning of one, anyway."

Mark saw his chance. "Better get rid of it, then," he said. "Must be early days yet. Your lot must know the right people." His family certainly didn't, he knew, and then the awful prospect of having to tell his mother and father came down on him like a black pall over his head. Things were really bad already. He couldn't do it.

But Sally was smiling. "No need," she said. "This is a new sprog and it's ours. I can't destroy it, Mark. I mean to love it, care for it like I've seen other girls caring for their babies. And you will, too, when you think about it. In fact, it could be the answer to all our problems."

He stared at her, amazed at what she was saying. He reckoned he was inches away from rock bottom already. No job, father hated him, mother permanently despairing. His so-called friends were mostly problem cases themselves, relying on drugs and drink to prop them up. He could see no future at all, let alone the rosy one that Sally seemed to be floating in.

"Sally," he said, "you're in fantasy land. We're about the last people in the world who could take on the responsibility of a kid!"

"You've forgotten my despised family," she said, now more like her old sharp self. "I really want this baby so much that I'll force them to help. I've worked it all out. I know how to handle Auntie. Trust me, Mark. It'll be a new beginning for us both."

He did not reply, but stood miserably in front of her, his head hanging down so that she could not see his desperate expression.

"I'm going to the doc tomorrow," she continued happily. "You can come with me, if you like."

He groaned. "Dad will kill me," he said. "Finish the job he's been working on for years."

"Forget him," Sally said. "We don't need him. You won't need him. I've got it all worked out," she repeated. "Now, I have to get back. If you want to come tomorrow, I'll see you in the surgery at nine thirty sharp."

Mark said nothing. He watched her until she was out of sight, then decided he would join the others, find himself a little consolation. But when he got back on his bike, he realised he couldn't do that. His head was spinning, and he headed for home. There was nowhere else to go.

Mrs. T-J was watching her favourite programme on television when Sally came into the long drawing room. Without turning her head, her great-aunt told her to sit down and be quiet, or else go up to her room. "I have to see who gets to the final," she said.

Ten minutes later, Sally was still there, hunched up in a big armchair. "Are you all right, child?" Mrs. T-J said, switching off.

Now or never, Sally thought. No use trying to soften her up. "I'm all right," she said. "Just feeling a bit sick, but I'm told that's normal in pregnancy."

The silence seemed to go on forever. Finally Mrs. T-J took off her glasses and rubbed her eyes. "We shall need to have the nursery redecorated," she said. "When is it due?" She stood up and held out her arms. Sally began to weep, and her aunt folded her to her ample bosom. "There, there," she said. "It happens from time to time in this family. I thought I'd be the last, what with family planning and so on. But here you are, and here I am with nothing to do except to look after you and the baby. I suppose the father is that rather dreadful Mark something-or-other?"

"Mark Brown," snuffled Sally, extracting herself from the lavender-scented embrace. "And I do love him, Auntie."

"Of course you do. For now, anyway. Come along, my dear, let's have a glass of sherry to celebrate. Then we have some arrangements to make."

Mark arrived home and parked his bike, banging the shed door, half hoping his parents would hear him. Maybe his father would come out of the back door looking for him, finally take him by the hand and lead him into the house, sit him down on the sofa beside him and ask him—no, plead with him—to forgive him and together they would begin again. A baby? Wonderful! Just what your mother would love. Don't worry about the money. We've got a bit saved. Time to let us help, son. You can rely on us.

Pigs might fly. As Mark pushed open the door, he heard his father shouting. He listened, and heard them arguing about who should look after the house while they were away on holiday. "That stupid little runt!" his father bellowed. "Couldn't look after a rabbit hutch!"

Mark crept on tiptoe up to his room and sat down on the edge of his bed. He could see nothing beyond a terrible blankness. No help, nowhere to turn. He did not trust Sally. You didn't trust her sort, if you knew what was good for you. He stretched out on the bed. His heart was beating fast and he was trembling, the old familiar feeling of panic overtaking him. There was one route of escape that he had taken many times. The trusty packet of pills was there in his bedside locker. He sat up, reached for a glass of water and counted out the usual number of calmers. He needed more. This time he needed twice as many. And maybe a few more, to guarantee respite. Only a few left now. Might as well make doubly sure. He lay back, carefully pulling the duvet over his head, and waited for oblivion.

FORTY-TWO

Greg Wilkins arrived at the door on time. Gran let him in, and ushered him into the sitting room, where Lois and Derek were reading separate pages of the local evening paper. They folded them up, and got to their feet. Derek extended his hand, and Greg took it. "Evenin'" Derek said. "Sit yerself down."

"I'll make some coffee," Gran said, and went off to the kitchen.

"Where are you staying?" Lois said. She had not seen him around in the village, and had heard nobody mention him. In Long Farnden, a stranger who spent longer than a couple of hours was noticed, discussed, and what was known about him generally passed around the network. But neither Gran nor Lois had heard a word about him.

"In Tresham," Greg said. "An old friend—widower—living in Sebastopol Street—found me a bed-and-breakfast place around the corner. Quite comfortable, but food is not quite what I'm used to!"

"I suppose you live on yams and kangaroo," Derek said. Lois couldn't tell whether he meant to be offensive, but Greg winced.

"You said you had something to tell us?" Lois said quickly. "About Rob, was it? Have you seen Josie?"

He shook his head. "Not since my first call on you. I thought I'd leave you to tell her. It may come as no surprise to her, anyway."

"What, then?" Derek was blunt. He had taken a dislike to this chap right from the beginning. He hadn't much liked Greg's brother Rob, come to that. Not good enough for his Josie. But, as Lois said, who would be?

"Well, as you know, I haven't seen him for a long time. But as a family we are great letter writers, and I was fairly sure I heard from a cousin that he had married a girl from Thailand working in Oz. Years ago, that was. Did he ever mention it? I suppose they must have divorced, or separated or something."

Derek was shocked. "O' course he never bloody well mentioned it!" he said. "D'you think my Josie would've had anything to do with a married man? Next thing, you'll be telling me there were children!"

Lois said nothing, waiting for Greg to continue, and to her horror she saw him nod. Yes, he said, he had checked with the cousin first to make sure his memory served him correctly, and then was told there were apparently two children. Nobody in the family knew anything about what had happened to them.

Lois sighed. "Well," she said, "we shall have to think about this. Maybe it would be best not to tell Josie. She has suffered enough, poor kid. And it's not going to make any difference to anybody, is it?"

Greg made a face. "It could," he said. "You see, apparently Rob had quite a bit of cash. Inherited from some relative on his mother's side. He must have salted it away somewhere. You didn't hear of an investment or similar?"

"No, nor would we have asked," Derek said. "That was his business, and Josie's. We're not ones to pry."

"Mm. Well, as Rob and your daughter weren't married, and Rob had these children, unless there was a will saying otherwise, all his money could go to them."

"And I suppose you are intending to be trustee for them?"

"I know what you're thinking, Derek," he said. "But I assure you all I want to do is to make things happen the way my brother would have wanted. I have no idea where these children and their mother might be, but I intend to find them. And to find out what my brother's intentions were."

Derek stood up. "In my opinion, Mr. Wilkins," he said, "you should leave all of that to Josie. She looked after him, stood by him, put up with his lazy ways, and, I sincerely believe, subsidised him with profits from the shop."

Gran came in bearing a tray of coffee.

"Mr. Wilkins has to go now, Mum," Derek said. "He won't have time for coffee."

Gran looked at Lois, who sighed and also stood up. "Just a minute, Derek," she said. "Don't you think it might be better if we all put our heads together and found the answers to Greg's questions? Information shared is always more useful."

Derek glared at her. "Up to you, Lois," he said, "but leave me out of it." He marched out of the room, slamming the door behind him.

Ten minutes later, Lois and Greg were sitting in Josie's flat above the shop. Lois had said that if they were really intending to get to the bottom of Rob's past life, they must include Josie. After all, she had known him better than any of them, Greg included.

"We came down here," Lois said, "because your father won't have anything to do with it, or at least, with Greg's part in it. You know what he is."

"Yeah, well." Josie was not too keen either on this so-called brother who had appeared out of nowhere. Rob had never mentioned him. Nor had he ever mentioned Australia. It didn't make sense, if he had nothing to hide. Now Lois broke the news that would change her mind completely.

"A wife!?" Josie's face paled.

"And two children," Lois said.

"I'm sorry, Josie," Greg said.

"But how did he manage to get a wife and two children in before he met me? He was really young when we first got together."

"Or so he told you," Lois said. "He could have lied about his age."

"Mum! Why are you taking this man's side against what we know about Rob? He was kind and gentle, and always willing to help. Remember that banner we put up to welcome you back from the lottery presentation? That was Rob's idea, and he spent days doing it."

Lois felt sick at heart. After all Josie had been through, to destroy her memories of her partner—and she was still grieving—was real cruelty. Perhaps Derek was right. On the other hand, if this man *was* Rob's brother and everything he said was true, then it would be just as hurtful for Josie to find out later that her parents knew all the time. She could see Josie was near to tears, and said that since none of them knew for certain, not even Greg, who had not seen nor heard from Rob for years, they should make some enquiries. And, of course, Lois knew just the person to help.

"Just as well you're still friends with your cop, Mum," Josie said, trying hard to smile.

"No harm in asking Matthew Vickers to help, too."

"Who's he?" Greg said. He was looking alarmed, and Lois noted this carefully for future reference.

"One of Josie's admirers," she said quickly. "Just happens to be a young policeman. And my cop is a detective inspector, so should be able to help. But I expect you've been in touch with the police?" she added. "Being Rob's brother, an' that?"

"Of course," he said. "Not that they are my personal friends, as it seems they are in your case." His voice was definitely chilly, and in a couple of minutes he said he must go, as he had promised to see his friend in Tresham in half an hour.

"Sebastopol Street, did you say?" Lois asked. "What's his name? I know quite a few people in Sebastopol."

"Must go," Greg said, not answering, and was gone, clattering down the stairs from the flat and out of the back door.

"Well, mother dear, and what do you make of that?" Josie said bitterly. "I'd say he got the wind up at the mention of police."

Lois had to admit that she was right. "On the other hand," she said, "it doesn't mean what he said was all lies. After all, if Rob had kept all that quiet, he must have had a dodgy reason for doing so, and maybe Greg himself is not great pals with the police in Australia."

"For God's sake!" said Josie. "We shall be in the hands of Interpol next! Why can't we just let poor old Rob rest in peace, and give me a chance to build a new life? You know this is all nonsense, Mum. That man is just hoping Rob had some money. He doesn't even know if there was any. But I do! Rob was a great spender, and not always on himself. He was a generous man, and we lived from one month's salary to the next, with the shop supplementing what he earned. Best go home, apologise to Dad, and forget the whole thing."

"Sorry, love. I'll be going now. And don't worry. I'm used to making it up with Dad. United we stand, an all that."

When Lois got back home Derek had gone to the pub, and she could hear the telly on in the sitting room. She did not want to face Gran's questions just now, and so went quietly upstairs and began to run a bath. Squeezing some exotic-smelling bath stuff that Jamie had given her into the steaming water, she submerged most of herself and began to think. Uppermost in her mind was the possibility that this man, brother or no brother, would not bother with such an elaborate foray into lies and fabrications, if that's what they were, unless he suspected it was worth his while. But if he'd been so anxious about finding his brother, why had he waited so long? Until after Rob was dead?

She reached out a wet arm and looked at her watch on the bathroom stool. It was still early by police standards. She did not need to look up the number, and dialled the direct line to Cowgill.

"Lois? Nothing wrong, I hope?"

"Only that the water's getting cold. I'm in the bath." Lois instantly regretted what she had said, and sure enough Cowgill replied that he would be along straight away with a kettleful of hot water to top her up.

"That's quite enough of that," she said. "Now listen." She told him the whole story, from Greg's first appearance to his hasty departure this evening. "Has he really been in to the cop shop?"

"I'm pretty sure he hasn't, but I'll check. This could be very important, Lois. What did he say his address was? Sebastopol Street? That's an odd coincidence. Your office there, and Dot Nimmo's house."

"And Hazel's friend who lives next door to the office. She's been there for quite a while. Between them, they should be able to give us a clue to the friend. Also, Greg's been around for long enough for one of them to have seen him in the street. Nothing goes past Dot's house without her knowing!"

"Useful for us," said Cowgill, who had a healthy respect for Dot Nimmo. "How is Josie?" he added. "You know my nephew Matthew is very fond of her? Do we think that is a good idea?"

"Take it from me, Cowgill," Lois said, "it won't matter what we think. They'll do just what they please. And a spot of romance is exactly what Josie needs right now."

Lois heard Derek's footsteps in the hallway downstairs. "Must go now," she said.

"Do you need any help? Someone to scrub your back?" Cowgill held the phone away from his ear. But instead of an explosion he heard a click. Dear Lois. Her timing was perfect.

FORTY-THREE

Dot Nimmo took Lois's call next morning, and immediately assured her that if a man called Greg Wilkins was anywhere in her part of Tresham, she would locate him. "Me and the Nimmo clan, Mrs. M," she said, "we can find needles in haystacks. Not that there are many haystacks in Sebastopol Street! Give us a couple of hours, an' I'll get back to you."

Lois grinned and sat back in her office chair. What would she do without Dot? She had nearly had to, when a hit-and-run merchant knocked Dot down and landed her in hospital, nigh unto death. That had been another occasion when Lois had been involved with Cowgill on a case. Her grin faded. Maybe Derek was right. Each time she had helped Cowgill, there had been danger to herself and other members of the family. An awful thought struck her. Had Rob been attacked and killed because of something she had done in the past? A revenge killing for getting a villain sent to the nick?

"Mum!" Lois yelled down to the kitchen for a strong coffee to boost her spirits. She told herself to use her common sense. It was extremely unlikely, surely, that she would be the subject of a revenge killing. And why Rob? Why not Derek, or one of her sons? Or herself? No, it didn't make sense.

"Thanks," she said, as Gran brought her a steaming mug.

"What's wrong with you, me duck?" Gran said. She knew the signs. Lois shook her head. "Nothing much," she said.

"Still no news from the police?" Gran handed her a shortbread, and said that she had heard something that might interest Lois.

Lois said dully, "What do you mean? Gossip from the girls?"

"Certainly not," Gran said. "Something Nancy Brown said on the phone just now. She was supposed to be coming round for coffee this morning, but rang to cancel it. Said Mark was ill in bed. She could hardly speak, and I reckon she was crying. I caught the word 'serious,' and then she was gone."

"Oh my God," Lois said. Here it was, happening again. Mark involved on the fringes of Rob's case, or even in the middle of it, writing that card, and now he was seriously ill. She must find out why, and check out Sally T-J, in case she was in on it, too.

"Not good news, Mum," she said, and drained her coffee mug. "I must make a call or two. I'll let you know, if you're thinking of supporting Nancy Brown at all."

"I tried ringing back," Gran said. "But there was no reply. Father out and mother sitting with Mark, I expect."

Sally T-J had arrived at the surgery early. She wanted to give Mark every chance to turn up and join her. Her aunt had offered to accompany her, but she had assured her she would be fine, and Mark would be with her. Well, maybe he would be. She reckoned that in spite of all his troubles, he was a nice kid underneath. Just as well, really, if he was the father of this squiggle she had inside her. She looked at her watch. It was nine thirty, and there was no sign of him. The surgery list was running late, as usual, and she picked up a magazine to pass the time. The pages fell open at a photograph of a half-naked model, and she was very pregnant indeed. Sally had a moment's panic. Would she really look like that?

Oh, where was Mark? She wished now she had let her aunt come with her. She had been to the surgery on her own many times before, with coughs and colds and a sprained ankle when she fell off her aunt's horse. But this was different! This was going to change everything for her. And for Mark! Where the hell was he?

Nancy and Joe Brown both sat in Mark's bedroom on chairs placed close together. They could have been miles apart. No word had passed between them since they had discovered Mark this morning. They had sent for the doctor and been told the situation. It was not a matter of life and death, but the lad was going to feel terrible when he woke up. He would need support, sympathy and a listening ear to find out why he had made a suicide attempt. It was often a cry for help, the doctor said. It seemed like hours had passed since they started their vigil, and by tacit agreement they had not moved. Nancy stood up. "Have to go to the loo," she whispered to Joe, and he did not look at her, but nodded.

Joe wondered if that little slag from the hall might know why his son had decided to take a handful of sleeping pills last night. Joe had strong suspicions that she was behind it. He knew the two of them had been spending a lot of time together, and if ever a pair was unsuited it was those two. His thoughts wandered on to when he and Nancy had found Mark seemingly nearly dead this morning, when his mother had taken him a cup of tea. A nagging voice told Joe that he should have known. He should have said good night to his son, made an effort to check that he was all right. But the lad often stomped in and went straight upstairs to his room, where he would lock the door and refuse to answer any approaches from his parents.

Thank God he hadn't taken enough to end it all. Maybe he hadn't intended to. Perhaps he just wanted somehow to draw his father's attention to the fact that he was desperate and needed help? Joe slumped further into his chair and covered his face with his hands.

FORTY-FOUR

Dot Nimmo stood in her small back garden and looked up at the sky. It looked like rain, and she remembered she had left her brolly at a client's house in Waltonby. She had been thinking about Mrs. M's call, and was glad she had a free morning. This afternoon she was due to clean for Mrs. Parker Knowle, who lived in Tresham, and was only fifteen minutes away from Dot's home. So that gave her plenty of time to think about the mysterious Greg Wilkins. Was he around here, for a start? He could be miles away, she told herself. But Dot had a nose for these things, and her instinct told her he was not far away. It was Dot's nose that had been so useful to Lois in the past.

Dot wondered if Hazel at New Brooms's office had been alerted, too. Perhaps she would pop in there first. No sense in the two of them going down the same route.

Hazel greeted Dot cheerfully. "What brings you out on the streets this morning?" she said.

Dot raised her eyebrows and said she'd be glad if Hazel would refrain from suggesting Dot had been out on the streets. "We Nimmos may have done some dodgy things," she said, "but I ain't never been reduced to goin' on the streets!"

"Come on in and calm down," said Hazel. "You know perfectly well I didn't mean that. Give me a minute to check the phone, then I'm all yours."

"Don't need that," Dot said. "Just wanted to ask you if you've spoken to Mrs. M this morning."

"No, I haven't. Why? Is something wrong? Nothing to do with Lizzie?" Hazel had left her small daughter safely with her mother-in-law, but you never knew these days.

Dot hastily assured her it was nothing to do with Lizzie. "Just checking. I have to call her myself later on. Thought she might have left a message for me on the office phone."

"Highly unlikely, I would say," Hazel said, "but I'll check."

There was no message, and Dot slipped out of the office and away before Hazel could ask any more questions. So it was just Mrs. M and herself on the trail of Greg Wilkins. That was how Dot liked it.

Lois worked all morning in her office, and when she began to feel hungry she shut down her computer and made for the kitchen. Unusually, there were no good smells of cooking emerging.

Gran's face was stern, and as soon as Lois came in, she went on the attack. "I suppose you don't care that you've upset your long-suffering husband, Lois Meade," she said angrily, and continued without a pause. "He was in a right mood after you'd gone down to Josie's last night. If you ask me, which you haven't, that so-called Greg Wilkins is up to no good, and the best thing you could do would be to send him packing, if necessary with help from your policeman chum. I agree with Derek. It's a good thing someone round here has got some common sense. Now, what d'you want for lunch?"

"Blimey, have you finished, Mum? Are you sure I'm allowed lunch?"

Gran sighed. "It's no good making light of it, Lois. You know you're getting in deeper and deeper. We wouldn't mind if you were any nearer finding Rob's murderer, but you're not, are you?"

Lois had to admit that Gran was right. "But that doesn't mean I'm going to stop trying. There's a lot we *do* know, and sooner or later it'll all come together."

"By 'we' I suppose you mean you and Cowgill?"

"And Josie, and you and Derek and anybody else who can help. Even Greg, though I agree with you that he's looking more and more unreliable."

Gran was somewhat mollified, and said, "Oh, I see, right then. I suppose we'd better just carry on. But for God's sake be careful, Lois. It's not just yourself you have to think about, you know. Now, d'you fancy scrambled eggs with cream and baby mushrooms?"

This was Gran's proudest achievement, and although Lois knew that it was not really the healthiest of meals, she accepted with enthusiasm. Then the telephone rang, and she disappeared to answer it in her office.

It was a brief conversation. Mark's mother was calling to say that he had woken up, been violently sick and looked pale and miserable. Would Elsie like to pop in and help cheer him up? It was probably best not to stay too long.

Mark Brown was propped up on pillows, looking pale and miserable, and the thought of Elsie Weedon visiting did nothing to cheer him up. He had surfaced with the memory of the desperate and awful thing he had done. His father had been sitting beside him when he woke, and had held his head over the bucket as he retched and retched. Through the unbelievable pain, he had still been aware of Joe's hand smoothing his hair.

When the nausea had subsided, the next thing he thought of was Sally. Christ! He had been supposed to meet her at the surgery! He had asked if she had phoned, but she hadn't. Without thinking, he'd asked Joe if he would ring the hall and tell her he was ill, and his father had been so surprised he had meekly left the room and made the call.

Then he shut his eyes and dozed until he heard women's voices in the hall. Sally? No, it was old women's voices, his mother and nosy old Elsie Weedon. He shut his eyes again, thinking he could pretend to be asleep. But it was too late, and the two women came in, his mother with her accustomed compassionate look fixed on her face, and his heart sank even further.

"Markie, how're you feeling, dear?" Nancy Brown was trying hard to stem the tears, and Gran took over.

"Now then, Mark Brown," she said. "What's all this about? You've not been living in Farnden for two minutes before you're in trouble. No need, you know. So what've you got to say for yourself?"

"How long have you got, Mrs. Weedon?" Mark said, stung by her accusing tone. His voice was getting stronger with each word. "And do you really want to know? You'd be the first person who did, and that includes your precious daughter Lois." He glared at her, waiting for a reply, and to his surprise, Gran burst into peals of delighted laughter.

"That's it, lad!" she said. "I knew you'd got it in you. Now you can shut up and rest for a bit while we do the talking. And don't interrupt. You can have your say when we've finished."

Nancy began to protest, but Gran was looking at Mark, and her soft heart lifted when she saw the glimmer of a smile on his pale face. "Carry on, Mrs. Weedon," he said. "Say what you've got to say, and make it helpful."

After what Gran considered a satisfactory time, she patted Mark's hand and got up to leave. She heard another voice in the hall, and looked back at the pale lad languishing against his pillows. "I hope you're feeling stronger now," she said with a smile, and stood aside as what appeared to be a human whirlwind entered the room.

"Mark! What the hell d'you think you're doing? How could you, without talking to me first?" And then Sally flung herself on the bed beside him, smothered him with kisses, and also burst into tears.

Gran gave Nancy Brown a firm push out of the room, shut the door behind them, and the two retreated downstairs. "A cup of coffee, Mrs. Weedon?" Joe Brown said, appearing from the kitchen. Gran said that would be very nice, and anyway, she'd been wanting a word with him for some time.

FORTY-FIVE

~

Athalia Lee and the other gypsies were cursing, looking up at a leaden sky, and this time it had nothing to do with Long Farnden village. They had become mired in a tidal flood swollen by heavy rain, now fast approaching their stopping place by the river Loare.

"It'll all be gone in a couple of days," the publican had said to George and Jal, but added that the mud left behind took a lot of hard work to clear. "My customers are saying you lot have brought bad luck to the village. You'd better be on your way as soon as you can," he had added mildly. He was not against the gypsies, and quite liked to see them arriving to and fro Appleby. It was a link with the past. There had been trouble with some of them, of course, like that rough pair with a killer dog, but they weren't around so far this year.

Though the publican did not know it, this was not strictly true. The dog, admittedly dead, had arrived mysteriously on its own, and Jal had sworn he had seen one of the brothers, Harry, he thought, in the nearby town on market day. "Got the usual junk stall on the fringe," he had said to George.

"Did you see Sid?" George had asked. Jal had said not while he was there, but the younger brother would have been around.

George had shrugged. "Ah, well. None of our business, as long as they keep well out of our way." He appeared to Jal to be dismissing the subject, but in fact he was worried, and pondered on the dead dog and absence of Sid for some while. Then the flood had threatened, and this had become more urgent.

Now he and Athalia were having a conference in her trailer. "How quickly d'you reckon we can be gone?" he asked, and she said it had been known to take as long as ten minutes. Then she laughed and said probably by the next morning, once they had decided.

"We shall be early in Appleby," she warned. "Still, we've done that before."

George nodded. "We'll get a good place for the trailers and horses. So shall we go tomorrow?"

"Have a walk down to the river, see how far the water's come up," Athalia said. "Then we can decide."

George went off to the pub to ask about tides, and discovered the best time, with the tide right out, would be now. He collected Jal, and the two of them set off to judge how long they had before the water reached their scrubby field.

It was an alarming sight. The deep channel where they had seen the dead dog was now full of water and lapping over the edges. "And that's with the tide out!" Jal said. He was a more nervous soul than George, and was all for moving on as soon as possible.

The Loare pathway, with its seats and promises of wonderful views and bird-watching, was now under six inches of water. "Another night of heavy rain, and this'll be halfway up our wheels," Jal said.

George laughed. "Cheer up, lad," he said. "You can swim, can't you?"

They kept to the higher ground, and reached the small bridge crossing the channel. It wouldn't be long before this was submerged, too, and they leaned over and stared at the swiftly flowing, muddy surge. Suddenly Jal shot back into the centre of the bridge. "George!" he said. "For God's sake, did you see it?"

George was looking grim. "Yeah. I saw it. Come on, quick, it's bound to get caught up in those reeds over there—yes, it has! Come on, Jal, we'll get it out."

Jal had absolutely no desire to get the body out of the water. "Leave it!" he shouted. "It'll get free again, and we won't have to have nothing to do with it."

He could have saved his breath. George was already off the bridge and splashing along the path. He reached the reedy patch and waded in. "Get over here, Jal!" he yelled. "I've got a hold, but it'll need both of us to get it out."

Reluctantly Jal joined him, and between them they heaved the bloated body out and on to dry ground. There they collapsed and sat down, George staring closely at the face, and Jal moaning quietly to himself.

"It's him, innit?" Jal said finally. "It's Sid, poor bugger. What do we do now?"

George frowned. "What d'you do, you mean. This is what you do. You go straight back to the telephone box outside the pub, dial 999, and tell the police to come here. Tell them it's an emergency, and tell 'em why. Then wait on the green so's you can guide them."

Jal looked terrified. "What're *you* going to do, then?" he squeaked.

"Stay here, o' course. We lost the dog, didn't we? So we don't want to lose poor old Sid. Nobody believes what we say, Jal, so we need the evidence. Go on, bugger off, and do exactly what I said."

"But what about the tide coming in?" Jal objected. "It'll cover him and you."

"Not yet," answered George. "Which is why the sooner you get going the better!"

After Jal had gone, George settled down to wait. He looked again at Sid's pitiful corpse. It was difficult to see any telltale marks on his head. There were plenty of marks where the body had bumped into obstacles on its watery journey, but impossible for George to tell exactly what had caused them. Still, once the police had got him, they had ways of identifying gashes and bruises.

The tide was on the turn, and George watched, now anxiously, as the water crept over previously dry grass. He turned to see if there was any sign of the cops, but only heavy, dark grey clouds hung over the landscape. He looked again at the water, and decided he had an hour or so yet in comparative safety. But unbeknown to him, the danger was coming from another direction. He was beginning to doze. It was almost dark under the approaching sky. His eyelids closed.

He was awoken by a voice in his ear.

"What you got there, then, Georgie boy?"

He leapt to his feet, and saw Harry, swarthy and unshaved, standing only inches away from him, and holding a gun.

"This 'ere belongs to me," Harry said, putting the toe of his boot under the arm of his dead brother. "I've always looked after 'im, an' you can help me look after him now," he added, and laughed.

God in Heaven! The man was mad, George realised with horror, and once more glanced over his shoulder in the hope of seeing Jal and the police. There was no one, not a single person in sight. His heart sank.

FORTY-SIX

Jal had so far failed. On his way back to call the police, he had been horrified to meet Harry, and though he tried hard to dodge him, had ended up dumped in a crumbling shed by the path, bound hand and foot to a metal post. The binder twine that secured him was tough, and he had rubbed his wrists raw in trying to break it. He was desperately worried about George. Harry had knocked Jal about a bit in an attempt to get George's whereabouts from him, but Jal had refused to tell. It was not, unfortunately, difficult for Harry to work out. There was only one path, and Jal had just come up it.

Athalia had begun to worry about George, and Jal, too. She looked up at the threatening sky, and thought they should be back now. Surely it didn't take this long to sum up the flood situation? She had seen the two of them disappearing across the marsh some time ago, and the light was almost gone now. It was treacherous ground, and whilst she knew George was skilled at negotiating difficult territory, in her imagination she saw them half submerged in sucking mud.

The other trailers and vans were quiet now. Many of the gypsies had gone off hawking or to meet up with others passing through the nearby town. There was nobody she could send after the missing two. Except herself. She turned around and looked for her boots. It was some time since she had ventured across that tricky ground, though she had been stopping here every year for half a century. She went down the steps from her trailer, and paused. She turned around and went back inside. A shiver of fear had sent her back, a feeling that something was seriously wrong. Her mother had claimed second sight, and although Athalia would not say she had inherited it, she still got warnings from somewhere, and they were always right. She took an old policeman's cosh from a drawer and put it in her deep pocket. Just as well her long departed husband had insisted on her keeping it handy.

Halfway to the now visible flood water, she passed the hut. A muffled sound came out of it, and she paused. Probably a rat. They arrived in large numbers in this weather, feeding on the detritus brought in by the floods. She was about to walk on, when the sound came again, and louder. She pulled open the rickety door and saw Jal. In minutes she had him free, and his story was told. "George?" she said.

"Back by the channel," Jal replied. "Waiting for me to bring the police. God knows what's happened by now."

"Get moving," said Athalia. "Let's hope it's not too late. Make the call, and then come back. George's life might depend on it, Jal, so run like the devil's on yer heels!"

George was still at gunpoint. Harry had ordered him to move the body of his brother into a clump of tall, rank grass and then break off and pile on top of the corpse tough, soaking reeds, until nothing could be seen of Sid. It was slow and arduous work, and every time George tried to take a breath, Harry prodded him with the gun and kept him going.

Where the hell were the police? And Jal? George could not believe he had chickened out of his mission.

As if reading his thoughts, Harry said, "Hoping for rescue from the polis? What d'ya think? That little sod Jal let you down, has he?" He roared with laughter, and told George exactly where Jal was, and where he would stay until released by Harry. "The sooner you finish that job the better," he added, and with another poke from his gun made it clear that if either George or Jal ever breathed a word of all this, he would see to it they would never speak again.

George straightened up finally, and looking past Harry, who was still keeping a close eye on him, he saw a figure approaching in the distance. He hoped to God it was Jal, and bent down to the concealed body of Sid. "There's a bit here where he's not covered," he said. "Another couple of minutes."

Harry looked suspiciously at him. "Get on with it, then," he said. "The water'll be up here any minute. No tricks, mind! We're not playing games, y' know. Get on with it!"

George bent to his task again, and Harry stood over him, never taking his eyes off him for a minute. Meanwhile, Athalia approached as silently as she could. George was still there! But what the hell was he doing? She moved like a sprite across the sodden ground, until she was standing close behind them.

"What the—!" Harry wheeled round, and saw Athalia. At the same time she was on him. She raised the cosh and with great accuracy and timing beat Harry about the head until he collapsed to the ground. George grabbed the gun as it fell, and heaved a sigh of relief.

"That's enough, gel," he said. "Don't kill the rotten sod."

FORTY-SEVEN

Only a week to go, and we'll be off with the raggle-taggle gypsies." Josie was standing behind the counter, talking to Lois while she filled her basket.

"Am I your best customer, Josie, love?"

"No. The vicarage buys enough chocolate to keep the shop going with no other customers. The Rev has a very sweet tooth, and now he's corrupted his wife as well."

"Talking of corruption," Lois said, taking down a packet of digestives, "have you heard about the Tollervey-Jones girl? Seems she's in the family way, and guess who is the father?"

"Yes, I have heard," Josie said. "And, as you know, I don't encourage gossip in this shop."

"But you've heard?" Lois said, grinning.

Josie nodded. "Seems the old girl at the hall has turned up trumps. She's encouraging Sally to have the baby, and offering to set the two of them up in an apartment conversion in the stable block. Not straight away, of course, but nearer the birth. Mark Brown is a lucky little devil. She'll probably find him a job as well. Talk about falling on your feet! And nothing's been done about the flowers label we found, has it?"

"You'd know better than me," Lois replied. "Your Matthew found them and took the whole lot back to the station."

"Except the one we found," Josie said. "I'm seeing him this

evening, so maybe I'll ask him."

"Probably best to leave it now, duckie," Lois said, and Josie knew by her mother's tone of voice that it was an order.

The door opened and the bell jangled. Dot Nimmo walked in and announced that she would like a word with Mrs. M. At once, if possible, she said, and just the two of them. Lois and Josie exchanged looks, and Josie said they were welcome to go up to the flat, if that would be suitable for Mrs. Nimmo?

Upstairs, as they settled in Josie's chairs, Lois said, "I hope this is important, Dot. I have a great deal to do this morning."

"Of course it's important, else I wouldn't be 'ere, would I?" Dot took a deep breath and began to describe what she had found out in her search for Greg Wilkins. "Not as easy as I thought," she warned. "He's no beginner, Mrs. M."

"Beginner at what?" Lois frowned. She was used to Dot's penchant for drama, but she really did not have time to wait for the story to unfold.

"Dodgy dealings," Dot said, with some satisfaction. "He's done it before. Gone in when families are bereaved, claimed to be a long-lost relative and conned them out of money. He watches the death notices in the papers. A right ghoul, my cousin over in Birmingham says."

Lois stood up. "Well done, Dot," she said. "I'll get on to Cowgill at once."

"I ain't quite finished," Dot said. "Better sit yerself down again. It don't get any better."

Lois sat down again. "Go on, then," she said, "but try not to take too long."

"Well, there was this woman over Solihull way, lost her husband, and hadn't got nobody else in the world. Apparently she was not an easy woman, and all the neighbours knew that her old husband had played the field. Mistresses all around town, so my cousin said. Then he dies. It were an awful death, lingerin' on for weeks."

"Dot," said Lois warningly.

"Yes, well, he died, and when it came to reading the will, his fortune was all split up round these women. O' course, the wife got her share. Anyway, she contested the will, got her own solicitor on to it, and it turned out the mistresses had been organised by a sort o' pimp. It was all a big scam, but when they came to arrest the pimp, he'd skipped the country, they reckoned to Australia. He was never found."

"And his name?" said Lois with sinking heart.

"You got it," Dot said, "Gregory Wilkins. At least, that's one of his names."

"But why Rob and Josie?" Lois said. "There was no fortune there, that's for sure."

"Yeah, well, maybe he thought he'd come back and keep his head down, start again in a small way. Most of these scam villains 'ave got no small opinion of themselves, Mrs. M. Believe me. They think they can outwit the cops, and sometimes they do. I bet that Greg is holed up in Timbuktu by now."

"So you reckon all this had nothing to do with the attack on Rob?"

Dot shook her head. "Not sure," she said, "but I'd say it were just a handy opportunity he couldn't resist. Probably noticed the story in the local, and thought whoever attacked Rob was after money, so he might as well have a go. That's my guess, Mrs. M."

Dot's guesses were based on years of experience in the subcriminal world, and Lois put great faith in her judgement. But she still found it hard to believe that anyone would risk a prison sentence for such a small likelihood of gain. Still, she would pass it all on to Cowgill and see what he had to say.

"Okay if I tell our friendly detective inspector, Dot?"

"O' course. He takes notice of you, Mrs. M." Dot smiled. "You're still a good-looker, Mrs. M, so don't let that daughter of yours take over. Now, I'm off," she added, and going dangerously quickly down the narrow stairs into the shop, she was out and into her car before Lois had had time to ask her what on earth she meant by that last remark.

Cowgill's reaction was puzzling. "Thank you, Lois," he said flatly. "It looks as if Josie has had a narrow escape. But then, if there really was no money involved, no harm has been done. I will, of course, follow up this man, and also alert the Birmingham police. I remember the case, but I seem to recall he'd never been caught."

"Right, well," Lois said, irritated that he sounded cool and not particularly interested. "I suppose it's pointless asking you if you've got any further with Rob's killer?"

Cowgill realised that Lois was, to use her word, snitched. She had obviously taken Dot Nimmo's story very seriously, whereas he always took the word of a Nimmo with a pinch of salt.

"Anything else to tell me?" he said. He listened carefully to what Lois told him about Sally's pregnancy and Mrs. T-J's reaction. Had it any bearing on Rob's case? He was still working on it, he told Lois. Anything else she could discover about Mark and his friends in the village hall gang could be valuable information.

"I rely on you, Lois, as you know," he said placatingly.

"Mm. I'm thinking. You know the night of the gypsy fire? Well, the gang was there, weren't they. Mark Brown was seen, an' he reckoned they were innocent and it was him what called the firemen."

"Go on," Cowgill said.

"Well, who *did* start the fire? And who told the gang when the fire was going well, and it was safe to sound the alarm? They are just a load of dropout kids, y' know, Hunter. They've never done nothing really serious. Just been in the nuisance stage they all go through."

"Maybe," said Cowgill. He was still thinking more along the lines of gypsy feuds, especially since he'd had a message to say there'd been a death and an arrest up north, in the place where the Farnden gypsies had gone after the fire.

"So who's bin pulling the strings?" Lois said. "What with all this to-do with Greg the conman, I've not been giving enough thought to that side of it."

"Any suggestions, Lois?"

"I'm working on it." She thought of advising him where to look for the gang's mastermind, but because she could not bear the thought of more trouble for Sheila Stratford, she did not.

FORTY-EIGHT

I'm off now," Sheila Stratford said. "I'll be back for lunch. It'll be cold, so there's nothing to be done except dish up. What're you doing this morning?" Sam was reading the local paper, and did not look up.

"Nothing much," he said. "I thought I might go over and have a look at that field of barley on the Waltonby road. Looks to me like it's got some kind of blight."

"It's not your responsibility anymore, Sam," his wife reminded him.

"So?" Sam said truculently. "Am I supposed to go into purdah? Not go near the farm where I've worked for God knows how many years?"

"No, of course not," Sheila said wearily. When was he going to stop acting like a spoilt child? "I just meant that it was not something you had to worry about too much." She sighed. "Well, I'll be going. Cheerio—see you lunchtime."

"Maybe not," Sam said. "If I'm not allowed to look at fields, I might go into Tresham on the bus and catch the four thirty back."

Sheila's mood deepened. Go to Tresham . . . and meet someone? Who? She was sure there was someone. She got into her car and drove off to her client in Fletching, trying to concentrate her mind on cleaning.

"Who was that on the phone?" Alf asked. He had come into the farmhouse kitchen to find Edwina replacing the receiver.

"Oh, that woman from WI headquarters, trying to persuade us to get a rounders team together for the county tournament."

"So will you?" Alf said, smiling as he pictured the ladies of the WI wielding a rounders bat. Heaven help anybody who got in the way!

"I'll have to speak to Mrs. T-J. She's in charge," Edwina said. "By the way," she continued, "I see we're low on several things we need from the wholesaler. I'll go in this morning and stock up. Library, too," she added, "my book's overdue."

"What about lunch? Shall I get something?"

"I'll make you a sandwich before I go," Edwina replied. You wicked woman, she thought, but not very seriously. Your poor husband has to exist on a sandwich, while you go off gallivanting with your lover. It was some time since she had seen Sam, and the thought of having lunch with him in that new place behind the library drove all creeping feelings of guilt from her mind.

"Have a good trip, then, lovey," said Alf. "I reckon I'll give Sam Stratford a ring, see if he can come over and give me a hand with a bit o' fencing."

Ooops! Edwina had a momentary pang of alarm. Why would he say that, out of the blue? She looked at him closely, but his bland face gave nothing away. She went out to collect the eggs.

The small café was almost empty when Edwina arrived. She looked around for Sam, but could see only one single lady sitting at the window looking out into the small passage that ran round the back of the library. The waitress came out with her order pad, and Edwina said she was waiting for someone and would order when he came. He shouldn't be long, she said.

"No hurry," the waitress said, smiling. "We're not exactly packed out, as you can see. The café has only just opened, so it's early days. Would you like a newspaper while you wait?"

Edwina read the headlines, and then turned to the crossword. She had solved several clues, and began to wonder if Sam was really coming. Perhaps Alf had persuaded him to do the fencing job. Maybe he'd made it impossible for him not to do it. There was something in Alf's eyes this morning when she said goodbye and set off in her car. Something calculating?

The café door opened, and the tall, bulky figure of Sam walked in. He saw her at once, and as he sat down, said, "Sorry I'm late, gel. Your hubby kept me talking, an' I didn't like to hurry away sayin' I'd be late for lunch with his wife." He chuckled and took her hand surreptitiously, at the same time looking round to check there was nobody in the café who would know him.

So that's all right, thought Edwina, and relaxed. The waitress reappeared, and took their order, and they were left alone. Suddenly neither could think of anything to say. It was different at the farm when Alf was out, or in the woods or up in the hayloft of the old barn. Familiar places were comfortable, and there was always some farming subject for them to talk about. Now, here in a big town, in a café remote from everything familiar, they searched for something to start a conversation.

In the farmhouse, Alf sat eating his solitary sandwich and thinking about Sam Stratford. They were troubling thoughts, so he switched to thinking about something else. Sheila had told him the latest gossip. The Tollervey-Jones girl was pregnant, and the old thing at the hall had extended a reluctant hand of friendship to that young liar, Mark Brown. Lucky lad. He was not stupid, and could have a useful life. He was surely clued up enough not to get a girl in the family way? Perhaps it was a clever move on Mark Brown's part. Now he was safely under the protection of the Tollervey-Jones umbrella. Untouchable. Or was he?

Alf rinsed his plate under the tap, washed his hands, and walked out of the kitchen, locking the door behind him. He had decided to tackle at least one of his problems this afternoon, and set off in his car towards Waltonby, where he intended to call on Sheila Stratford.

Edwina had discovered that she couldn't eat her omelette and chips. Her appetite seemed to have gone completely. Fortunately, Sam was having no such trouble, and happily dealt with Edwina's plateful as well as his own. It was this that made them laugh, and finally got the conversation going.

"You like cooking, don't you, Edwina?" Sam said. "I bet this is not up to your standard. D'you fancy anything else, love?"

She shook her head. "Sorry, Sam. I expect I'm a bit nervous. You know. . . ."

"No need to be sorry. We'll find another place with better grub. This is handy, because we're not likely to meet Farnden folk here. Anyway, have some pud? They got ice cream. That'll slip down easy, as my mum used to say."

"I don't remember her," Edwina said. The past was probably a safe subject. "Were you an only?"

"Yep. And Mother's pride and joy, as a result. It wasn't always easy, especially as the other mothers wouldn't speak to her outside the playground, an' when the word got around, some of the other kids took it out on me at first. Like they do. I hated my mum then. Still, I was bigger and stronger than the others, so I soon showed 'em who was goin' to be boss. They forgot about it in no time."

"Why was your mum ignored?"

Sam hesitated. He had spent his life trying to hide it, but he supposed Edwina could keep it to herself. "She was from the bloody gypsies," he said. "She was fantastic to look at, and my dad meant to have her, come what may, silly fool. They were married secretly in a registry office, an' I was born six months later. And no, I wasn't premature!" His laugh was hollow, and it was Edwina's turn to take his hand.

"Nothing wrong with that, was there?" she said. "Happens most of the time in villages. There's one family in Fletching with five daughters, an' every single one of 'em was five months gone by the time they got married! Sailed up the aisle in purest white empire-line dresses, carrying all before them!"

She had to explain what empire-line was, and then Sam saw the joke. He looked at his watch. "I should be getting back," he said. "Your Alf made me say I'd look in later to help him finish the fences. I've really enjoyed this," he added gallantly, and signalled for the bill.

"Me, too," lied Edwina. She was relieved to know they'd soon be out in the streets. She felt like a squirrel in a trap, waiting to be discovered. They made their way to the door, where two people were entering, and Edwina's empty stomach gave a painful lurch.

"Good morning, Mrs. Smith! And Mr. Stratford . . . how nice to see you. Marjorie and I thought we'd try this new place. Any good?" It was Father Keith Buccleugh and his wife. The vicar was a professional, and managed to ease his way past the embarrassed couple without turning a hair. Not so his wife. Marjorie faked a sudden sneeze, and with a handkerchief up to her nose she nodded at Edwina and bolted for a table.

"Well, Keith?" she said. "And what d'you make of that?"

FORTY-NINE

Lois and Josie decided to go to Appleby in the New Brooms van, it being the newest and most reliable of the family vehicles, and also, said Lois, it would be good for publicity. She had read in her researches on the Internet that fifty thousand people visit Appleby during horse fair week, and surely some of them might need a cleaner?

"Mum, these are Romany people," Josie had said. "They don't have cleaners doing their trailers once a week. And they're always on the move, most of them. Besides which, huge numbers of tourists come from countries abroad. Are you planning New Eurobrooms?"

"Why not?" Lois replied, and changed the subject. "We'll start early, then we can stop on the way for coffee and lunch an' that. I said we'd check in at the hotel around five." Derek had said that they must stay in the best hotel, in the town centre. He didn't want them wandering about up side roads, he said. And when Lois had been shocked at the price of a twin-bedded double room, Derek had said what was the point of winning the lottery if you couldn't stay in a good hotel once in a while? He had found the name of the old county town hotel, the Appleby Arms, and booked them in.

The next morning, Gran and Derek waved the two of them off, Gran with a frown, and Derek with a cheery wave.

"Take care of y' mother, Josie!" he shouted, as they moved away down the street.

"You'd think we were going to darkest Africa! Did you see Gran's face?"

"Yep," Lois said. "She was always like that when I was a girl at home. Anxious all the time I was away anywhere. I reckon that's why I went off the rails."

Josie looked sideways at her and smiled. "You mean when you met Dad?"

"Never you mind," Lois said. "Now, when shall we set the satnav going? I know the way to the M6, and then it's straight on for miles."

"It'll be useful when we get off the motorway and head for Appleby across the moors." Josie was determined to use her latest acquisition. She had had fun using it to go to Tresham and villages around, sometimes obeying the confident woman's voice, sometimes not performing a U-turn when instructed. When she was delivering groceries on wet, grey days, she sometimes had a conversation with Mrs. Satnav, telling her there was a much better way, cutting off corners and negotiating lanes where grass grew down the middle of the road.

As they sat in a rush-hour jam around Wolverhampton, Josie said suddenly, "Hey, look, Mum! Look at that wonderful shiny trailer! That must be gypsies on their way."

Then they began to see more of them, including a traditionally painted, curve-topped old caravan safely anchored on a flatbed truck with an entire family crammed into the lorry cab. Lois wondered irrationally if they would see Athalia . . . or George. . . .

If only she had been able to tell them she and Josie were coming, she was sure they would at least have looked out for them. As it was, Lois would have to keep her eyes open. She remembered Athalia's surname was Lee, but had no idea of George's. She was convinced that if she could talk to them away from Farnden bigots and Tresham cops, they would have more to tell her about poor old Rob.

Mrs. Satnav guided them to Appleby by a main route, and Josie, looking at the road map, said that when they returned home she had found a much more interesting-looking route. "Sorry, Mrs. S," she said, as they drove into the yard, where old stables had been converted into guest rooms, "but don't worry. We're very grateful."

"You want to watch it," Lois said, getting out of the van and stretching her arms up in relief. "You'll be talking to Mr. and Mrs. Sidelights next."

The receptionist greeted them warmly, and showed them out into one of the rooms overlooking the market square. It was spacious and elegantly decorated, and Josie flopped down on the bed, closed her eyes, and said, "This is the life, Mum! Wake me in an hour with a glass of champagne and a soupçon of caviar."

"A what?" said Lois. "Now, get up at once and help me unpack. We'll go and get a cup of tea in the town, and then have a walk around. It looks as if it's all happening already." Cars had indeed been nose to tail over the bridge that crossed the river Eden, and Josie had seen small children playing in the shallows on a sandy bank.

It was early evening by the time they began their stroll around town. "It's a great place, isn't it?" Josie said, snapping away with her camera at the wide main street with its monuments top and bottom. There was a steady incline from the marketplace up to the top, with beautiful old houses, offices and galleries and shops, lining the road.

"Shall we look in the church?" Lois said. She loved old churches and graveyards. "All the history of the town lies there," she told a sceptical Josie.

"Do we have to, Mum? Can't we just walk along by the river and see what's happening? That's where the action is, I reckon."

Lois gave way, thinking she could always indulge herself with a mooch round the church on her own. She was reminded of Derek saying he wanted them to stay together all the time. What nonsense, she thought, looking at the happy scene. The strong wind had dropped and the evening sun shone benevolently. But this was their first evening, so she said, "Right, lead on, Josie. I'll have a look at the church tomorrow." She knew from when Josie was a teenager that her daughter was a great companion, but not for too long. Then she needed to get away by herself for a while.

"What did you say?" Josie hopped back on to the pavement to avoid being run down by a trotting pony and trap, driven by a fiercely handsome, bare-chested young man with dark curly hair who yelled at his mates on the side of the road as he passed.

"Nothing," said Lois. "Just watch where you're going, and stop ogling the raggle-taggle gypsies."

They walked on over the bridge, and turned left on to a footpath leading along the riverbank into a stretch of tall trees. They passed a slipway into the river, where horses were being led down to be washed, ready for selling among the dealers. There were children everywhere, small brown imps, fearless in the water.

The river under the bridge looked treacherous to Lois, and she noticed police and RSPCA officials mingling among the gypsies here and there. Sandbanks stretched out almost to midstream, and then the fast running channel was suddenly deep enough for young lads to ride bareback with no safety gear whatsoever, driving their horses on until the animals swam, with wild eyes and only heads visible. More imps, their clothes soaking wet from the river, clung precariously to the backs of cars and trucks, as the nose-to-tail traffic edged forward along the road.

"You know what Gran would say," Josie laughed. "It'll all end in tears!"

Lois smiled back at her daughter. This was really nice, she thought, being away from home and all its attendant responsibilities and worries, with her only daughter, who looked brighter and prettier than she'd seen her since the—But no! This was a holiday, and until she found Athalia and George she would not brood on anything else but enjoying themselves.

They strolled slowly along the riverbank, listening to the Romany language being spoken. "You know what, Mum," Josie said. "I feel like we're the foreigners here. It's rather humbling, isn't it."

"Not humbling for the residents of Appleby, apparently," Lois said. "They're all advised to lock up their daughters, cars, garden statuary, an' that. Some of them curse at the loss of trade when they shut up shop for the week. I suppose it's necessary," she added, looking at a family picnicking under a tree, "though it all seems peaceful enough now."

"Ah, but," Josie began, and then was aware that her mother had stopped and was staring back along the road that ran parallel to the footpath. "What is it, Mum?" she said.

Lois did not answer for a moment, and then said, "That was one of the gypsies we saw at Farnden! I'd know him anywhere!"

"Not the ones with the dog!" Josie said.

"No, the one who introduced me to the old woman when I thought I'd run over *her* dog. I'm not sure, but I think his name was George." She was sure, of course. She was absolutely certain that the tall, strong figure sitting sideways on a minimal racing trap, waving to friends at the wayside, was indeed George. He was wearing a bright check shirt, enabling her to follow him with her eyes as his horse sped along with its odd-looking trotting action, weaving its way through the traffic.

Josie frowned. "Aren't they endangering the public, driving like that? Where are the police?"

"Everywhere. You must have noticed. But it seems Appleby hands over the town to the gypsies for the fair. It's been going on for more than three hundred years, you know."

"Doesn't mean it's safe now. Supposing a child ran across in front of that man? It wouldn't stand a chance."

Lois refused to feel depressed. She recognised her daughter as a child of the health-and-safety age, and wondered what had happened to a sense of adventure and learning to cope with risk by encountering it.

"What about the hunt at home?" she asked Josie. "They mill around on the roads, and their followers in Land Rovers are a menace on the narrow lanes. Nobody persecutes *them*." But even as she said it, she knew she was wrong. Hunting with dogs was banned, and the hunting folk were keeping a low profile, desperate not to attract attention to the fact that they were carrying on regardless.

"Forget it, anyway," Josie said. "We're here to soak it all up.

The romance, the tradition, the danger and the spectacle! Stand still, Mum," she added. "I want to take a picture of you up to your ankles in empty tins and plastic bottles, just to see if Dad mistakes you for a gypsy!"

They walked on through the shadowy trees and out into a camping place. Lois could not believe her luck when there across the field she saw the trap with the horse still between its shafts, with George in close conversation with a man half his height, wearing a cloth cap and carrying a stick.

FIFTY

Lois did not approach George. She had decided to make her first contact with him when Josie was off doing something on her own. It was a small risk, she knew. She might not be able to find him again in this huge crowd, but as all the gypsies from Athalia's lot would be here, she would be sure to see at least one of them, and ask about George. Best of all would be to meet Athalia herself. Although the old woman had warned her off from wanting to be friends, she reckoned she could persuade her that here, miles and miles from Long Farnden, there would be no harm in it.

She and Josie walked back across a small iron bridge and on to the footpath going along the opposite side of the river. This bordered the leisure part of the town. A playground for small children had its usual huddle of subteens, up to no good. "Part of growing up, Mum," Josie said, reading her mother's expression. "Not that different from your own depraved childhood."

Lois laughed. "That's quite enough of that, miss," she said.

They walked past the scout hut, the wide open sports field, and admired an attractive row of cottages on the far side. Josie tried to imagine the town without the horse fair, and thought how pleasant it must be to have a holiday here. But Rob would have been bored out of his mind. He was an indoor man, she remembered, continuing her train of thought. So in that case, what was he doing *walking* along a road on his way back home late at night?

Lois glanced at Josie, whose pace had slowed. She knew at once what had happened. Josie's head was down, and she was frowning.

"Penny for 'em," she said.

Josie looked up. "Nothing much," she said, and seeing disbelief on her mother's face, she continued, "and do you really need to ask?"

"Not really," Lois said, linking her arm through Josie's. "Let's try to leave it behind for a few days, duckie. Come on, time for supper soon. I don't know about you, but I'm hungry."

This hotel is *so* comfortable and pleasant, thought Lois as they sat down at a table in the dining room. I could stay here for ever, away from Farnden and all my worries. She knew she didn't mean it, and supposed that was what holidays were for, to escape and return home more able to cope.

They ordered their meal, and looked around. It was early, and only two or three other tables were occupied. The waitress was foreign, but her English was adequate, and they had a conversation about her home in Poland and the boyfriend she had left behind.

"I don't suppose gypsies would be allowed to stay here," Josie said. "Can you imagine them sitting respectably at a table talking in hushed voices and minding their manners?"

"Of course not," Lois answered. "The whole point of the fair is to be together with all their . . ."

"Tribe?" suggested Josie.

"Friends, I was going to say," Lois said. "They want to be with their own. A lot are related, and only see each other at these fairs. Appleby is like the Grand Prix. The big event of the year. You wait 'til we see the races an' the campsite."

"How come you know so much about it?"

"I did my homework," Lois said proudly. "Googled up all the Web sites. Your mum is no slouch, you know." She patted Josie's hand and smiled. Then both she and Josie turned to look at the entrance to the dining room, hearing a familiar voice.

"Well, if it isn't Mrs. Meade and her sidekick!" Alf Smith, with an odd expression on his face, approached them and stood looking down, first at one and then the other. "And what brings you here, may I ask?" he said.

"Same as you, I expect," Lois said, quickly gathering her wits. "We're having a break, come to see the fair and shake the dust of Farnden off our feet for a few days. Is Mrs. Smith with you?" She did hope he wouldn't ask to share their table, but he shook his head.

"No, she's not interested in gypsies. Quite the reverse, in fact," he said. "She's looking after the farm while I'm here. Getting up to mischief, I dare say. While the cat's away, etcetera."

Was he joking? Lois thought. He didn't smile, and excused himself without further conversation, walking across to a table as far away as possible from theirs.

"Blimey, that's a turnup," Josie whispered. "Didn't know he was that keen on his gypsy friends."

"He claims his great-grandmother was one of them," Lois said softly.

"Why ain't he camping up with the rest of 'em on their site, then?" said Josie sourly. She had not forgotten his set-to with Sam Stratford in her shop, and had no neighbourly feelings towards Alf Smith.

After supper, Lois and Josie decided to have a wander around the town. "Leave your handbag in the room," Lois said. "Best if we have nothing on us worth stealing."

"I thought you didn't believe all that stuff about the gypsies thieving?"

"There's good gypsies and bad gypsies, just like everybody else," Lois said. "Better safe than sorry, as Gran would say."

The town was jumping. Crowds ambling along the roads made it impossible for traffic to do more than crawl. Loud-voiced men, women dressed for a festival, the ever-present wild children and dogs, all filled the town, transforming it into something—as Josie said—very un-English.

There was a police presence larger than any Lois had seen anywhere. Policemen and policewomen on every street corner, cruising round in cars, gathering at well-known hot spots, anticipating trouble. By a Caught on Camera van, a knot of police officers talked together, and then suddenly they all laughed. Friendly badinage between gypsies and police reached up to Lois's open window, and she felt a strong urge to be part of this festive atmosphere.

The hotel receptionist had given them a key to the front door of the hotel, which was firmly locked. She looked worried when they said they were going for a stroll. "Stick to the middle of town, then," she said. "We get a lot of hangers-on this week, bad 'uns who use the fair as an excuse to break the law, knowing that it'll all be blamed on the gypsies. Keep together, anyway. Most of our residents spend the evening in our pleasant lounge, watching television and having drinks. Can't I persuade you?"

Josie would have been happy to be persuaded, but Lois thanked the receptionist kindly, and said they would be careful. She was sure they would be fine, with all those police about.

FIFTY-ONE

Edwina Smith was not as excited as she thought she would be at the idea of Alf being far away for a few days. She had got up early and seen him off to Appleby, assuring him that she would look after everything on the farm. "And Sam will come over and help with all the things you arranged with him," she said innocently.

That would be tomorrow morning, quite early, Alf had said, as he left. Now it was evening, and she wondered if he had arrived at his hotel. She looked at the clock. Nearly time for Alf's favourite programme on television. She had had bread and cheese for lunch and a cheese and pickle sandwich for supper, and had indigestion. Perhaps she would go to bed early, stretch out and ease her stomachache. She went through to the empty sitting room and switched on, ready for the show.

Sam and Sheila Stratford were watching the same episode, and instead of sitting separately, Sam settled on the sofa and beckoned Sheila to join him. "Come and cuddle up," he said, and put his arm around her.

At last! thought Sheila. Here's my old Sam back again. It had been such a long time since he had shown her any sign of affection, and she impulsively kissed him on his cheek. He smiled at her. "Why do we watch this old rubbish," he said. "Not exactly the everyday story of country folk, is it?"

"Nor the everyday life of our dear young Queen," she said, and began to giggle.

"Funny how you remember these sayings from years ago," Sam answered. "My mum was a royals fan. She watched the Queen's coronation on my gran's little 'ole telly. It was covered with a fancy cloth when it was switched off."

"My gran's telly was kept in a cupboard," Sheila said, snuggling closer.

Sam roared with laughter. "God," he said, "how long ago that was. Seems like another life. An' yet in some ways, only yesterday."

They were quiet for a few moments, and then the familiar soap tune came up and Sheila said, "D'you reckon that Karen will leave her hubby?"

"Dunno," Sam said. "Be a right fool if she did. He's not a bad bloke, compared with some."

Derek was not watching television, although Gran had settled for an hour or so's viewing with a cup of tea after supper. He said it was a good opportunity, with Lois away, to fix the overhead light in their bedroom. It was lethal, he said, with bare wires visible.

"And you an electrician," Gran had said.

Now he came back and fidgeted about the room, passing by the screen so often that Gran said finally, "Oh, for goodness sake, Derek, settle down, do."

"What d'you think they're doing at this moment?" he said, by way of an answer.

"Enjoying themselves, I should hope," Gran said. "There's been enough fuss and bother organising it all. Mind you, that Floss did a good job in the shop today. I've told her to ring me if she has a problem. I reckon she's too good to be a cleaner. And now she's married she'll need more money than Lois pays."

"She likes working for New Brooms," Derek replied, slumping down into the armchair that was usually Lois's. "Like one big family, Lois always says." He looked at his watch. "D'you think they've had supper in the hotel?" he asked.

"Derek Meade!" Gran said, losing patience. "Forget about them! There's safety in numbers, and Lois is not going to put her only daughter in any danger, is she? If you don't want to watch telly, for heaven's sake read the evening paper. It's still on the mat in the hall."

Derek got up thankfully and fetched the paper. "Usual rubbish," he said, before he opened it. He turned at once to the sports pages, and it was not until the programme had finished that he sat up suddenly and said, "Gran! Look at this! Here, at the bottom of the page."

"Tresham market trader arrested in the north." The headline meant little to Gran, until she read on and learned that the market trader had had a stall in Tresham market with his brother. She had seen it herself on a market day when she went in to town shopping with Lois. But they had agreed that it was all junk, and Lois had said they were just fly-by-nights. Something to do with the lot that camped here, on Alf Smith's land. Probably never paid any rent for the market pitch, Gran guessed.

"I remember them!" She looked at Derek in alarm. "Nowhere near Appleby, is it?"

"Doesn't say exactly where they were. But read on. See what he's supposed to have done."

The story was brief. The body of the younger brother had been found, possibly drowned in nearby floods, and the older one had been arrested. "Police are pursuing their enquiries," the story said. "And there's a missing dog."

"I reckon they were among them gypsies that were here," Derek said. "Alan Stratford said he'd walked round the wood behind them, and saw the same pair as I did them with the pit bull terrier. They'd more or less told him to clear off, he said."

"I wish Lois and Josie would ring us," Gran said. "Just to let us know they're safe."

"I thought you said we should forget about them, let them get on with enjoying themselves," Derek said.

"Yes, well," Gran muttered. "As long as they're safe."

Floss and Ben had gone to bed early. They had a telly in their bedroom, and were propped up on pillows watching the news.

Floss had enjoyed her day in the shop, with one or two new customers from the development over in Waltonby. Josie stocked such a good variety that Floss reckoned you could buy all you needed and not have to go out of the village at all. She was trying this out herself, as her Ben had decided that supermarkets were the root of all evil. Bankrupting the farmers, he had said. And making people buy more than they needed with their cheap offers and buy-one-get-one-free enticements.

The local news started with a story about kids from Fletching school who had done a cycle ride for charity, and Floss said she knew one of the boys they could see wobbling about on his bike and giving his neighbour a push so he fell off. "That's young Braddon," she said, "his folks farm over at Fletching. A trouble-maker, apparently. Funny how you can tell quite young."

"I wonder if we'll spot it in our own. . . ." he said, looking sideways at her.

"Ours will be perfect," she said, "*when* they come along."

He turned to her. "Shall we give them a helping hand?" he said, sliding down the bed beside her and disappearing under the duvet.

"Hey! Stop it, Ben! Wait! Look at this—it's about them gypsies who were camped over at Farnden. D'you remember all that fuss, with them being moved on? I'm sure that one who's been arrested was over the fields one day with one of them dogs—you know, the dangerous ones you're not supposed to keep. Ben!"

Ben surfaced, his face flushed, and said never mind about flaming gypsies, how about a bit of the other.

Floss giggled, and turned off the news. Much later she remembered the story about the arrested man. The young one had come to the door once, she was sure, asking if they had anything to sell. She had shut the door in his face, more or less, and now wished she hadn't. It must have been him that ended up dead in the mud up north.

Hunter Cowgill was also watching television. He had eaten a solitary supper and picked up a thriller he had borrowed from the library. But the author's account of police activity was so wide of the mark that he wondered if she was thinking of some other country, a police state some thirty years ago maybe. He turned to the front to look up publication date and saw that he was right. Published in the seventies, and not reprinted. No wonder! Not only were the police sorely misrepresented, but the plot was so convoluted that he gave up, throwing it to the floor.

Now he was watching the news, and nodded sagely as the story of the drowned man and his arrested brother came up. He knew about it, of course. He wondered if Lois was watching. Perhaps he would give her a ring, draw her attention to it.

"Hello? May I speak to Mrs. Meade, please? Inspector Cowgill here."

Derek had answered the phone, and his heart sank. "What's happened!?" he said. "Is Lois all right? And Josie?"

Cowgill said, "Sorry? What did you say? Surely you would know better than I if Lois and Josie were all right?"

It occurred to Derek that Cowgill did not know they were in Appleby, and he relaxed.

He explained that they had gone to the horse fair, and would be away for a few days.

"Where are they staying?" said Cowgill, his voice suddenly sharp.

Derek told him, and gave him the number. "What d'you want her for?" he asked suspiciously.

"Nothing important, thanks Derek," Cowgill replied, and cut off the call at once.

FIFTY-TWO

Lois and Josie set off from the hotel, past the crowd sitting outside the pub and over the bridge, where families were walking slowly back and forth in the evening sun.

"We could be in the south of France, not the remote north of England," Josie said.

"With the same weather for once!" Lois took her daughter's arm in an excess of affection, and Josie squeezed it and then gently disengaged it.

"Well, now our climate's supposed to be changing, perhaps we could do the same? Maybe play boules round the back of the village hall? We could suggest it to Dad, get him to propose it to the parish council."

"Not quite British, though," said Lois. "And what about when it pours with rain every evening for weeks, like it did last summer?"

"There's brollies," Josie objected. "You can get lovely holiday designs, like the ones people bring back from Monet's garden an' that."

"Can you see old Ivy Beasley under a Monet umbrella promenading down the High Street in the rain?"

"Why not? She's a game old thing. Probably lead the way."

Lois gave up. "Let's go and look at the field where the camp and the stalls are. Where everything happens," she answered, expecting a refusal. After all, the sun was beginning to sink and the camp field was the heart of it all, and after a few beers they must all be in fighting mood.

But to her surprise, Josie said it was a good idea, and they started up Gallows Hill. Privately Lois had decided that she was most likely to see George or Athalia when they were all gathered together on the field.

From a long way off, they could hear the music, loud and exciting. Josie said she reckoned the stalls would all be packed up for the night, so perhaps not so many people would be up there. They could just have a wander around and then come again tomorrow with money to spend.

Eyes followed them as they entered the field. It was full of activity and with so many camp fires burning, there was a marvellous smell of wood smoke and charred meat. Everywhere there were vans, trailers, tents, and dozens of small tinkers tearing around with noisy shouts in a foreign tongue. Several times, a group of them stopped dead at the sight of Lois and Josie, staring, as if the two women were creatures from another planet. A row of stalls ran from the entrance into the field, and they walked slowly along. Many were still trading, and most of the stuff for sale was to do with horses. There were beautiful leather harnesses, and brightly coloured carts for racing, horse blankets and newly decorated traditional wagons, with their owners sitting proudly chatting, puffing on pipes.

Josie stopped at a stall selling jewellery, and after a conversation with the seller, bought a bracelet with tiny hanging pendants bearing pictures of Christian saints. Lois agreed it was pretty, but doubted if it had been a traditional craft of the Romany people. "More like Taiwan," she said.

A gypsy woman approached them and said directly to Josie that she could see she'd had a lot of sadness lately, but good things would happen by the end of the year. She offered a gypsy wish for a fiver, and Lois tried to pull Josie away. Josie did not move, and stared at the gypsy woman. "I'll have a wish, then," she said. The woman gave her three blue glass beads, and patted her on the hand. "Good luck, my dear," she said.

"Mum!" Josie said suddenly. "Look! There's that bloke you were staring at this afternoon. He's one of them gypsies that were in the village, isn't he?"

Lois tried to look nonchalant, and said, "Where?" But Josie said, "Oh, come on, Mum. You don't fool me. You're here with a purpose. You think this lot can give us some clues about what happened to Rob. Well, you don't have to keep it a secret from me. I was his partner, don't forget. Let's do it together, shall we?"

Lois sighed. "All right, then. Let's see if we can get a conversation going."

They approached the half circle of vans where Josie had seen George, and, sure enough, Lois saw Athalia in her usual place, sitting on the steps of her trailer, gazing out across the field. She saw Lois and quite deliberately looked the other way.

Not a good start, thought Lois, but approached with a big smile, nudging Josie to do the same. "Hello, I was hoping we might see you here," she said, stepping forward to where Athalia sat, now glowering at her. Lois ploughed on. "This is my daughter, Josie, who you might have seen in the village shop when you were stopping in Farnden?"

Athalia was a good woman, and felt confused. She had decided that the less she had to do with people from that village the better. And although she had liked Lois on first acquaintance, she judged it was best for both not to pursue a friendship. Bad things had happened in Farnden, and she and George had decided not to go there at all next year, in spite of Alf Smith's encouragement. Athalia had known Alf for many years, and had been fond of him, but he had changed. She was not sure about him anymore. One of their family had said they'd seen him in Appleby, going into the big hotel. Athalia hoped he would stay clear of them. Too many puzzles were unresolved.

But then she looked at young Josie's smiling face, and remembered that the girl's partner had been attacked on the road, left to die in a ditch. She relented, although she also remembered that the gypsies had been the first to be suspected of the crime. She stood up and extended her hand. "Pleased to meet you, Josie," she said. "I didn't come to your shop. We got our shopping in Tresham. More anonymous in a supermarket for us. We might get stared at, but they let us buy their goods! How're you doing now, gel?"

This last was addressed to Lois, who nodded and said she was fine. "We're takin' a few days break, me and Josie," she said. "I've always wanted to come to the Appleby fair, so here we are. Your lot doin' all right? I read about them two who were with you in Farnden. Sounded nasty."

Athalia's eyes narrowed. "Nuthin' to do with us," she said. "They didn't come along of us to here. Though we saw them on the way." She didn't mention that their encounter was closer than that. Less said about that the better.

Lois felt George's presence before she saw him. He was there behind her, and spoke close to her ear. "Slummin', are we?" he said.

She whipped round and faced him. "That's a nice welcome, I'm sure," she said angrily. "Come on, Josie. 'Bye, Athalia, we might meet up again in the next day or two. Have a great time."

"Hey, hey, hey!" George said. "No need to be so hasty. I was only joking. Evenin', miss," he added, nodding politely at Josie. "Must be your daughter, Mrs. Meade," he said. "She's the image of you."

"When young," Lois said sharply. "Anyway, Josie," she added, "we must be getting back."

"You'll be quite safe here with us," George said. "Have a beer. We got crates of the stuff in the van."

Athalia looked at him closely. She missed nothing that went on with George, and realised with a sinking heart that the poor man was attracted to Mrs. Meade. Now what? she thought. Since his wife had gone off, Athalia had taken him under her wing, and thought of him as almost a son. This must be stopped, and at once.

"Mrs. Meade was getting back to her hotel," she said. "You can see the light's goin', George. Not safe for two beautiful young ladies to be alone in Appleby on a fair night."

"They won't be alone," George said, fetching a bottle and four glasses. "I shall escort them back to their palace."

"If the pumpkin coach don't turn up first," Josie said, and all except Athalia laughed, and she went back to her seat on the trailer steps. George fetched two chairs, and Lois and Josie sat down, with George on the grass at their feet. They sipped their beer and watched the scene, listening when a song broke out somewhere on the field.

After a while Athalia relented, and began to tell stories of past days, when travellers, real gypsies, were welcomed, and had stopping places where they could spend several weeks. "Nowadays," she said bitterly, "we get a reputation for being dirty people, not clearing up after us. But, Mrs. Meade, when the police come and want you off the site and on your way with no time to do anythin' but pack up a few belongings, it ain't no wonder things get left."

"I hope you don't mind my asking, Mrs. Lee," Josie said, "but how can you keep really clean living in a caravan and always moving on?"

Lois held her breath, expecting a blast from Athalia. It didn't come, and Athalia chuckled. "Different way of life, Josie. We think we're cleaner than you *gorgios*. We'd never wash dirty socks in the same bowl as scrub the veg. And in the old days, we never had no toilets. Ugh! Fancy all that in one place! We used the woods and the hedges in a proper way. Now, o' course, we got toilets and showers an' all that in these fancy trailers."

Suddenly, shouts of a fight came from across the field. Raucous voices joined together to cheer on one side and then another. George got to his feet. "Time to go, ladies," he said. "Athalia will tell you more another time. Somebody should collect her memories before it's too late. Come on now, follow me."

On the way back, George chatted about nothing much, filling them in on gypsy ways. "We've always had fights, but shake hands after." With a bit of prompting from Lois, he asked if they'd got Rob's attacker. When she said not, he stopped and looked at her. "Do *you* think we did it?" he asked seriously. Lois shrugged. Josie said that until they found the guilty person, they had to suspect everybody.

"Even the respectable citizens of Farnden?" George said. "Like that lot in the pub on quiz night? One or two there would have done us in on our way home. Think on it, Mrs. Meade," he added.

When they were safely back in their hotel room, Josie said, "Mum, shouldn't we ring Dad?"

"If you like. Yep, let's ring him and Gran. They're probably imaginin' all kinds of disasters. Then we've got to think, like George said."

FIFTY-THREE
⟡

Derek heard the telephone and looked at his watch. There had been several calls during the evening, and none of them had been from Lois and Josie. Now he had no great hopes of it being them this time.

"Dad?" It was Josie's light, clear voice, and Derek felt a tear come to his eye. How stupid, he told himself. The girl's a grown woman now. And anyway, Lois was there and would see her safe.

"How's it goin', me duck?" he answered in a husky voice. He cleared his throat, and added, "has yer mum run off with the raggle-taggle gypsies yet?"

"No, I have not!" Lois's familiar sharp voice was so reassuring that Derek relaxed, and sat down on the hall chair. "So havin' got that out of the way," she continued, "how's everything at home. Any problems with the girls? Is Gran managing?"

"No problems with New Brooms," Derek said. "Except, o' course, they sweep cleaner when you're around. And as for Gran, she's in her element, bossin' me and everyone else who comes in sight. Douglas and Susie rang from Tresham to see how you were getting on, and Gran told them she didn't know, but all at Farnden under her supervision is runnin' like clockwork."

"Oh, well, in that case shall we stay another week?"

Derek's voice changed instantly. "Certainly not," he said. "If you want the truth, we're all missin' you and Josie a lot. Come home soon, gel."

Josie took the phone again and chatted to Derek and Gran, and told them they were having a great time, taking lots of photos to show them when they got home. "Cheerio, then, Dad," she said at last. "Here's Mum."

"'Bye, Derek," Lois said, and as an afterthought, "Love you."

"Now," Josie said, flattening out on the bed, "let's have a review. You first, Mum."

Lois had an uncomfortable feeling that her daughter was taking over, but reminded herself that it was Rob they were talking about. Josie's Rob. "Right. First of all, Athalia was not at all pleased to see us. To see me, I should say. Still, that was fair enough. She told me in no uncertain terms that I should stay away from the Farnden gypsies. I expect it would have been all right if they hadn't got the blame for Rob's murder. Then, o' course, there was the fire."

"But she came round later on, with those great stories," Josie said.

"Yeah, but did you notice how she clammed up when I said we'd read about those two brothers? I reckon she knew more than she was saying."

Josie was silent for a minute. Then she said, "You're right. And those two were the most likely candidates for attacking Rob. I suppose the police checked for dog bites?"

"Dunno. That's one thing we can ask Cowgill or your Matthew when we get back. I expect the autopsy shows up all that kind of stuff."

"Anyway, what else?" Josie yawned.

"Only one thing, really. Probably the most important. When George told us to think on about village people. He actually hinted at somebody in the pub that night. You know George and his mate were stopped and threatened on their way home after the quiz?"

"Who by?" asked Josie, wide awake again.

"A gang—some of them kids, some older. There was a man in charge, Athalia told me soon after. But nothing seems to have come of that."

"Another thing to ask the cops, Mum. You know who I'm thinking of, don't you? The man who hates outsiders and particularly gypsies?"

"Sam Stratford," Lois said grudgingly. She dreaded stirring up more trouble for Sheila. The poor woman had not been at all happy lately.

Josie nodded. "And yet he's not a bad bloke really. He'd do

anything to help if he thought you were in trouble." Then she remembered his spat with Alf Smith, and mentioned it, asking Lois if they'd always been enemies.

"Not really enemies," Lois said, and laughed. "They used to be rivals for the favours of several of the village girls, and Sam always won. He was a great looking bloke in his youth, and Alf was always a bit of a runt."

Josie said innocently that it couldn't be that. They were elderly men now. Lois laughed again, more loudly. "They wouldn't like to hear that!" she said. "Wait 'til you're their age, my gel, and you'll see there's life in the old dogs for years."

"Anyway, we're getting off the point," Josie said. "Who else, if not Sam? Alf?"

"Goodness, no. He's been the gypsies' friend for years. They've stopped on his land every year. He's fond of Athalia Lee, too. And she of him, I think. No, not Alf."

"Who, then? And if it was the same gang that attacked Rob, what would any of them have against Rob?"

"That's it, isn't it," Lois said. "I reckon we know now that there was another side to Rob. Most of us have secrets, usually in the past. Is there anything that might have happened before you met him? Something that made him an enemy?"

Josie bit her lip and frowned, thinking hard. "Well," she said, "he didn't talk about his family or friends he had before he came to Tresham. He didn't make friends easily, that's true. But he was always happy to be just with me, at home. He seemed grateful. . . ." She choked, and put her hands up to her face.

"Don't fret, duckie," Lois said quickly. "That's enough for tonight. Shall we go down to the bar and have a nightcap? Stone's ginger wine is the thing. Gran swears by it. Come on, shoes on, and lets go and chat up the locals."

As they went downstairs, Lois reflected that maybe because they were away from home, Josie seemed more able to talk about Rob, though she was sure that there were still things that Josie was not telling her. She remembered then how Josie as a teenager had been able to keep her secrets forever, if necessary. People didn't change that much, she reckoned. What was it Derek said? "Softly, softly, catchee monkey." She must bear that in mind.

The bar of the hotel was not as crowded as Lois expected. There were a few farmers talking comfortably about sheep, and one or two married couples clearly on their regular night out.

"I suppose the locals keep away from the town centre on fair nights," Josie said. She looked around and saw over in the far corner a familiar figure with a newspaper hiding his face. Alf Smith. Why wasn't he up on the field with his precious gypsies? He'd seen Lois and herself, she was sure, and obviously did not want to join them. She said nothing to Lois and led the way to the opposite end of the bar.

"Mrs. Meade, isn't it?" A large, overdressed woman had approached them, and smiled broadly at Lois. "You're a long way from home, dear, aren't you?"

Without being invited, the woman, Mrs. Westonbirt from Waltonby, a New Brooms client, sat down heavily in the elegant hotel chair and began to talk at once about the gypsies and how colourful it all was, and how she'd always wanted to come to Appleby, as her ancestors had been gypsies, though her mother had always denied it.

"So glad to see you here," she enthused, as Josie and Lois sat glumly, not able to get a word in, as the monologue continued. "When you're a woman on your own—my dear husband passed on five years ago—as you know, of course, Mrs. Meade—it is not easy to come into a bar for a drink without inviting attention—even in these days of women's lib!"

She paused only to take a sip of her gin and tonic, and then told them in detail all that she had seen and done that day. Finally, after what seemed to Lois and Josie like hours of relentless burbling, she stood up with difficulty and said it was time for tat-tat to bo-boes—"In other words, dears, up the wooden hill to Bedfordshire! I shall look out for you at breakfast tomorrow—perhaps we could sally forth together?" She walked out of the bar, pausing only to order morning tea and a newspaper from the receptionist.

Silence fell over Lois and Josie. "Not sure I remember how to speak," Josie said at last.

"Nor me," Lois said. "What was that about tat-tat to whatsit?"

"God knows," said Josie. She noticed that Alf Smith had gone. It must have been while Mrs. Westonbirt had them fixed with her beady eye.

"Shall we have another?" Lois said, picking up their empty glasses.

"Why not," said Josie. "Then it'll be time to go tat-tat to bo-boes," they chorused, and laughed with relief.

FIFTY-FOUR

What time d'you think Mrs. Westonbirt appears for breakfast?" Lois was standing at the hotel bedroom window looking down on the sunlit marketplace. There were only a few people about, local shoppers with bags of food, out early to escape the crowds. A stray dog lifted its leg against the gate into the churchyard, and Lois remembered she had promised herself a wander around looking at tombstones.

"Not very early, I guess," Josie said. "Must take her all of ten minutes getting out of bed, the great lump."

"She wasn't always that size," Lois said gently. "I expect it was comfort eating after her husband died." She could have bitten her tongue out. Josie's face fell, and she said she herself had found it quite easy to do without extra food after Rob died. In fact, she said, she would have been quite happy to give up eating all together, and it was only because Gran had force-fed her that she was not now a confirmed anorexic.

It was like walking on eggshells, Lois thought. Just when she thought they were getting on well together, she had to say a stupid thing like that. But then Josie came over to her and patted her on the head. "Sorry, Mum," she said. "I'll get used to it. Meanwhile," she added, heading for the bathroom, "bags me first in the shower."

Athalia Lee was up early. It was a habit she could not break. All around her the field was sprinkled with rubbish, and she wondered whether to set out with a sack and clear at least some of it. She decided in the end to collect over a good patch of grass around their own trailers and tents. The whole place would be heaving with people quite soon, and her work would be wasted. She knew it took days for the Appleby council to clear the town after the fair was finished. Still, they did well financially from the visitors, and though there were always grumblers who said the fair should be stopped, the council would have none of it.

"Morning, Athalia," said a voice behind her, and she straightened up, knowing without turning round that it was Alf Smith. "How are we this fine morning?" he asked.

"Fine, thanks, Alf. D'you want a cuppa?" she added. She still felt warmly towards the man who had followed them up to Appleby, who had told her so many times about his dream of being a gypsy on the road. So many evenings she had spent sitting on her trailer steps, discussing with Alf the plight of gypsies and whether things were getting better or worse. She was sad when she and George had agreed that they wouldn't stop in Farnden again, regretting that Alf was not the cheerful, outgoing bloke he used to be.

"Who's looking after the farm?" Athalia said, handing Alf a mug of tea. Did y' wife come to Appleby, too?" She knew perfectly well that Edwina had not come. She was well aware that Mrs. Smith did not have her husband's interest in gypsies. In fact, she would probably have sent for the Tresham police to see them off, had it not been for Alf.

"The wife's taking care of everything," he said, "with the help of Sam Stratford and a nephew of Edwina's from Fletching."

"Sam Stratford?" Athalia could not hide her surprise. "Thought you and him didn't get on? You said he used to bully you at school."

"School was a long time ago, Athalia," Alf said. "I can't say I really like the man, but he's useful. And we're grown men now," he added.

"Grown men sometimes act like kids," Athalia said, and Alf began to wonder if she knew something she was not telling.

"You're a real old wise woman! Tell me fortune, can you?"

Athalia did not smile. "Yes, I could tell yer fortune, Alf," she said. "Me mother was known for it. Used to set up here on the field with a board up outside her wagon. Fortunes told, crystal ball, reading hands, all that. People came from miles away. Mostly women."

"I bet she told them all they were goin' to meet a tall, dark stranger and be rich and famous," Alf said.

Athalia shook her head. "No call for you to mock, Alf Smith," she said. "Some of them women used to come out of me mam's wagon crying their eyes out. She only told the truth of what she saw. Could be quite a difficult job sometimes. Lots of times she wouldn't tell the bad bits."

"You goin' to read me palm, then?" Alf said, thinking he hadn't had much fun yet on his visit to Appleby.

"D'you mean it?" Athalia was serious.

"Yeah, come on. Here—I've finished me tea." Alf followed Athalia into her trailer, where she sat on one side of a small table with Alf opposite her. She took his hand and stared at it for a while without saying anything.

"Come on, then, gel. What can you see?" Alf said impatiently. He saw in some alarm that Athalia was frowning. She did not answer him, but got up and looked out of the trailer door.

"What's the matter? What did you see?" Alf was really worried now.

Athalia turned to look at him, shaking her head. "I lost the knack, Alf," she said. "Mind you, I was never as good as me mam. Now, it's time I did some work, so why don't you get round and have a word with the others. I'll see you again."

He did as she suggested, and walked off. She had said she'd lost the knack, but he knew that she was lying. There had been something bad. A giveaway in his own hand, and his old friend Athalia did not want him to know.

The sunshine was now warm on Lois and Josie as they set off from the hotel. It was a beautiful calm morning, and they had agreed to go their separate ways. Lois planned to wander around the churchyard and inside the church, and Josie said she would be quite happy walking along the riverbank and maybe she would sit on one of the seats and watch the children and the horses.

"Sure you'll be all right on your own? You know what your dad said," Lois asked.

"Of course, I shall be fine. What could happen in bright sunshine in the middle of town with thousands of people about?"

Lois had to admit that Josie was unlikely to come to any harm. They arranged to meet at the church gates at eleven thirty, and then they parted.

Lois walked towards the sandstone church door, deciding to look around inside first, then take her time in the graveyard. Inside it was very quiet. The light filtered through the jewel-bright stained glass windows above the altar, and she walked slowly up the aisle towards it. Nine hundred years, she thought, people had been going to and fro in this church, being baptised, married, carried to the graveyard. It was too long a time to contemplate. Must have been like a different planet, thought Lois. Just about all they would have had in common was eating and drinking, having sex and getting born.

But when she began to think about it, she realised how wrong she was. All the basics were the same. Just the trimmings were different. She walked back down the aisle, and ran her hand over the smooth, cold stone figure of a seventeenth-century lady, stretched out on her grand tomb, hands clasped in prayer. She would have quarrelled with women she didn't like, fancied men she couldn't have, had indigestion, got constipated and taken the remedy of the time. Did she plead a headache to her husband when she didn't feel like a spot of the other? Lois patted the chilly forehead. "You weren't the first, ducky," she said, "nor the last, not by a long chalk."

"Just a woman, but a good one," said a voice behind her. She whipped round, and saw George standing behind her.

"Bloody hell!" she said, glancing up towards Heaven in apology. "You made me jump. I didn't hear you come in. How d'you walk without makin' a noise?"

"Practise," he said. "All us wicked gyppos know how to move silently. Where's Josie?" he added, looking round.

"Gone off for a walk by the river," Lois said. "We're meeting outside at half past eleven." She looked at her watch. "I plan to look round the graves for a bit, and then it'll be time to meet."

"Not a good idea to let her go alone," George said quietly. "You get funny people coming to Appleby."

"But surely nobody would want to hurt Josie?"

George did not answer. He sat on the edge of a chair by the door. Athalia had told him about Alf Smith being in town, and now he was uneasy. He knew she had been hiding something to do with Alf. She said it would be best to avoid their old friend at the moment. "Alf?" he had said. But wasn't Alf their longtime supporter and champion? Athalia had grunted and said she had seen danger in Alf's hand. Then she had added that it would be as well to warn Mrs. Meade and her daughter. "No doubt you'll be seeing them," she had said sourly.

He had tried to get her to say more, but she had clammed up, and more or less sent him packing into the town to find the Meades.

"Let's skip the graves, then," Lois said, frowning. She suddenly had a stab of fear, and made for the door. It was like a bucket of cold water thrown over her. For God's sake! She didn't know this man! He was a gypsy, a traveller, and she really knew bugger-all about him and his people.

"Hey, wait for me!" George shouted, and Lois paused. He took her arm. "Why don't I wait by the gates," he added, "and you go up to the bridge to see if you can spot her in the crowds. If she turns up here, we'll wait until you come back. Just go up and take a look along the riverbank. You're more likely to spot her."

Lois walked quickly, pushing her way along the crowded pavement, deaf to the angry looks and curses as she collided with other people. She reached the bridge and looked down. It was the same idyllic scene. Lithe young men were washing the black and white horses in the river, then leaping on their backs and guiding them into deep water. Children were chasing about on the sandy banks stretching out into the river, and all along the grassy edges were families strolling, shouting to each other, sitting down to rest, drinking and eating and taking no notice of anybody but themselves.

"There she is!" Lois said aloud in relief. Josie was ambling along the footpath, coming back towards the bridge. Lois ran along and down the steps, meeting her where the horses' ramp led down into the water.

"I'm not late, am I?" Josie said.

"No, no. Just thought I'd come and meet you. Had a nice walk?"

"Didn't go far. I was more interested in watching all this carry-on. They're brilliant on the horses, aren't they?"

As they watched, a bullet-headed young man led his horse down the ramp and into the water. He splashed around with the children for a bit, and then he jumped on to the horse's back and tried to kick it forward into the deeper part of the river where a current ran strongly. The children crowed and urged him on.

"Doesn't want to go," said Josie in a worried voice. "Look at its eyes, Mum. It's terrified!"

The man got angry and yelled at the horse, pulling at its head with the halter, kicking it forward. Finally it gave in, and all Lois and Josie could see was its head, the rest of its thrashing body submerged.

"Is it swimming?" Lois said anxiously.

"Dunno," Josie said.

Then the head disappeared. The man was swimming now, desperately pulling on the halter, and suddenly other men were in the water, all of them pulling and pushing until slowly, slowly the inert form of the horse was dragged up onto the bank.

"There's George!" Lois said, grabbing Josie's arm. "Look, he's trying to revive it. They're giving him space."

"It's dead," said Josie, and choked. Lois took her hand and tried to move her away, but she shook off her mother and stood still, staring at the group of gypsy children gathered round, looking solemnly at the drowned horse.

"That bloke!" Josie said suddenly. "The one who drowned it! He's running away!"

"George!" shouted Lois, pushing her way through the crowds of gypsies. "He's gone up to the road! Quick, catch him!"

"Catch him! Catch him!" shouted the children, chasing after George, and they all disappeared towards the road, making slow progress because of the swelling crowds.

Finally Lois persuaded Josie to go back to the hotel, where they found George waiting. "I was too late," he said. "Seems he had a friend with a car, and they buggered off before anybody up there caught on to what happened. You all right, Josie?" he asked, noticing her chalk white face. He made to put his arm round her shoulders, but she pulled away from him. "Don't touch me!" she spat at him. "Sodding gypsies! I want to go home," she yelled at Lois. She rushed away from them and disappeared into the hotel.

"Better go after her," George said. "I'll hang around here in case you need me. God, I'm sorry," he added, "there'll be big trouble now."

Lois nodded. "'Bye then," she said. "Might see you."

FIFTY-FIVE

Lois made her way up to the hotel bedroom and found Josie stretched out on her bed, a pillow over her head, racked with sobs.

Lois said nothing, but settled down in a chair and waited. After a while, the crying stopped and Josie sat up, scrubbed at her face with a tissue, and said that she'd be ready to go in half an hour.

"Fine," Lois said. "I'll just have to pay the bill, and we can be on our way."

"D'you mean that?" Josie said suspiciously.

"O' course. That was one of the most awful bloody things I've ever seen. Just thinking about it makes me feel sick." She hesitated, then said, "And you know what was the worst thing about it?"

Josie nodded. "That bloke who drowned his horse—him running away."

"They'll get him," Lois said. "Sure as anything. If the police don't, the travellers will. Rough justice, that'll be."

"Mum," Josie began slowly, "d'you have any idea what we're getting into? Don't you feel it? Under everything goin' on here? Put one foot wrong, and really bad things could happen to us."

"Us?" Lois said, raising her eyebrows.

"Yes, *us*," Josie said firmly.

"I hate to say this, Josie," Lois said pleadingly, "but what could be worse than what happened to Rob? Isn't that why we're here? You're right about things going on under the surface, and I *know* we're on the right track. I can't even put it into words, but if we go home right now, we shall lose it."

"And the police?" Josie said angrily. "Do we assume they're doing nothing—leaving it all to the great detective Meade?"

"Of course not," Lois said. "I expect we shall hear from Cowgill soon, wanting to know what we're finding out and not telling us anythin' about what *they're* finding out. But that's the way it goes. All that matters is Rob, isn't it?"

Josie got up from the bed and walked to the window.

"Everything's gone quiet," she said. "Even the gypsy kids."

"Naturally. Horses is their life, and sometimes their livelihood."

Neither said anything more for a few minutes. Then Josie turned around and faced her mother. "All right, then. We stay. So what next?"

"First of all," Lois replied, "we get out of this room. Come on, best foot forward."

Along the corridor in his room, Alf Smith was also staring out of the window. He had been crossing the bridge when the horse was drowned, and for a moment his attention was redirected from his own worries to those of the gypsies up on the field. The continuing existence of the fair was not only ensured by the respect for tradition from most of the parish councillors, but also because with the RSPCA watching, the travellers made sure there was no cruelty to the horses. The reverse, in fact. All the horses were at their peak, well fed and endlessly groomed, so that there would be good sales when the time came. Now this! It would be hard to face the critics now.

Alf's mind wandered on, thinking of Athalia and George, and wondering where they would go after the fair had finished. Athalia had been talking about a permanent site in Yorkshire. She reckoned they could get a place, now that she was getting old and George was speaking about a regular job. But Alf knew that Athalia wouldn't last long on one of those permanent sites, with mains running water and toilet facilities and all the things that local authorities held dear, but not taking into account the gypsies' need to be free to go when and where they chose. It was not, he knew, a gypsy conspiracy to avoid council tax and the law in its many guises. Which came first, he wondered, the fact that they had been moved on for so many generations, unwanted outcasts, or because they *needed* to travel, a deep-down, nomadic urge.

Alf's attention was taken by a couple of figures emerging from the hotel. Mrs. Meade and her daughter, of course. What the hell *were* they doing here? He could not believe that it was just a holiday break. As far as he knew, neither Lois Meade nor her daughter had previously shown the slightest interest in horses. As he watched, they reached the monument in the square, and he saw a figure he recognised step forward. George. Yes, it was him. They stood talking for a few minutes, and then walked off together.

So Lois Meade knew George, and therefore also Athalia. Come

to think of it, Alf remembered seeing Lois talking to Athalia on the camp in Farnden. George, Lois Meade and her daughter, all talking to each other in a friendly fashion? What would they talk about now? The drowned horse, of course. And what else? Reading palms, telling fortunes, more than likely. Telling how Athalia read Alf Smith's palm this morning, and did not tell him what she saw?

Alf shook his head as if to clear away unwanted thoughts, and strode out of his room and down the corridor to the lift. He might be needed up on Gallows Hill, and set off purposefully out into the market square.

"Where are we going?" Josie said, as they left George and walked in the opposite direction from the bridge, leaving behind the sad scene.

"Anywhere except by the river," Lois said. "We need to clear our heads. We'll go up there and see what's behind those gates. Looks as if it might be interesting."

They walked slowly, admiring elegant houses and little alley-ways that ran between them into mysterious-looking courtyards. "There's a baby shop," Josie said. "Maybe we should take a look."

"Who for?" Lois said.

"Dougie and Susie."

"Blimey! They're not wed yet!"

"So?"

Lois stared at Josie. "What are you saying?"

Josie laughed. "Don't you fancy being a grannie?" she said. "Come on, let's go and have a look."

Before they disappeared into the shop, Alf Smith, halfway across the market square, had seen them turn away from the centre of town, and decided to follow them. His unease was growing, and by the time he saw them inside the baby shop, it had turned into near panic. The more he thought about it, the more certain he became that Athalia had seen the truth he was hiding, and had told George, who would be sure to have told them. He walked down the passage by the side of the shop, planning to accost them when they emerged. He thought no further than that, and had no idea what he would say.

He saw a sturdy little stone building, its door half open, and a key dangling from the lock. There seemed to be nobody about, and no windows overlooking this part of the passage. He would just step inside and wait. It was obviously a storeroom, and there were piles of boxes stacked up against the back wall. He would see them through the open door, and positioned himself to get a good view.

His heart was pumping, and he felt dizzy. Blast! Maybe he would give Edwina a quick call while he waited. He'd promised to keep in touch, and had not so far spoken to her. There was no answer for a minute or two, and he was just about to give up when a voice said, "Hello? Who is that?"

It was a man's voice and Alf recognised it. It was Sam Stratford, and he could hear Edwina's muffled laugh in the background. He said nothing, feeling himself sway. He put the mobile back in his pocket and leaned against the wall. So Josie's lad had been right. He shut his eyes and tears squeezed out from under his lids, coursing down his cheeks.

FIFTY-SIX

Who was it, Sam?" Edwina sat at the kitchen table, drinking tea and sobering up from the comical story Sam had told her about an elderly teacher at the village school when he and Alf were young. She had been standing on a chair trying to kill a wasp with a rolled-up newspaper when her skirt suddenly descended round her ankles, leaving her in a shiny green silk petticoat halfway to her knees. The kids had been quiet as mice, terrified to laugh.

"She just bent down, pulled on her skirt, and got on with the lesson," Sam remembered. "She was a marvellous old gel. Don't make 'em like that anymore." Then the phone had rung, and Sam had answered it, Edwina still laughing.

"It was Alf," he said, completely solemn now. "Nobody said anything, but I'm sure it was Alf. I just know it was."

Edwina frowned. "How could you possibly know?" she said.

"Could have been a wrong number, or been cut off, or anything."

Sam shrugged. "It was him," he repeated. "Bugger it. Just when we'd decided to call a halt."

Edwina nodded. "These things come to a natural end, don't they." All the colour had drained from her face and she avoided Sam's eyes.

"If you wait long enough," Sam replied philosophically.

They were both silent, until the phone rang again.

"I'll get it," Edwina said, pushing her chair back so hard that it fell with a crash on to the stone floor. She held the receiver with a shaking hand, and said, "Hello? Oh, hello, Sheila. Yes, he's here. He's finished hedging. Do you want to speak to him?" She handed the receiver to Sam and picked up her chair.

"On me way, me duck," he said. "Edwina says do you want any eggs? Right-o. I'll bring a dozen. See you in a minute."

He turned to Edwina, who was pale and shaking. "Don't worry," he said. "It'll be all right, you'll see. I'll get hold of Alf later. He gave me his mobile number in case anything went wrong on the farm. Leave it to me. I'll put him straight."

The Appleby baby shop was crammed full of lovely little garments in all shades of blue, yellow and pink, and Josie drooled over them. Lois looked at her and thought that it was time her daughter settled down and started a family.

"Look, Mum! How about this one? It'd be fine whether it was a boy or girl. Don't you love it?"

The woman in charge smiled broadly. "An imminent arrival?" she said.

"What?" Lois said. "Oh, no, we're just looking really. My son and his fiancée are getting married in the autumn, and Josie here thinks we should be prepared!"

"More than that, Mum," Josie said. "I shouldn't have spoken out, I know. But Doug and Susie won't mind. There's one on the way. Only just, but definitely on the way."

"Oh," said the woman, disconcerted. "Ah, well, um . . ."

Lois decided to put her out of her misery. "Oh, that's great!" she said. "Don't know what y' father will say, but I think it's really great! What's more, it'll save the expense of a white wedding . . . that should please him!"

All three laughed, and went into action. The yellow garment was joined by another couple of white ones, and an irresistible teddy bear.

Alf looked at his watch. What the hell were they doing? He shifted his position and passed his hand across his eyes. His vision was blurred and he blinked hard. Then the shed began to revolve around him, and a sudden excruciating pain like the clutch of Lucifer himself struck his chest. He crumpled to the ground in agony.

When Lois and Josie finally came out of the shop, carrying full bags, they were laughing and talking. "Hey, Mum, I need the loo," Josie said. "Too much excitement! I'll just nip in and ask her if they've got one handy." She disappeared into the shop, and Lois turned to go back to the hotel. No point in lugging all this stuff any further. They could dump it and set out again.

She glanced down the passage to see if there was an obvious toilet. A door ajar there, looking like it might be one. She could do with that herself. She began to walk towards it, and then stopped. Was that a man's hand . . . on the floor just inside the door? Oh, lor', maybe she should go back. She glanced round, but there was no sign of Josie, so she approached cautiously.

"Oh my God!" she yelled. Now she could see exactly what it was. The hand was Alf Smith's, and he was lying unconscious on the dusty brick floor.

The ambulance arrived promptly, and the paramedic asked Lois if she was Alf's wife. No relation? Lois shook her head, but explained that she knew him well and of course she would go with him to the hospital. Josie could take the shopping back to the hotel.

It was a nerve-racking journey. With sirens blaring, they made their way out of town and to the hospital. Lois could just see Alf's face, waxy and still, as the paramedics held on to him. Was he dead? She daren't ask, but then one of the men turned to her and said, "Signs of life, dear. Don't fret."

What seemed like hours later, Alf was sleeping fitfully with a nurse in constant attendance, and Lois was told she must leave now and get some rest. Edwina had been alerted, and would be there as soon as possible. Lois had no idea when this would be, and felt completely exhausted. Josie had driven over and was waiting to take her back to the hotel. "Straight to bed, Mum," she said.

"No, not yet. Something I must do," she said.

"What? Can't I do it for you?"

Lois shook her head. "No, it won't take long. You can come with me." They parked the car, and walked out of the hotel courtyard towards the market square.

"Where're we going," Josie asked anxiously. Her mother's face was drawn and pale, but she was striding out with that look on her face. No arguments, it said.

"The camp. I have to tell Athalia. She and Alf were very close, and he'll want her there."

"But his wife . . . ?"

"She can't be up here for quite a while. Athalia can be there in half an hour."

"But they'll never let an old gypsy woman into the intensive care ward," objected Josie, wondering if her mother had flipped. It wouldn't be surprising. It had been a terrible shock.

"You don't know Athalia," Lois said, and they walked on in silence. Finally Josie said, "Mum. If you're right, why don't I go back and get the van and bring it up to the camp. If Athalia, or whatever her name is, will have a go, then I could take us straight over to the hospital. It'd be quicker."

"Well done, love," Lois said. "We'll wait by the entrance."

It was as Josie had guessed. Lois strode in with Athalia and, remembering the way, headed straight for Alf's room. "Absolutely not!" the nurse said, barring the way at the door. "We are expecting Mr. Smith's wife, and he must be kept absolutely quiet until she arrives. How did you get up here? It is strictly out of bounds!" She looked suspiciously at Lois. "Weren't you with him when he came in?" she said.

Lois said that she was, that she was a close friend of Mr. Smith and knew that this lady—she put her arm around Athalia's shoulders—was the one person in the world he would want to see more than anyone. The nurse hesitated, and Athalia saw her chance. She slid quietly round the nurse and was by Alf's side in seconds.

Before the nurse could do anything, Alf opened his eyes and said, "Athalia. You knew, didn't you. Stay with me, gel." He reached out a wavering hand and took her thin brown one, then closed his eyes again, and Lois saw the ghost of a smile on his face.

FIFTY-SEVEN
ⰣⱲ

The nurse brought a chair for Athalia, and retired to the corner of the room, a thunderous expression on her face. She had cautioned Athalia fiercely that she must be absolutely quiet. The smallest sign of distress from Alf, and she would be out on her ear. Athalia had given her a strange look, but whispered that she understood.

Half an hour passed, and to Lois and Josie waiting downstairs it seemed longer. "Looks like she's being allowed to stay. What the hell is Edwina going to say?" Josie asked.

"It'll take her at least three hours to get here, and that'll be long enough. I'm sure of that."

"Long enough for what?"

"For Alf to settle his mind," Lois replied. "He's been a troubled man for a while now." She had had plenty of time herself now to order her thoughts, and was pretty sure they were close to answering questions that had been haunting them all. If only Alf can make it. She crossed fingers on both hands.

As far as Athalia could see, things were going well with Alf. His breathing was good, and she could feel the pulse in his wrist was regular. He was holding her hand quite firmly still, and suddenly she felt him squeeze it. His eyelids flickered, and then opened and he looked straight at her. The nurse was there in an instant.

"I'm fine," he whispered, as she fussed about him. "I need to talk . . . to this lady. Not much, not for long. Promise . . . very important," he added.

The nurse was in a quandary. Signs were iffy, and his condition could change any minute. She looked at the gypsy woman, who sat so calmly, like a refuge beside the bed. Alf was still holding on to her hand, and the nurse finally decided that he would probably be more upset if she refused his request.

"No more than a sentence or two, then," she said, and retired to her corner.

For a moment neither Athalia nor Alf said a word. There was an almost visible bond between them, the nurse thought, and shivered. Gypsies gave her the creeps, and she prayed that the doctor would not suddenly appear.

"Tell me, then, boy." Athalia's voice was barely audible, and she bent close to Alf's head so that he would not have to exert himself.

"It's what you saw," he whispered. "Not me heart. Not that. I've known about that for some time."

"No, not that. This morning, Alf, it was in your hand. I saw the lad. Rob, that one. Tell me, dearie." Athalia stroked his hand, which was still holding on to hers.

"He was on the road. Thumbed a lift . . . I took him to the Green Man. He drank to drown his sorrows . . . so he said. Too much, Athalia. He had too much."

"Quiet now. Rest a bit," she said, and began to hum under her breath. After a minute or two, she whispered, "And what happened then?"

"Got him in the car to go home. He started on about Edwina. . . ." A tear ran down his cheek, and Athalia brushed it away with a soothing hand.

"No hurry," she said. "We got all the time in the world."

After a few seconds, Alf seemed to gather all his strength and said, "He was yelling at me. Laughing. Said Edwina was gettin' it regular . . . with Sam Stratford. He tried to take the wheel . . . I stopped the car. But he wouldn't stop . . . yelling an' laughing."

The nurse got up and came over. "That's quite enough now," she said. "I think you must go now and let him rest, Mrs. er . . ."

Athalia ignored her. "Go on, boy," she said. "Nearly there."

"Got him out of the car. Lost me temper . . . he fought like a tiger . . . drunk . . . kicked him in the ditch. Left him there to cool off . . . didn't realise . . ." All his energy, summoned with such difficulty, was spent.

"That's it, then, boy," Athalia said. "All done." She stroked his hand again, and, leaning forward, kissed him gently on the forehead. The hand holding hers slackened. "'Bye, Alf," she said.

As the nurse rushed forward, Athalia stood up and with quiet dignity walked away.

Edwina finally arrived and although drained with tiredness and anxiety, almost ran into the hospital, where a nurse was waiting for her.

"Where is he?"

The nurse took her arm. "We'll go and see him," she said gently. "But first, just a private word. I'm so sorry, Mrs. Smith. We did all we could."

FIFTY-EIGHT

Lois and Josie sat with Athalia in her trailer, silently watching while she made a large pot of tea in her best Crown Derby teapot.

"He won't be long," Athalia had said when they arrived back from the hospital. She had insisted they come in with her, and then excused herself for a few minutes, "To put the word out, and wait for George to come."

Lois had dutifully switched her mobile off in the hospital, and now she remembered. Almost as soon as she switched it on, it rang, and she answered it.

"Lois? Where the hell have you been?" Not Derek, she realised quickly, but Cowgill, and clearly very annoyed or worried about something. . . .

"I can't talk now," she said firmly. "I'll call you back later."

"You're all right? And Josie?"

"Of course we are! Have to go now. 'Bye."

"Lois! Hang on a moment. I'm on my way. Ring my mobile number. Have you got it?"

"Yes. 'Bye."

Athalia looked at her closely, but said nothing. Then George appeared, and came in, shutting the trailer door behind him.

"Poor old Alf," he said, sitting down and accepting a cup of tea from Athalia.

Josie was beginning to feel nervous. It was cramped and stuffy in the trailer, and she tried to catch Lois's eye. But her mother was looking straight at Athalia, and after a moment said, "Now then, is it time to tell us?"

Athalia nodded. "He would have wanted it," she said. "That's what he wanted, to have it all sorted out."

The others sat quietly, and Athalia began. She spoke slowly, thinking back carefully to what Alf had told her, making sure she got it right. When she had finished, George saw that Josie and Lois were stunned, and he repeated softly, "Poor old Alf. It weren't really his fault, was it?"

Josie snapped. She stood up and her face was red and hot with anger. "Of course it was his sodding fault!" she said. "Even if Rob was drunk and stupid, Alf had no cause to beat him to death! Come on, Mum!" she added. "Let's go home and leave this lot to think what they like. I've had enough!" she shouted, and was in tears again.

Lois put her arm around her, and gently sat her down. "We will go home, duckie," she said, "and now we know what happened it will be easier. But just sit quietly for a minute, and make sure there's nothing else you want to say."

Athalia had turned away, and when she turned back Lois could see that she, too, had tears streaking down her lined face. But she brushed them away and silently took Josie's hand. To Lois's surprise, Josie left it there, and all were still. Then George spoke again, this time directly to Josie.

"Your Rob," he said. "He was a good bloke, mostly. But like the rest of us, he weren't perfect. I heard things in the pub. If you don't know nothing about his other side, you sit there until you're ready to go. There's no need for you to say more. Take it easy, gel."

Josie sniffed, and looked at Lois. "There is something, Mum," she said finally. "I never told you and Dad. Rob didn't want you told. He'd been in trouble before I met him. Nothing serious, and I don't think it got as far as the cops, but he'd lost his temper in a pub in Tresham and went for a woman who was making fun of him. She was a tart, he said, and I didn't want to know any more. Anyway, it was all hushed up, but she was quite badly hurt."

"Josie! Did he ever hurt you?"

Josie shook her head. "Not really," she said.

"What d'you mean, 'not really'?" Lois's voice was sharp.

"Well, he grabbed my wrist once and twisted it. But I calmed him down."

"You said you'd tripped and fell on it!" Lois said. "Oh dear God," she muttered, and put her head in her hands.

George said, "Don't fret. It'll all be sorted out. I expect the cops are on the way?"

Lois didn't reply, but saw Athalia nod and realised she had guessed where Lois's call had come from. There was nothing more to be said, and after thanking Athalia for the tea, Lois and Josie walked back to the van. George stood in the background and raised his hand as they drove off. Athalia did not wave.

"Sorry, Mum," Josie said suddenly, when they were nearly back at the hotel. "Sorry for everything."

Cowgill arrived later, and found them in the hotel. He looked at their faces, and felt guilty at having to grill them right away for what they knew. The police investigation had moved on a good way, of course, but he did not know exactly what Alf's final involvement had been. Before he talked to anybody else, he needed to find out what Lois had discovered.

He soon realised that both she and Josie were totally exhausted. He sighed, with Derek's voice still ringing in his ears. Lois's husband had called him before he left, giving him a blast about making use of his wife and daughter. Apparently news of Alf's collapse had gone around Farnden village network at record speed. Edwina had seen to that, ringing Stratfords to say she had to leave.

"So where shall I begin?" Lois said wearily.

"Can't it wait?" Josie asked Cowgill, but he shook his head.

"Sorry, no," he said. "There is some urgency about this now."

"You'd better ask us questions, then," Lois said. "No point in my going over what you already know."

"First of all," Cowgill said, taking charge, "I'll tell you what I know about Alf. He had been a friend of the gypsies for years. Allowed them to camp on his land, and this was not popular with the village. His wife, Edwina, was on the side of the village, and was a longtime friend—possibly more?—of Sam Stratford."

"Sam hated the gypsies. It was him who encouraged a gang of kids to harass them," Lois said, knowing now that she had no hope of protecting Sheila. "And also, he was probably knocking off Edwina on the side."

"Well put, Mum," Josie said, seeing the note taker smile.

"So what made Alf come to the fair, leaving Sam Stratford a clear field?"

"God knows. Maybe he was testing them? He could have had some plan, and it didn't work out. Or perhaps it did," Lois said. She closed her eyes, seeing again Alf on the floor of the storeroom, tear streaks still on his face.

"Mum? Are you all right?" Josie said, and turned to glare at Cowgill.

"Don't worry love," Lois said, "it's best we get this over, then we can go home. This is the most important bit," she continued. "So listen carefully, Inspector. Alf knew all about Sam and Edwina. I don't know how long he'd known, but in hospital, just before he died, he talked to the gypsy lady, Athalia Lee. It was so sad. . . ."

Cowgill glimpsed a Lois he had rarely seen. Her face crumpled and she sniffed, searching in her pocket for a tissue. "Take your time, Lois," he said, desperately wanting to gather her up and comfort her, but he maintained his official demeanor, softening only to give her a large handkerchief. "As you say, we'll get it all done, and then you and Josie can go back to Farnden."

Lois straightened up, cleared her throat and told him about Alf's confession to Athalia, how he had been taunted by a drunken Rob until he lost control. "Alf may have had suspicions before, but Rob confirmed it that night. Oh yes, he made sure Alf knew for certain that Sam was having a passionate affair with his wife. No wonder the poor bloke lost it."

"So Alf *killed* Rob?" Cowgill said.

"Alf was doing him a favour. Rob was paralytic. Alf intended to give him a lift to see him safely home, but when the idiot wouldn't shut up, Alf tried to push him out of the car. Maybe he thought the night air would sober him up. Rob resisted and they fought. Alf kicked him into the ditch, and left him. I don't know if he meant to kill him, but that's what happened."

There was a moment's silence, then Cowgill said he had one more thing to ask, and then that would do for the moment. "When you found Alf round the back of the baby shop, was he able to speak at all? Did you hear him say anything?"

"No, nothing. He was out cold," Lois said.

"But his mobile phone, Mum," Josie interrupted, "don't you remember we found it on the ground beside him. It was still switched on, though there was nobody at the other end. Your chaps will have it, Inspector. It'd be interesting to know who he was talking to. Maybe Edwina? Something she said caused his heart attack?"

Cowgill said that this was a useful point to follow up. Then he thanked them both, and was about to wrap it up when Lois said she had a question for him. "What happened about them two ugly gypsy brothers who weren't in the camp proper? They were prime suspects for Rob's murder at one time, weren't they?"

"Ah yes, them," Cowgill said. "Yes, it did seem likely. They were seen around the pub in Tresham that night. The dog had had a go at somebody. But there was no obvious motive. Now it looks like it was just coincidence. We also reckoned they had a hand in the fire, but can't be sure. Why would they want to foul up their own camping ground? Once again, no apparent motive. We still don't know the answer to that one, but are working on it. It could've been a careless accident, or that gang of kids.

"Anyway," he continued, "the brothers left the others and went off on their own. Ended up in Lancashire, and one of them killed the other. A quarrel, apparently, over a dog. The killer was arrested and spilled out a whole lot of stuff about being on the site in Farnden. He said his brother had seen Smith's wife and another man hand in hand, and blackmailed her. He blamed his brother for everything. Nasty business, but we'll get at the truth." He stood up and said that was enough for today. He dismissed his assistant and walked over to the window, looking down into the square, saying nothing more.

Josie began to feel uncomfortable in the silence. "Mum, I need the loo," Josie said, looking from one to the other. Lois nodded, and contemplated Cowgill's back. She looked at her watch, and waited.

Finally Cowgill turned to her. "All right?" he said.

"Yep, more or less."

"You know what I want to say, don't you, Lois?"

"I can guess. But go on. Say it anyway."

"Right. This is it. I'm not sure I can allow you to involve your-self in future cases," he said formally.

"*Allow* me? Since when did I need your permission?"

He looked away again. "All right then, how about this?" he said in a muffled voice. "You mean more to me than solving a few diffi-cult cases. I can't stand seeing you upset, nor can I bear the thought that I might be sending you into danger."

"Well, tough," said Lois, taking his hand and turning him to face her. She kissed him lightly on the cheek, and added, "because I intend to carry on. Besides, if you shut me out, who will cheer you up on gloomy mornings?"

FIFTY-NINE

The story of Alf Smith's death was now the main subject for conversation in the village, and when Lois and Josie returned next afternoon in the New Brooms van, curious eyes followed them all the way down the street.

Derek was standing by the gate, and his face lit up as they approached. He waved them in, and the minute Lois got out he hugged her tight. Then it was Josie's turn, and Lois said lightly that they must go away more often. Absence certainly makes the heart grow fonder, she and Josie agreed, and followed Derek into the house where Gran was waiting. In spite of reminding herself that she was a grown woman with a family and a business, Lois was nervously anticipating what her mother would have to say. Gran's first words lived up to expectations.

"I should think that'll teach you to think more carefully before you go off gallivanting without your husband!" she said, banging cutlery down on to the kitchen table. "And taking your only daughter with you, getting her into your silly games!"

Derek saw that Josie was near to tears and Lois had a mutinous look, so he said that what had happened in Appleby was in the past, and anyway, until Lois told them all about it, they were just relying on gossip and rumour. Gran sniffed and tutted, but put a large fruit cake on the table, set out the best cups and saucers and plates, and made the tea. When they were settled, Derek took Lois's hand and said, "Now, me duck, let's have the whole story. We're all very sorry about poor old Alf, and his Edwina is a real mess."

Lois told herself that she had yet to find out if Edwina deserved to be a real mess, but began to explain what had happened. When she reached the part where Alf had had his heart attack and was carried off to hospital, she asked Josie if she'd like to tell the rest. But Josie shook her head. "You carry on, Mum," she said. "It's your party."

This brief remark pulled Lois up short, and for a long time afterwards she pondered on just how much she really rated these jobs with Cowgill. Still, this time the reason had been family, finding out who had attacked Rob. Was this the whole truth? She decided to think about it more seriously next time Cowgill got in touch, and was shamefaced at her prevarication.

"I don't know about Josie," she said, "but I began to have a nasty idea that Alf had some secret reason for being in Appleby. Something to do with us. He sort of shadowed us around the place. Why was he really there? I know that he had this thing about having gypsy ancestry, but he didn't look as if he was enjoying himself much. I reckon he suspected we were on to something."

"Well, what *were* you on to?" Gran said impatiently.

Lois told them then, all about Athalia and George, and Alf's confession to his old gypsy friend, and Athalia relaying what he'd said to her.

"I can't believe that Alf Smith murdered our Rob for no other reason than being teased about Sam Stratford and Edwina!" Gran shook her head. "Him and those gypsies!" she said.

Josie cleared her throat. "It had nothing to do with the gypsies, Gran," she said. "Rob had gone off after a row with me, and Alf gave him a lift into Tresham and kept an eye on him in the pub. By the time they were on the way home, Rob was drunk witless. And when he was like that, he was a different person. I've seen him out of control a few times," she added, biting her lip.

Lois frowned and wished she could do something, anything, to spare her daughter this ordeal. But it had to be told, and it was probably better for Josie to tell it.

"There was this time, Dad," she said, now looking straight at him. She continued with the story of her twisted wrist, and Derek pushed his chair back and clenched his fist. "I'll . . . I'll . . ." he began, and then sat down again, remembering that there was nothing now he could do to Rob.

"That still doesn't excuse Alf Smith," Gran said. She came from an unforgiving generation, living by stricter codes. "And anyway," she added, "is it true about Sam and Edwina? D'you know the truth, Lois?" she asked.

"Not for certain," Lois said. "I know Sheila has been very upset lately, but she was poorly and it might have been that. But I shall find out. Sheila's one of my girls, and I owe it to her."

They were quiet for a while, digesting what Lois and Josie had recounted. Then Josie said, "It's rough justice, if it *is* true, isn't it?"

"What d'you mean, duckie," Derek said.

"Well, if Edwina was carrying on with Sam, and it has led to the death of her husband, who wasn't a really bad man, then she's got her desserts, hasn't she?"

Lois did not answer, but asked Derek if he had heard whether Edwina was back home yet. Derek said he did not know, but Gran said she had been told that Edwina would be back tomorrow. There would be the funeral to arrange, and then all the enquiries.

Josie said, "Then it's just beginning for her, isn't it. For me and Rob, it's finally over. Maybe we should remember that, eh, Mum?"

Lois managed a smile. "You're a great girl, Josie Meade," she said. "Me and your Dad, we couldn't be more proud of you."

"And me!" Gran said loudly. "Now," she added, "who's going to do the dishes while I feed the dog. You haven't said hello to her yet, Lois."

Jeems was released from the scullery, and bounced all over Lois and then Josie, and Lois could not help feeling that now they could start again, especially Josie. She made a mental note to contact Edwina Smith tomorrow, and then have a talk to Sheila. But for now tomorrow was another day, and she gave Jeems a hug. "Let's go walkies," she said. "A breath of Farnden air is just what we need."

SIXTY

In the event, it was Sam Stratford who knocked at the Meade's door very soon after breakfast. Gran opened it and was shocked. Sam looked a good ten years older, and she noticed that his hand shook as he asked if Lois was in.

"Yes, she's back," Gran said. "But she's only just sorting herself out, Sam. Couldn't you come back a bit later?"

He shook his head. "I've got to go to Tresham later," he said. "I really would—"

"Morning Sam," Lois said, coming through from the kitchen. Then to Gran she said, "It's all right, Mum. I need to talk to Sam anyway."

Gran disappeared, looking disapproving, and Lois showed Sam into her office. When they were settled, Lois said, "Now, Sam. Do you want to tell me what's been going on? Don't forget I've known you and Sheila for years. I've always reckoned on both of you as my friends. No secrets between us, eh?"

"If only," Sam said. "Everybody has secrets, Lois," he added, then continued, "I just need to put you in the picture before you get the wrong end of the stick from other people. Now I'm retired, we need Sheila's money from New Brooms, and I don't want her getting the push because of me."

Lois bridled. "I'm not likely to do that!" she said. "You can't think much of me if you think I'd do a thing like that."

"It doesn't much matter what I think," Sam said. "But Sheila thinks a lot of you, and so I want you to hear the truth of it all from me." He paused, and then said, "I warn you, it ain't easy for me. I don't come out of it very well." He looked weary, and Lois could see this was a big effort for him. "It began a long time ago," he said by way of introduction. "Edwina and me were at school together, sort of a twosome. But then we went our separate ways, and I didn't think nothing more about it. She married Alf, an' Sheila and me got together. I never thought much of Alf, but we got on. Then I was working in Junuddle one summer. It were hot and I'd stopped under a tree for some shade for a bit. Edwina suddenly appeared. She was takin' some tea to Alf across the fields and havin' a walk at the same time. We sat down and had a chat, and then— p'raps it was the heat—we were kissin' and it didn't stop there. It all came back, all that we'd had at school an' that."

"But that wasn't the end of it?"

Sam shook his head. "It were like a drug. The more we had the more we wanted. Sometimes it was bloody dangerous, with Alf around or comin' back any minute. I told Edwina we should stop an' she agreed, but somehow it carried on."

"So would you say that's why Alf had a heart attack and died in Appleby?" She needed to know whether Sam realized what he had done.

"Edwina reckons he'd found out. He was different, she said. An' that night Josie's bloke was beaten up, Alf had come home in such a state. Wouldn't talk to Edwina for a couple of days."

"Oh, Sam," said Lois. "It'll all come out when the police have finished. What a stupid shame. Two families messed up."

"An' a drunken young fool who couldn't keep his mouth shut," Sam said. "That's what I reckon, anyway."

Sam seemed to have nothing more to say, but Lois had another question.

"And what about the gypsies, Sam? Who caused that fire, and who got a gang of kids to do his dirty work for him?"

Sam sank lower into his chair. "Yeah, well," he said. "It was a bit of fun at first. Gave 'em something to do, an' I was all for getting them dirty gypsies out of the village. I could never work out why you liked 'em, to tell the truth. Anyway, that Mark Brown was the ringleader, an' I suppose I encouraged him, though it weren't him what started the fire. It was one of the younger ones, Mark told me. The kid did it to show the rest of the gang what a big man he was. He started it with several boxes of matches and paraffin he got from his dad's shed. Crept in and out like a shadow. The grass was dry as a bone, and two of the caravans were old wooden ones. They went up like tinder boxes. He was terrified when he saw what he'd done, and confessed to Mark. He wouldn't tell me the kid's name."

"The police will get it out of him," Lois said. "Young Mark Brown is going to need all the help his future mother-in-law Mrs. T-J can give him, that's for sure. Another thing," she added, "did you know about that bunch of flowers Mark left for me at the roadside where Rob was killed? With a charming message on the label?"

Sam nodded. "I was mad at him about that. Wouldn't tell me what he wrote on the label. Was it bad?"

Lois stood up. "Sam Stratford," she said. "God knows what's going to happen to you, but I'd like you to know just how much trouble you have caused. No doubt the police will sort you out, but I'll have my say." She spared him nothing, angry on Sheila's behalf as well as her own, and then pushed him out without ceremony.

"But Sam was my best friend," Derek said plaintively. "God, it just shows you never really know people."

"So are you going to see Edwina?" Gran said to Lois.

"No, no need now. What a silly woman! And not just silly, neither."

"Frailty, thy name is woman," said Derek, surprising them all.

Before Lois could answer that men weren't that great, they heard footsteps coming up the drive, and then Douglas and Susie appeared, grinning like Cheshire cats through the window.

"Have a good time, Mum?" Douglas said, as they came in hand in hand.

"Wonderful," Lois said flatly.

"Great! Now we've some news for you. Hold tight to Dad—we don't want him blowing his top. Susie and me, well, we're going to have a baby. In the autumn, end of October. So we'll bring the wedding forward, if that's all right with you."

Lois waited, but could not stop the smile spreading across her face.

Derek took a deep breath, and before he could explode, Lois said. "That's terrific!" and kissed them both. Then she kissed Derek on his scarlet cheek, and said, "Save us all a white wedding, that will."

"If you think I'm skimping on my eldest son's wedding, you're wrong," he said stiffly, and, grasping Douglas's hand, shook if firmly. "Well done, boy," he said, and only Lois knew what it cost him.

Sixty-One

The next day was comparatively quiet, with Gran keeping visitors at bay. In the evening, they all collapsed into armchairs in the sitting room to watch undemanding television. Lois drifted off to sleep, and was woken by the doorbell ringing insistently.

"I'll go," Derek said. "They'll get sent packing, whoever they are. Disturbing people at this time of night." He went off muttering crossly. Lois heard him open the door and start to speak loudly. Then he stopped, said something more softly and they heard footsteps coming back to the sitting room.

"It's Edwina," he said. "Can she come in, Lois? She's in a right state."

Gran stood up, arms akimbo. "I should think she is!" she said, but Lois got wearily to her feet. "You'd better come in," she said to the ghostly figure hovering in the dark hall.

Edwina scuttled in, looking round the room to see who else was there.

"There's only me and Gran and Derek," Lois said. "If you've got something to say, you can say it now. We all know about poor old Alf, anyway."

"I'm sorry to butt in on you like this," Edwina squeaked. She cleared her throat. "It's just that I can't stay in the farmhouse any longer by myself. I thought you could tell me a bit more about what happened in Appleby."

"You got to learn to cope by yourself now," growled Gran. "Unless, o' course, you can get company from Sam Stratford now and then."

"Mum!" Lois said. "You don't kick a man when he's down, surely."

"It's all right," Edwina said. "I deserve it. Me and Sam, we killed him, didn't we. Or as good as." She pushed her hair back from her face. It looked as though no comb had touched it for a day or two. "D'you know any more, Mrs. Meade? Did he get together with his gypsies? Were they with him when . . .when, you know . . ."

"When he had his heart attack?" said Lois. "No, me and Josie found him. But Athalia Lee was with him in the hospital. She was the nice old lady he used to talk to when they camped in your thicket."

"D'you know if he told her anything before he . . . died? Before I got there?"

"Yes, he did," answered Lois. "But I'm not at all sure I should tell you. It was a private conversation, but Athalia said he'd wanted me to be told. And as he knew about me and the cops, he'd be sure I'd pass it on. As far as I know, he didn't mention any message for you. I'm sure he would've," she added, seeing Edwina's face, "but he didn't have much time."

Edwina was silent for a minute, then said in a low voice, "He knew, didn't he?"

Lois nodded. "Yes, he knew."

"The police are coming tomorrow morning," Edwina said. "I suppose I shall hear the full story then. Seems they have to investigate it. He did have a heart condition, you know," she added hopefully.

"So he did," Lois said. "Now, if there's nothing more, Mrs. Smith, we're all tired and it's a busy day tomorrow. I'm sure if you go home now you'll be all right. It's surprising how sleep comes, just when you're sure it never will."

She took Edwina's arm and escorted her out of the room. "Good night," she said, and started to shut the door. Was that a car drawing up outside their house? "Oh, God, who now?" she said, and waited. A tall figure came up the drive, tipping his hat to Edwina on her way out.

"Sorry to bother you, Lois," Cowgill said. "Could you possibly spare me a few minutes? One or two important questions I need to ask. I really am sorry." He waited, and Lois looked at him. His face was so familiar, and, after all this time, somehow endearing. She remembered what a stiff and starchy cop he had been when she first knew him, disapproving and cold. He'd changed quite a lot. And he loved her. She knew that, and could not deny that it pleased her. But he was such a right-thinking old thing. She had never felt threatened. Derek was another matter. He was deeply suspicious, but knew his Lois too well to play the heavy-handed, irate husband.

"Well?" Cowgill said, wondering why she didn't answer. "Can I come in? Was that Edwina Smith I passed in the drive?"

It was Edwina Smith, Lois acknowledged. Edwina's world had fallen apart, and all as a direct result of a stupid affair with a child-hood sweetheart. But who was she to say it was stupid? Frailty, thy name is woman, Derek had said. And so it is, she said to herself.

"I'll just ask Derek," she said. "I'm sure it will be all right. Even Gran won't chuck out a policeman." She grinned, put out her hand and he took it, kissed it lightly, and followed her into the house.

Postscript

Nearly a year later, a newspaper cutting arrived in the post addressed to Lois, with a handwritten message scrawled across the top.

Me and Athalia are in York now. Show this to Josie. Nice knowing you. George Price.

Man Finally Sentenced for
Death of Horse at Appleby

At last year's 300-year-old Appleby horse fair, crowds of gypsies and tourists witnessed a horrific drowning of a horse, which subsequently intensified opposition to the fair from many quarters.

After extensive searches and delays, a man aged twenty-two was found and sentenced to twenty-eight days in jail. He was banned from keeping all animals for five years. The judge said he had shown irresponsible recklessness, when, after purchasing a piebald horse, he had taken it into deep water in the River Eden, where it drowned. It was said in his defence that he had not intended to be cruel to the horse, but that the halter had not been fixed correctly.

RSPCA and police officers had witnessed the event, and said later that they were grateful to George Price, spokesman for the travelling community, who gave them valuable co-operation in official investigations.